THE COURTESAN'S FORGOTTEN PRINCE

THE COURTESAN'S FORGOTTEN PRINCE

Megan Mackie

The Courtesan's Forgotten Prince
Copyright © 2025 Megan Mackie. All rights reserved.

Cover & Typesetting by Autumn Skye

All rights to the work within are reserved to the author and publisher. No part of this publication may be reproduced, stored in a retrieval system, or transmitted in any form or by any means, electronic, mechanical, photocopying, recording, scanning, or otherwise, except as permitted under Section 107 or 108 of the 1976 International Copyright Act, without prior written permission except in brief quotations embodied in critical articles and reviews. Please contact either the Publisher or Author to gain permission.

This is a work of fiction. All characters, organizations, and events portrayed in this novel are either products of the author's imagination or are used fictitiously.

Paperback ISBN-13:
Hardcover ISBN-13:
Ebook ISBN-13:

DEDICATION

To all women who just want to be seen as they are.

Contents

Characters ix
Settings..xi

Chapter 1..1
Chapter 2... 6
Chapter 3...11
Chapter 4...17
Chapter 5...23
Chapter 6...29
Chapter 7...34
Chapter 8...39
Chapter 9...45
Chapter 10 51
Chapter 11 57
Chapter 12 62
Chapter 13 67
Chapter 14 72
Chapter 15 78
Chapter 16 84
Chapter 17 90
Chapter 18 95
Chapter 19 100

Chapter 20	106
Chapter 21	111
Chapter 22	117
Chapter 23	123
Chapter 24	129
Chapter 25	135
Chapter 26	140
Chapter 27	146
Chapter 28	152
Chapter 29	158
Chapter 30	164
Chapter 31	170
Chapter 32	175
Chapter 33	181
Chapter 34	186
Chapter 35	192
Chapter 36	198
Chapter 37	203
Chapter 38	209
Chapter 39	215
Chapter 40	220
Chapter 41	226
Chapter 42	231
Chapter 43	237
Chapter 44	242
Chapter 45	248
Chapter 46	253
Chapter 47	258
Chapter 48	263
Chapter 49	269
Chapter 50	274
Chapter 51	280
Chapter 52	285
Book ClubQuestions	291
Author Bio	293

CHARACTERS

THE CRIMSON COURT

Lydia, aka The Virtue of Beauty: Heroine
Georgiana, aka The Queen of Virtues: The madam and mentor that Lydia works for in the Crimson Court.
Street Mother: a lesser madam/street urchin mother to Lydia. Deceased.

THE UNDERCOURT

Damian, aka Imperial Prince Regulus Dominicus Damian Justinian II: The surviving eldest son of the previous Emperor. An Imperial Prince who has been disinherited because of the affliction of his face. Now serves as a shadowy figure, protecting his younger brother.
Alexandros, aka The Imperial Phoenix: Alexandros is a Phoenix who can take on the appearance of a man and is bonded to Damian. Pretends to be Damian's secretary.
Imperial Butler Walter Kinley: Damian's butler and longtime caretaker. Husband to Edith Kinley and grandfather to Kitty.
Imperial Housekeeper Edith Kinley: Damian's housekeeper and longtime caretaker. Wife to Walter Kinley and grandmother to Kitty.

Kitty aka Catherine Kinley: Ladies' maid to Lydia. Granddaugther of Walter and Edith

The Baker: an ally of Damian's, also one of the providers of food for the Undercourt.

IMPERIAL COURT:

Xander, aka Emperor Magnus IV, : Damian's younger brother and the current Emperor

House Laon, a house whose loyalty to the Imperial family is questionable.

Bertie, aka Emperor Regnus the VI: the former emperor and father of both Damian and Xander. Deceased.

Lady Regina of the House of Laon: Damian's former fiancé.

House Cathor, a house who familial ties to the Imperial family, is considered a rival family.

Sciom Lord Dominique of the House of Cathor: A Scion of House Cathor, running the house despite his unwell father is still alive.

Scion Lord Petre: Cousin to Damion and Xander, from a line that cannot inherit.

Viscount Louis of Coralus: Noble friend of Xander.

Lady Chrysanthemum: a lesser noblewoman in the Imperial Court.

OTHER:

Queen Regina Emeralda of the Southern Kingdom: a monarch from a rival kingdom, promised in marriage to Emperor Magnus to end the war between the Empire and her kingdom.

SETTINGS

World: The Imperial City of Arcadium; a fictional land at a time analogous to Victorian times.

The Crimson Court: the red-light district where the highest most illustrious courtesans live and work.

The Undercourt: A sunken city beneath the Imperial City that has created elaborate tunnels of ruins. The term also refers the open secret of the Imperial network of spies.

The County of Summberbourne: The traditional lands of the Crown Prince's wife; it is the prize offered to Lydia for five years of service and will make her the Countess of Summerbourne.

The Imperial Opera House.

She wore her scars as her best attire. A stunning dress made of hellfire.

— Daniel Saint

You are not the darkness you endured. You are the light that refused to surrender.

— John Mark Green

CHAPTER 1

THE OFFER

"It is completely up to you, darling," the madam, Queen of the Virtues, declared with a flutter of her fine fan.

Lydia, the courtesan known as the Virtue of Beauty, re-examined the letter in her hands. The penmanship was elegant with the sweeping letters the nobility used. The quality of the paper also spoke volumes of the sender: not just money but influence as well to get such fine grain. Yet, there was no embossment on the page declaring from which House it came.

Very curious.

Lydia lifted it closer to her nose and took a breath in. Hints of cedarwood. A fairly popular if common scent favored by men of the capital city. No real hint there.

It was all very intriguing.

"Ten thousand marks," she said out loud, looking over the enclosed amount listed in the brief letter. "That is an exorbitant sum for one night's company."

"Indeed. I am almost tempted to take the offer myself," the Queen of Virtues said, arching an eyebrow at it. "But the letter stipulated it was for the Virtue of Beauty specifically."

Lydia nodded, noting that. Her reputation had been gaining traction over the past year. This letter was just another sign of her accomplishment in the Crimson Court of the Capital City. She looked over the additionally enclosed conditions on the second page of the letter. "I am not to see his face at any time?" She hesitated.

"Speak your thoughts frankly, my dear," the Queen urged.

Lydia blinked at the letter, trying to process those requested thoughts. "Well, it will certainly make some activities ... a challenge. But I suppose I do spend much of the time with my eyes closed."

"It is also stated that you are not to speak to anyone except your patron," the Queen confirmed.

"That is easily done, but do you have any notion why the great secrecy?" Lydia asked as she set down the letter on the small table between them, safe within the Queen of Virtue's private boudoir.

"I have my theories, yes, but I would keep my own counsel on them."

Lydia understood the reasoning behind that. The clientele the Crimson Court attracted were often members of the actual Imperial Court. Even idle gossip could have dangerous implications. It left Lydia with her own speculations of whom this mysterious client could be. Possibly a cabinet minister or someone under great public scrutiny. All clients enjoyed discretion, many of them had official spouses and in-laws to consider. But this letter hinted at something more. She supposed it was possible the client was sickly or dying, and it was a last wish. She had given such comforts before. Lydia found those clients rather sweet.

"This decision is yours alone, of course," the madam added, neutrally.

"I would be honored to be of comfort," Lydia said after a moment more consideration.

"Beautifully answered." Then the older woman smiled. "I think I named you well, my dear."

"All of your Virtues are beautiful," Lydia answered graciously.

The Queen of Virtues, Georgiana, snapped her fan closed to give Lydia a reproachful expression. She was still elegant with a mature beauty in her own right. It was rumored amongst the other courtesans that her last patron had been the late Emperor himself, and after his passing, she refused to take another because of her broken heart. It presented like a beautiful fantasy, but Lydia felt sure if the rumor were true, a sizable trust would have been bequeathed to the Queen of Virtues: more than enough to retire, giving Georgiana more comfort than could any memories of love for the rest of her days.

Elegantly, the Virtue of Beauty bowed her head at the madam's reproach. "Forgive me, Madame. I'm not sure what I said, but if it offended you, I am the soul of regret."

Georgiana's face continued its imperious stony expression for a few seconds more before it broke into a warm, motherly grin. "Oh, Lydia, my darling. The embodiment of a Virtue is more than simply a pretty face." She set her fan in her lap and extended a hand toward the nearby tea set to perfectly pour two cups with exacting elegance. Lydia focused on her movements, enthralled by the older courtesan's artistry.

"You are my Beauty because of your manner and heart. Despite the darkness you have endured in the Night and the world you have found yourself in, you have not let it touch you or bring your spirit down. It is a divine gift you have, for you remain beautiful to everyone who is fortunate to encounter you."

Lydia nodded her head, acknowledging the compliment with the grace she had been taught.

Georgiana sighed. "My dearest hope for you, my dear, is to see you with a wealthy patron who will treat you with the honor and respect that you deserve." The Queen held out the prepared cup of tea to her Beauty with a steady hand, having dressed it exactly how Lydia liked it without asking: heavy and dark with a dollop of honey. Lydia received it graciously, smoothly taking it without a drop escaping the cup. "I know my girls talk amongst themselves. I like the mystery, but I wish to confirm something to you and only you. Can you keep my secret?"

Lydia understood the request for the test it was. One aspect of a courtesan's role is to hold the secrets of their patrons, not only as lovers but also as companions and sometimes confessors. A courtesan's honor was tied to holding such secrets in trust, and the greatest gift a courtesan could bestow on another was to impart a secret of their own. Her heart sped up at the request.

"Yes, Madame," she said, barely containing her excitement under her façade of grace.

The Queen of Virtues smiled knowingly and took a sip from her own cup, drawing out the suspense for her listener. "I was indeed the courtesan to the late Emperor."

Now Lydia failed to contain her delighted smile, and her chagrin at having guessed wrong. "I knew it," she said jubilantly instead, and both women laughed.

"Yes, but I tell you this secret not just for your gratification, or the bragging rights of a past conquest. I tell you this because I want to stress..." Now the older woman hesitated, licking her lips a moment as she searched for words. The fact that she deliberated made Lydia sit up and pay even closer attention, for the Queen was never one to be at a loss for words.

"Love ... is not forbidden to us," she finally said, taking the younger woman much by surprise. "I wish you to remember that."

Lydia's eyes went wide at the implication. "You *loved* the Emperor?"

A wistful, happy sadness washed over the older woman's face. "And he *loved* me."

And Lydia understood what the true secret was that the Queen imparted.

Georgiana set down her teacup and held out her hands to Lydia, which she followed suit and took. "I love you like one of my own daughters, child. Truly. And I wish to see you happy and secure. I am not saying that this commission tonight will be that person for you, but I want you to keep your mind open to the possibility of your future with someone who will make you happy."

"A patron is security," Lydia said, a bit confused by what her Queen was saying. "I mean no disrespect, Madame, but we are courtesans." Lydia had seen too many times how such notions of love were poison to the mind. They lived in a world where favors were exchanged for money, and to be fooled into believing anything more could arise from that was dangerous. Love was a sad fairy tale for little girls who had to grow up too soon, and it was the first story to die.

Her incredulity was not lost on the Queen of Virtues. She withdrew back behind her mask and nodded to the request letter on the table. "If you are taking the commission, a carriage will arrive for you tonight by the fourth bell. You should prepare. I will send your reply back this hour."

"I am more than eager to take it, Madame. Thank you," Lydia said, looking over the offer one more time. It did not yield more details, but it only whetted her curiosity more.

"Naturally, your safety is guaranteed," the Queen of Virtues said, fluttering her fan once more toward her face.

"Naturally," Lydia acknowledged. It was the reason she had joined the Queen of Virtue's Crimson Court, for the protection it afforded. No one of the Imperial Court would dare cross the Queen by harming one of her girls. To do so would spell their own disgrace above, and every client welcomed in the Crimson Court was taught that lesson early and clearly, or was not invited at all.

The Beauty of the Virtues stood and nodded to her Queen. "Thank you, Mother," she said as she bobbed a curtsy then hurried off, her mind reeling with delight at the interesting mystery that awaited her that night.

CHAPTER 2

A MYSTERIOUS DOOR

Lydia loved the scarlet color. Maybe it was a cliché, an expected shade for a courtesan to wear, but she loved it. The soft velvet skirt beneath her fingers felt delicious and imbued her with a feeling of desirability that no other cloth seemed to. Her whole self felt truly beautiful that night, which, in turn, created an armor that she needed in order to do what she must that night.

Her client may be noble, but she was no shrinking commoner. When she was a child, that steel had earned her abuse, but as the Virtue of Beauty, it was indispensable when dealing with and serving this particular clientele.

Adjusting her hair, she let her soft ringlets of black slip through her fingers, releasing a little of the perfume added to it by her clever maid. The jewelry she wore were gifts from other nobles, lesser ones who needed to prove something with their gifts. Greater nobles were stingier with their favors, mostly because their power and status made them feel like they didn't have to prove anything to anybody. She had only entertained one such noble before. It was hard to tell what to expect from this night, but the carriage offered some clues.

Not only were the seats covered and stuffed thick and soft, but also beautiful curtains had been hung on the inner walls and gray fur covered the floor. When the carriage had arrived to pick her up, it had seemed much more conservative and standard on the outside, like a geode, hiding its opulent secrets within. The brocade curtains were drawn over the windows for discretion, but a small flat carpet had been laid out for her to step across, presumably to preserve the beautiful furs within from inadvertently dirty slippers. Though, it didn't matter because she removed her slippers immediately so she could delight in the feel of the fur beneath her toes. All in all, the ride had been very smooth and comfortable. She could imagine falling asleep to the gentle rocking of the carriage very easily. There had even been a small cupboard on the side, with glass bottles of refreshing water, sweating condensation.

"Whoever this patron is, he has spared a lot of expense to impress me," she said to herself softly. "The real question now is, is he old, ugly, or infirm?"

She giggled to herself and leaned back to enjoy her ride of luxury, peeking out the windows as the carriage went past. The dark streets were quiet as most, both laborer and gentry, were retiring for their evening meal. Already, she could see the quality of stone that made up the streets had improved. Men in top hats escorted ladies carrying muffs, their worlds right and wonderful and perfect. She had a contempt for them all even as she envied what they had.

Then all at once, her view of that small slice of privileged life vanished. She yipped out loud as she startled back from her new view of a solid stone wall, moving quickly past, made visible only by the lights hanging at each corner of the coach. She leaned forward to look through another window and saw the same thing. The coach moved quickly through a narrowly constricted stone tunnel at speed.

"How are the horses not startling at such close quarters?" she asked herself, marveling at the sight. If she hadn't been looking out the window, she wouldn't have even noticed; the horses had not changed speed at all.

She almost leaned forward to speak to the driver, but she remembered at the last minute the warning in the letter of commission. No contact with the driver nor anyone else who was not her client for the night. A thread of apprehension slipped through her as she sat herself back against the comfortable cushions.

Now a whinny echoed out from the horses as the carriage slowed. Just beyond the crack in the curtain, the wall fell away. The carriage came to a full stop with a final whinny. She held perfectly still as the driver and footman both jumped down from the driver's seat. The door opened next to her, and she saw the footman bend over to pull out a small set of steps for her to use as she disembarked. Then he offered his hand. Through the small door, she saw another, larger one, made of ornate wood with torches blazing on either side.

Realizing there was no turning back, Beauty rolled her shoulders back and set her hand in the footman's offered one. Stepping out, she got a sense of the cavern all around them. Echoes of bats clicked and squeaked above. She did not flinch from them but stared in wide-eyed wonder. The space went twenty feet up easily, and the wall she faced looked as if hands had carved it flat. The large door set within seemed even eerier for it.

Before the door stood a man, clearly not her client. His posture spoke of breeding and training that only noble servants had. He also held a tray before him. As she crossed the few steps between them, he held out the tray to her. Upon it rested a mask.

It was beautiful, painted gold and cream, with stylized feathers around the edge wrought in silver. It wasn't until she picked up the mask that she realized ... it wasn't painted. The weighted thing was all made of gold, lying heavy in her hands. The backside was covered in finely carved ivorywood. Two black ribbons had been laced into the edges of the mask, clear indications of what she was expected to do with it.

That was when she noticed that the butler wore a mask too, a simple domino one of black. His eyes watched her patiently, waiting.

She slipped the mask on and tied the ribbon snugly behind her head. The mask fit incredibly comfortably.

Satisfied, the butler turned and opened the door for her. If she thought the entryway with its single door mysterious, the room beyond it was a wonder. A large room, it had everything in it she could desire for a night of pleasure. A grand bed sat to one side, large enough to fit a whole family and complete with a canopy and curtains. A large fire burned on the other side with chairs sitting before it. In the middle between these two stood a dining room table, laid with many covered dishes.

And at the far end, a man stood up as she entered. From the smoothness and confidence of his rise, she knew he was a gentleman raised. But that was all she could tell about him.

He wore a long cloak that covered his body, like the robe of a high priest. The hood hung over his face, more akin to an executioner's hood, obscuring any details except the most general of shapes. The most she could deduce was a noble brow and some well-defined cheekbones.

Upon his rising, the door behind her closed. Without hesitating a second, she spread her skirt out on either side of her and curtsied. "Greetings, Your Grace," she said diplomatically.

He visibly flinched, even underneath his shield of cloth. His gloved hands went behind his back, taking a defensive stance. "You know me, lady?" he asked, the warning a heavy undercurrent in his voice.

She shook her head, unintimidated. "Not at all, Your Grace. Your secrets are still safe from me."

His shrouded head cocked to the side a little. A small tell. She'd intrigued him. And if she were honest with herself, he had intrigued her, going so far as to even enshroud his face from her.

"If you do not know me, why do you address me so, lady?" he asked.

"It is worth my life to be able to count up the measure of a man in a glance," she said, coyly. "There are not many who would have so much to risk that they would hide their face from me as you have and to such an extent. You have much at stake here, thus you must be of the upper echelons of the upper echelons, which would make you a Duke," she cocked an eyebrow the same amount he had tilted his head. "At the very least."

He grunted, and she imagined that if she could see her patron's eyebrows, they would have pinched together. She waited, letting him study the companion he had acquired at great expense. This was always the tensest moment. Many men and some women who sought her company all came with preconceived ideas of what a courtesan would be like, all of them far from the truth. The trick was determining with the information provided, what sort of fantasy they sought and fulfilling it as best she could.

"What is your name?" her patron asked.

"Beauty, Your Grace, Virtue of the Crimson Court," she said, curtsying again.

"No, no," he said, waving a hand at her. "Your real name."

That question took her aback. She couldn't help herself. She broke out laughing.

CHAPTER 3

AN EXCHANGE OF NAMES

Maybe it was all the tension, but Lydia found she couldn't stop once she got going. She could even see that her patron was not amused as she was by her outburst of humor, but that just made the situation seem even more absurd, feeding her mirth.

"Have I said something amiss, lady?" he asked, sounding unsure of the situation. She could imagine, whoever he was, he was not someone who was used to being unsure about *any* situation.

"Please forgive me, Your Grace," she chortled, covering her mouth with her fingers, trying by sheer force of will to master herself. "It just struck me..." She cleared her throat before continuing. "You wish to know my true name while covering my face and obscuring your own." She gestured with a hand toward the door. "My coming here was even ensconced in secrecy, and they brought you a lady to share the night whose whole purpose is to present a fairytale larger than life for your pleasure, whose whole purpose in this world is to grant you such a thing. And you wish to know my true name?"

He stood there, taking in her words, and again, she knew she had said too much, but even if this night failed, she already had quite a story to tell ... if she dared.

"Beauty, then," he agreed, nodding once as if concluding negotiations. He gestured to the chair at the other end of the table. "Please would you join me, Virtue of the Crimson Court?"

"As Your Grace pleases," she agreed, curtsying once more, a small bob this time, not to tease him, but to show him her respect.

"You do not need to address me as such," he said. "I will call you Beauty and you may call me..." He hesitated a moment.

Offering a lie he hadn't prepared for, Lydia thought.

"...Damian," he said at last. "Please address me as Damian. I wish ... an evening with a true companion." The longing in his voice was not for lust, and it actually touched Lydia's heart and piqued her interest.

"That sounds lovely, Damian," she said graciously, giving him a warm smile that touched her eyes in turn.

Damian's covered head nodded once, and the masked butler stepped forward to uncover the dishes. A feast lay before her, and Beauty's eyes went wide.

The main attraction was a roast on a silver platter. A tray of oysters waited beside it along with a tureen for soup, dishes with braised leeks and asparagus as well as prepared cymbal berry compote, imported from the southern coast. Even more exotic, the final cover to be removed was a platter piled with a pyramid of bright oranges. All of it smelled divine.

Beauty gasped at the display before her. Courtesans rarely attended feasts and certainly not ones so richly laid out as this. There was enough presented to feed at least a half dozen people. Once all had been revealed, the butler went to her chair and pulled it out for her. She sat graciously, while her patron waited by his chair for the butler to return and help him into his own.

Then the butler proceeded to serve them. When the wine had been poured, her host held up his glass in one of his gloved hands.

"I thank you, lady, for joining me tonight," he said.

"And I thank you for this fine feast," she saluted in turn.

He moved to bring the glass to his lips, and she did the same as protocol prescribed, but he did not drink through or under the cloth draping his face.

"You will not be partaking, My Lord?" she asked, settling on that style since he still called her "lady."

He seemed to accept it. "My current requirements would make such a thing untenable," he pointed out.

"I would not judge you," she countered.

"I thank you for your courtesy, but I will not subject you to my visage—"

The butler cleared his throat at that, arresting his master's words.

Curious, Lydia thought.

"But please don't let me prevent you. Please enjoy," her host insisted.

Not needing to be told twice, Lydia did just that, using her cutlery in the way Georgiana had taught her to eat as elegantly as any noble. Grateful that she had learned, despite the fact that this sort of formal dining never came up in her time as a courtesan, Lydia felt confident enough to enjoy the meal before her.

A thought occurred to her, that her madame may have offered this training, and insisted on it actually, for this exact scenario with the person sitting across from her. She would not put it past the wily Queen of the Crimson Court to have been grooming her for this one specific someone. She had seen her do it before.

"Share your thoughts with me," Damian asked, and she realized she had gone too far inward.

"I am just savoring, My Lord," she said and cleared her mouth with the wine.

"You laughed earlier, and I would ask you a question about that," he said.

"I am sorry for that—" she started to amend, but he waved his hand away.

"Please don't apologize," he said impatiently. "Just be yourself."

"Uh... as you wish," she said, not really sure what to say otherwise. "What did you wish to ask me?"

"What... what does one..." he stopped and blew out a frustrated breath. "When one hires... engages one of your profession... what is typically expected?"

"Whatever you are interested in, which I believe you said was conversation," she teased. "In all honesty, it is not the request I get the most often, but one I do enjoy."

"And what topics do you gravitate to?" he asked.

She tilted her head. "You are allowing me to select the topic?"

"Please," he said.

Well, he did ask. "I like to study people."

"Yes, you said your life depended on it, I believe."

"My life and my livelihood." She picked up her wineglass and imbibed from it. *What am I doing?* she thought. *This is not a safe topic. I should have picked art or horses or something,*

The pause for that thought went on too long. "I also find horses engaging. Do you own any fine horses?"

"Yes. What did you detect in any of this that made you think I was a prince?" He gestured to the room around him. "I went to a lot of trouble to prepare things as comfortably and discreetly as possible, yet you sussed out my rank within seconds of seeing me, even through..." He gestured to his covered face and body. "...all this."

Again, the butler cleared his throat. He had his back to them, preparing something at the sideboard. The hairs lifted off the back of Lydia's arms. She hadn't said prince, but if he was a prince... There were many princes within the Empire, a couple of Archdukes above them, with only the Imperial Princes ranking between the Archdukes and the Emperor. A Duke would be at the bottom of the highest Echelon she knew. She had been too cavalier, and she knew better. Mistakes were dangerous.

"The men I have known in the past..." she started. "It is pleasing to them to be thought of as higher than their station, at least within the room with me."

He grunted at that. "The King of one's world as it were," he said.

"Yes, indeed," she agreed. There was no tension in her shoulders; conveying anxiety would be like blood in the water, but she felt momentarily safer.

"Then why did you not address me as 'Your Highness,' or even 'Your Excellency?'"

Curses! she thought, so he was higher ranked than she had thought. This patron seemed determined to trap her. "I am a loyal subject to the Imperial Crown. I would never go that far, even for a client."

"Hmm, somehow I don't believe that," her patron said, though he sounded bemused.

"I am not seeking to deceive you, My Lord or would you rather Your Highness?" she countered, as she took another bite of her roast, remembering to taste it this time.

Calm down, she internally ordered herself. *Georgiana would never put you into a situation where you were in danger.*

Except that wasn't entirely true, and she knew it. The rich and powerful of their empire, even if they would not get away with it in the end, by the time they met their justice it would not matter. She would already be dead. Little good it would do her then. And she did not wish to be another dead whore in the gutter.

He ignored her question about titles. "By your own admission, everything you do is to deceive. To create a fantasy to entice and beguile your client," he said.

Gods, she wished she could see his face and read his expressions. His voice had all the training of his kind, giving nothing away but pleasantries, hiding the trap underneath it all.

She had been sorely underprepared for this patron. The majority of her clients having been only interested in one thing, she had very little she needed to do to keep herself safe. They usually did most of the talking during the evening. Even the shy ones. This was different, and she did not like different.

"I have offended you," her patron suddenly said. His shrouded head looked away, and he cursed softly under his breath. "I'm making a mess of this aren't I?"

He stood then, turning away from the table to go toward the fireplace. "This was a mistake," he said to those flames.

Lydia didn't dare move a muscle, watching that back for a weighted moment, her heart pounding. She glanced over at the butler, who glanced back at her at the same moment, still holding a tray with prepared trifles waiting to be served.

Then her host turned his head toward her. Through the shroud hanging off his features, she could see his silhouette backlit by the fire, a shadow man with a fine profile.

"I will leave you."

Chapter 4

HE DESIRES STILL

"I will leave you," he said and turned, moving to one of the curtained-covered walls. He pulled aside the curtain to reveal another door hidden underneath. "See that she returns safely," he said to the butler.

"My Lord!" she called after, standing up alarmed.

Then he regarded her again, his head bowed. "Do not concern yourself. You will be fairly compensated in full. I apologize for putting you through this." And he turned once more toward his exit.

"My Lord, please wait!" she said. Her tone turned more commanding than beseeching, but it worked. Her patron hesitated, his back to her as he hovered in the doorway. The problem was she did not know what she planned to say to him. "Why—why are you leaving like this?"

"You do not have to fear, lady," he said. "You have done nothing wrong. The fault is with me and not your lovely company—"

"I would say the same, sir. You have nothing to fear from me," she said.

His whole body flinched, and she knew she was right.

"I am the one who must apologize," she said. "I originally supposed that the masks and the secrecy were to protect your identity, but this level of..." she hesitated.

"Speak!" he barked, then amended, "Please, lady."

"Shyness," she said carefully, "this denotes to me shame. You are ashamed of your appearance and the risk of censure by my eyes is too great for you to bear. Censure, I assure you, you imagine it to be far worse than I could possibly truly think."

"You have no idea," he said in a soft, self-condemning growl. "My visage has sent great men to blanching."

"Then they weren't very great at all, if they would be frightened by scarring or disease. I have seen plenty of both, My Lord, and it does not frighten me," she said with honest strength and resolution.

Her words touched him. She could see it in the way he turned back the merest inch, gravitating toward the slightest string of hope that maybe he would be accepted.

Her guess filled in the piece that had made her so apprehensive. Georgiana had chosen well amongst her Virtues, and she understood her purpose now. This was a man of means and title, who had lost something he could never regain amongst his peers. This understanding gave her comfort and strength, quieting her own fears.

"The various battles needed to keep this Empire safe have claimed many souls, and left others with broken bodies," she said. "Bodies that feel the need no less for companionship and acceptance. I have served such before."

His shrouded head turned full to look at her and she extended her hand. "Please, join me."

"Why would you stay, when you know that you will be compensated anyway?" he asked carefully. "Why would you want to?"

"Yes, I understand, but now I am curious."

"Of the freak under this cloth?" he sneered.

"Of the man, who despite every reason, still desires to hope," she said, smiling. "You called for a courtesan, not merely a piece of flesh from the street. I will hold your confidence as a priest and give comfort to you as an angel would, if you will only let me. Please, let me fulfill my purpose."

"Please," he said, his voice shaking. "Do not ... offer such to me, lady. My heart will not bear it if it proved false."

There was nothing to say to that, so she only continued to extend her hand and wait. It was his move on this board they played upon. At last, he stepped back into the room, letting his escape fall closed.

Beside her, the butler audibly sighed with relief.

Her mysterious patron returned to the table but did not immediately retake his seat. Instead, he set his gloved fingertips to the table. "All this was done," he started, clearly still wrestling with himself, "in a misguided bid to impress you."

"I am suitably impressed. The mystery and romance of it have been intriguing. I would like to hear your story."

"Even if it is not a particularly pleasant one?"

"What else do we have to do this evening?" she asked, already knowing the answer. She gestured to his chair. "Please join me. Eat something. This is entirely too much food for simply me."

"I would not put off your meal, lady," he said, disparagingly, but he did reclaim his seat, and Lydia counted that as a victory.

"In regards to me, you guessed rightly," he said. "I am, or was, a scion of the Imperial House."

"Our late Emperor was very prolific," she said, using the code commonly used in regard to his numerous children, both legitimate and illegitimate.

"My father was an immoral hound dog who jumped any bitch in heat whenever it suited him," her patron said harshly.

Lydia plucked up her wine glass to drink and cover her expression. "Such a thing to say of one's own mother," she said under her breath, but the silence in the contained room seemed to carry her words to him anyway.

"Yes, it is. You are right," he conceded, which surprised her. She was coming to like this patron more and more.

"The gods know I am a hypocrite in my thinking. I am my father's son well enough," he said just as disparagingly.

"I don't believe that," she said, cutting another bite of her roast. Now she tucked in with gusto since she was more assured now than before of her security. Though she did really wish he would eat something.

"And what is it you believe, lady?" he asked, again fingering his wineglass, looking more at ease than before with himself.

"That we are not bound by the sins of our parents, not if we don't let ourselves be."

"If only that were true, but my face would prove you wrong for it," he said.

"And you deepen your mystery still."

"Do you like fairy tales?" he asked abruptly.

"I have heard many," she said diplomatically.

"That is a judicious answer."

"Like I said, my stock and trade are in the creating of such flights of fancy. I would be remiss in not knowing the classics." At last, her plate was empty, and the butler came up beside her.

"Would you like more?" her host asked, in place of his silent servant.

"No, thank you. I think I am ready for that decadent trifle I saw before," she said, gesturing to the sideboard where it waited.

The butler nodded and went immediately to fetch it.

"Are you going to tell me a fairy tale?" she asked.

"If I was much of an orator, I would like to, but my simple facts will not do the story justice. But do you believe in curses?"

"I do, otherwise there is no justice in the world," she said, bobbing her eyebrows as she stuck a decadent mouthful to explode in her mouth. "Many a back alley crone makes her living fashioning such."

"Imagine if you will a young prince, handsome and master of his fortune."

"What prince would be worth his salt in a story if he were not handsome," she agreed.

"He had everything he could desire. Friends and boon companions. His health and intelligence."

"And all the women he could want to fill his bed, more than willing."

"Indeed," he agreed, lifting his own glass to take his own uncomfortable drink, only to remember too late the curtain before his face. Instead, he awkwardly put the glass back down. "He was not in want of companionship. All that was required of him was to be the face and voice for his people. Someone they could look up to and admire, to symbolize the Empire in all its glory."

"I think I do know where this story is going," Lydia said softly. Everyone knew the official story, and the rumors.

"Yes. And then. All of that went away. By some means outside of his control, his face and body were twisted and became something hideous. Something that could no longer represent the Empire. Or maybe it represented the Empire too well," he said the last as a dark, bitter afterthought.

Her patron lapsed into silence again, and despite not seeing his face, she felt he stared at the table and no longer at her. Using her tiny spoon, she scraped out the last bite from her dessert flute and set the spoon to the side of the glass. With silent perfection, the butler swept it away.

"And now the prince exists alone, in the dark and shadows. With no one to touch him or offer him company," she added. "A forgotten prince."

"Yes, the curse is quite complete. Any man who once called him friend has indeed forgotten his name and any woman abhors his touch."

"And yet, he desires these things still," she said softly.

"And yet, he desires these things still," he agreed.

She stood up from the table and looked to the butler. "Thank you," she said. "You may go now."

Normally, such a thing was a breach of protocol, but the butler's eyes seemed grateful to her. He bowed once at the waist and left out the door his master had almost taken before. Once it clicked shut, she turned and went to the bed. She didn't need to see her patron's eyes to know they followed her every movement.

She slipped her shoes off beside the bed and turned.

Chapter 5

THE FIRST TRYST

As much as Beauty loved her dress, it was made slightly differently than a typical woman's gown. Slipping her fingers across herself, slowly, seductively, she caught one of the hidden strings inside and pulled, undoing the tie. The dress opened itself like a rose blooming, slipping from her body as slowly as her arm had moved. It seemed like a magic trick, letting the cloth hug her curves as it dropped away.

Her patron was just as slowly leaning toward her as it dropped. She could feel his hungry gaze from across the room.

Underneath the dress, she did wear undergarments, but the minimum required. For one thing, she did not wear nearly enough petticoats to be considered decent, only the one to keep from being itchy. That she slipped down once the dress had pooled at her feet. She wore a chemise under her corset, but the side sleeves were already dipping low down her shoulders and the chemise itself was of the shorter variety. She kept both of those on. And the mask he had provided her, of course. Other than that, she was as the gods had made her.

Leaning back in just the short chemise and corset, she slid herself up onto the bed, flashing him a peek just below the chemise of her naturalness. The room's dimness added to the mystery. Out of the darkness, he appeared, like a shadow out of the night. She kept her eyes slit open to watch him.

He positioned himself before her knees, hesitation, maybe reverence, in his every move. Still, she waited. She was more than willing, this whole experience brought wetness and excitement to her as the tension between them built.

"Take off your gloves," she whispered throatily. She had bared so much of herself, it was only fair.

His hesitation bordered on frustrating, but at last, he complied, lifting his hands up to peel the gloves away one at a time. As he dropped them on the floor, she arched her back and his fingers reached for her. Gingerly, they touched her knee and even that little bit of contact sent shivers through her.

"Oh gods," he breathed, and his hands almost retracted. She didn't let them, reaching up to grab his wrists. His skin felt cooler to her touch, but she was near feverish. What a delight this night was turning out to be.

Taking control, she guided his hands, encouraging them up her thighs to the pooling of the short chemise. What she revealed and what she still concealed played into the visual tease she presented to him. Drawing him forward forced him to bring his knee up onto the bed, into the space between her legs. She brought her feet up to press into the mattress. Even at this close distance, the cloth covering his face only wavered, but did not reveal his face. She didn't need to see it, she didn't need all his secrets at once.

On their own accord, his hands continued up over her covered stomach, then over the mounds of her generous breasts. The corset hugged them to her body, but she had laced it looser than was fashionable so that one, she could breathe comfortably on her back, and two, if her client desired, he would be able to pop them out the top without her having to take it off.

Indeed he did desire, caressing over the tops of her mounds, seeking out more flesh. She moaned as his fingers found her aching nipples just as they cleared the upper edge of the corset. He groaned in response, returning her natural call. His body curled over hers, and she wondered for a moment if he had already completed his journey so easily. It wouldn't have been the first time, though she would have been disappointed. She was all excited herself.

She could see him breathing heavily, and she raised a hand to cup his face through the cloth. He froze, his desperate gasps halting sharply. Her hand found the outline of his jaw and cheek, whatever the substance of him, the outer edges were very pleasing.

"Come," she whispered and pulled him in even closer.

Letting her legs fall apart, she felt the scrape of the cloak he wore against the sensitive skin of her inner thighs. Releasing his face, she slid her hands down his shrouded body, at last parting the cloth.

She was not surprised to find clothing underneath, but at least like her, he had chosen to dress simply. Expertly, her fingers sought out the clasp holding him back and was delighted to discover that he had wisely done as she had and wore next to nothing underneath. Tugging up on his buttoned shirt she found his skin, cooler than her own but warmer than his hands. Like her, his gentle nether hair felt coarse but clean.

Finding his girth, she wrapped her hands around him and pulsed.

He groaned out louder, nearer to a cry of completion, but she could tell again that he resisted it.

Such discipline, she thought admiringly. This was no virgin she dealt with, this was a man with some skills in love, just long starved.

The thought became even more validated when he shifted to the side of her body, instead of plunging into her. She didn't know what he was about until his own fingers found her lower lips. He parted them with a stroke, and she shivered as he tested her waters.

"I want to hear you," he begged.

Accepting the invitation, she let out a full-throated cry of her own. Maybe it wasn't entirely in earnest, but it had a wonderful effect on both of them. Her inner lips moistened even more, and his finger rolled in a circle, the pad of it seeking out the measure of her flower petals. Crying again, this time in more earnest, she pressed up her pubic bone to brush against his obliging hand.

"Yes," he breathed, enjoying her music. "God, it's been so long." He continued to play her, and she allowed him to, relaxing into the act. Her pleasure grew more intense with each stroke and exploration. He reached his finger in and found the spot to the front that sent an aching need through her, to clench and drive against the obliging digit. Soon he had two and then three fingers inside her, seeking out more spots, and she encouraged such daring exploration. This was a man who had come to enjoy her fully, not just a simple fuck and flee. It was akin to finding a dance partner who could in fact really dance.

"Do you wish to cum now?" he whispered, his breath barely touching her ear through the cloth, but warm all the same.

"Not yet," she answered breathlessly; though it had been a tough debate, she didn't. He was eliciting great pleasures from her, but he did not quite reach the deepest spot within her. She longed for that feeling of fullness that she could grip against and ride to final completion.

"I want to feel you within," she whispered. "Please, My Lord."

"My lady angel," he whispered back, so full of hunger it was near a groan.

He shifted again, bringing himself back to the place between her legs. His own were still bound together by his trousers, the cloth of his robe sliding along her body, making it awkward for him to move.

"Dammit," he muttered, as he tried to get himself into alignment, and clearly embarrassed by his lack of suaveness in that moment.

She wanted to laugh but knew it would be interpreted wrongly. His antics were charming and sweet. Instead, she lent assistance, reaching between them to help direct his generous girth to the right entrance.

"Here, My Lord," she whispered, gently, and he looked up into her face. She still couldn't see him, the covering still holding to its function, yet she could feel the intensity of his eyes. His lower head entered her folds, and she gasped and arched... at first for show and then in truth as he filled her all the way to the hilt. The sensation rocked inside as he reached the place where she ached and pressed into it.

"Oh fuck yes!" she called out, then blanched at the breach of decorum, the piercing of the fantasy.

But this time *he* laughed, satisfied chuckles that thumped against her chest as he held in place. Then he moved, shifting out to drive back in, creating a rhythm that she could join. This was no mere thumping of rabbits copulating in an urgent hurry. This was music. This was a continuation of the dance, and her partner knew the steps. He dipped and swirled while she clenched and shifted, giving as good as she was getting.

"Dear Lord!" she called as pre-tremors rippled through her, pumping wetly around his strong erection. "Don't stop!" she ordered when he hesitated after an initial gushing.

"Yes, my lady," he murmured as if she were the patron and he was in service to her.

He continued on, and she felt herself mounting toward a conclusion. Whether it was the right thing to do or not, she no longer cared. She wanted this, wanted to feel a relief she had not in a long time. The fact that he was driving it made it all the sweeter.

Her voice rang out unabashedly as she climbed the mountain toward the heavens. She was so close and so mindless of the need to complete that she dared to slip her own finger down between them, finding her pearl. Lightning struck the mountain. She swore something crude as it hit, but she had no memory of what it could have been. Her entire being exploded.

As she crested and coasted down, she became aware that the man above her still drove hard, only steps behind her. Dreamily, she looked up at his form, his back arched, his head thrown back. And with each thrust, the curtain hiding his features moved clear, unrealizing as she stared up into the face of Death.

CHAPTER 6

A NIGHT OF MIRACLES

Her patron completed moments later, arching down as hard as he had been arching up. The cloth obscured the skull-like visage beneath once more as he shuddered through his last tremors of ecstasy.

Lydia looked away, turning her head to the side as she waited for him to catch himself up, hoping her face did not reveal any true feelings about what she had just seen. After working so hard to gain his trust, such a breach was unthinkable. The passing thought, that she had copulated with Death himself, or even a demon, whistled through and out the way it came. She knew this was a man. A desperate man who had done her no harm and had in fact been far kinder than so many others. Taking a breath in, she ordered her body to relax and sink.

Her patron shifted off of her then, curling onto his side as he gasped for breath. Again, the cloth lay over his face, outlining his features. He had a nose and mouth, a cheek and jawline... a complete face. She could not have seen a Death's Head like she thought. It had to be a trick of the light and shadow.

Bringing her legs together, she pulled her shorter chemise over herself and waited for him to collect himself.

After several moments, her patron's hand came up to cup her face, making her gasp involuntarily herself. He retreated an inch, but she recaptured his fingers and pressed them once more against her skin, in defiance of her stupid, superstitious feelings.

"My apologies, My Lord. I had drifted into the realm of twilight," she whispered.

"Don't apologize, sweet lady," he whispered back. "This is more than I dared hope for."

She gave him a gentle smile and closed her eyes. *He is a man. Just a man. He feels like a man. There is no hint of brimstone about him.* She breathed in. A scent of male musk and their own lovemaking, for sure. The fire beyond added smokey wood and the remnants of their meal. All normal, earthly things.

She returned her focus to her patron.

"You are a man who knows his lovecraft," she murmured.

"What happens now?" he asked, his thumb tracing her eyebrows. "Typically?"

"Well... Usually, my patron rolls over and goes to sleep. You seem to have much more stamina than the usual," she said, and another thought occurred to her. *Would he desire to go again?*

"It has been so long," he said, clearly not hearing her thoughts, thank the gods.

"I imagine you had a great many lovers?" she asked, turning herself so she more or less faced him, pillowing her arm under her head since they were a good bed length away from the actual pillows.

"A great many," he agreed. "It was something I felt quite accomplished about, being a great lover."

"I applaud your efforts," she said, mirthfully. "I cannot speak of how often I am the one who has to take the lead."

Her patron chuckled. "Did you have one of those rods like the governesses have? In which it instills correction?"

She laughed as well. "You jest, but you would be surprised what gets requested from one such as me."

"Really?" he asked, as surprised as she said he would be.

"We all have our needs," she said. "No different than you, My Lord."

He sobered at that. "Quite different from me."

She decided not to keep arguing that point and pursued another. "So there has been no other to touch you as I have since..." she brushed her fingers against the cloth and the face hidden underneath. "Since this happened to you?"

"None could stomach the sight of me, and even in this covering, none would tolerate my touch. This ... solution was a last hope."

"That must have been very difficult for one so used to touch," she said, truly sympathetic.

"Every man wished to be my friend and every woman my lover," he said with macabre humor as if he were reciting something commonly said of him. "Yes, it was very hard to find myself alone."

"Show me," she said softly. She did not expect to say it, but the words could not be taken back. Instead, she leaned in, reaching for his shroud.

"No!" he barked and turned, rolling himself off the bed and away into the safer shadows. She sat up, pulling back up on her corset to tuck her breasts more securely within.

"My Lord, wait!" she called after him. "I apologize for my forwardness. I only want to assure you, there is nothing—"

"Please lady!" he called, swinging his hand out toward her before her bare feet could slip from the bed. "Please do not pursue me."

"I only wish to assure you, you are safe here with me."

He laughed maniacally like a madman would, and she hesitated at the end of the bed.

"On a night full of miracles, I will not be fooled into believing that such a *complete* miracle as that could even possibly be up for offer," he sneered. "You are an excellent liar, but please take care. I am not one to be treated as a complete fool!"

"My Lord, please—"

"Enough!" he roared, his anger dangerous.

Lydia froze, heeding the warning, understanding the danger. She had pushed him too hard, and he had power. Real power. And as she believed before, maybe he would pay for whatever harm was done to her, being blacklisted alone when he had such desires and needs would be torture enough, but it would not matter to her if she were dead.

"This is enough," her patron bellowed and grabbed a cord that blended into the curtained walls. Tugging hard, a bell somewhere sounded. The hidden door opened, and the butler reappeared. His master stood before the door, and the butler bowed to him smartly, before glancing over to Lydia.

Despite her profession, she scrambled for her dress to hold it in front of herself for modesty's sake. Usually, being seen in such a state by men was nothing to her, but her emotions were raw and vulnerable, and she wished more to cover her distress than her skin. The butler wordlessly looked away and spoke softly to her patron.

"See to it," he snapped, not taking the care of his servant to curb his voice. He exited then, a shadow of cloak and hood, through the door and was gone.

Angry tears actually beaded in Lydia's eyes as she turned her back to the butler and pulled her dress up over herself. Unfortunately, the trick of the string that secured it was difficult to manage on her own, especially with her hands shaking.

"Could you please, sir, help me with this," she said, turning back to the waiting butler.

He said nothing, but nodded once and crossed, all the while keeping his eyes downcast.

"Please just loop and tie it here," she said, indicating with a finger what she meant.

He followed her instructions, and soon, she was returned to her original state of dress, though her hair had been undone by her recent activities. Pulling the carved pins, she let it fall over her shoulders.

"I am ready to return," she said softly, as she stepped into her slippers still by the bed.

"Very good, ma'am," the butler mumbled so automatically she was sure he hadn't realized he had spoken for the first time at all.

Yet, he hesitated a moment, turning himself back toward her, clasping his hands behind his back. "Thank you, for trying," he said.

The gratification took her aback a moment. "I don't know if I helped," she said earnestly.

The butler only grunted, having violated the rules to say that much, and turned to lead her out of the room through the door she came in. The carriage still remained, and she was helped in by the butler himself, the footman and driver rushing to reprepare the horses to take her home.

Lydia wrestled with her feelings as she rode back in silence. She had done her best, she knew that. Going over every interaction, every exchange, she couldn't be certain what she could have done or said differently with so many unknown variables.

"If only someone had warned me sooner so that I knew more of what I was getting myself into," she muttered softly. She understood his desire for anonymity, but it had not helped her to succeed. And yet, succeed she had, in truth. She had lain with him, and he had enjoyed the experience as much as she had. It really had been the minimum required of her, so why did she feel so utterly unsatisfied by it? Never had a patron left her feeling so resolutely heartbroken. Angry and disappointed, yes. Ill-used, for certain, but heartbroken? It was far worse than any of those.

"And I did what was asked!" she hissed at herself.

But still, her heart did not care for her argument.

Chapter 7

A DEEP DARK DECISION

Damian lay on his back next to the deep, dark pit. "If I threw my regret within, it would not even begin to fill it," he muttered aloud. The dismal dark around him did not reply.

"Don't start writing poetry. You're abysmal at it," a cheeky, reedy voice did.

Turning his head up from where he lay on the rough, ruined ground, Damion saw his friend sitting on one of the broken ledges. While Damian wore a loose shirt with trousers and no shoes, not too far off from a common tramp, Alexandros wore the finest in suits with a crisp white shirt and a smart bowler hat on his head. His black shoes, which were naturally polished to a shine, were pressed together side by side. One would think he was a gentleman out for his lunch on a park bench, rather than someone sitting on top of a pile of rubble deep underneath the Imperial City.

He gazed down at Damian lying there with his hands folded neatly on his lap. "I should know, I *was* a poet. And a playwright. And a soldier. And a butcher, baker, candlestick maker."

"You do not have to be here you know," Damian said with disgust, lying back to stare up into the darkness above.

"From what I understand, and granted that is limited as there is still so much in the world to learn, you seemed to have had a very good time enjoying her company. I simply do not understand why you are letting how it ended taint the entire experience," Alexandros said airily. He took off his bowler and started brushing at it with his sleeve.

"That's because you are a fool," Damian said uncharitably, throwing his arm over his eyes. "And so am I."

"Well, I for one, am happy with the experiment. I think we can conclusively prove that there *is* a female in the world who is not going to have a problem with whatever it is you say is wrong with your face," Alexandros declared as he adjusted the hat back onto his head.

"What good is that when she will never come back again? Not after how I screamed at her like a deranged madman."

"I have noticed that, often, if you can throw enough money at someone, they can get over anything." Then he shook his shoulders like a bird resettling his feathers. "Except me of course."

"Why am I taking advice from you when you fly into a panic attack any time you have to meet someone new?" Peeling himself off the cold stone ground, Damian stepped up close to the edge of the pit.

"If you jump down there again, I'll just pull you back up. I can do it, you know, but I really like this suit, and I would wish you would be more considerate of me," the well-dressed man said.

"I am always considerate of you."

That earned him a snort.

"And how do you know she will never come back again? Did you ask her?"

"I do not need to. I wouldn't return if I was able to." He started walking along the lip, like he had many times before.

Alexandros simply watched, unworried, which was ironic considering how many things in life his secretary did, in fact, worry about. Somehow Damian's life was never one of those things, no matter what ended up happening to him.

By the time Damian got to the end of the lip, where the rubble of the city-that-was blocked any progress, he had made up his mind.

"Send the letter."

"Oh thank the gods." Alexandros popped up onto his feet. "I'll get it out immediately. Oh, and also..." Going into the inner pocket of his coat, the secretary pulled out an envelope sealed with a familiar wax seal. "She has sent another one."

Damian took it and immediately threw it into the pit.

Alexandros sighed as he watched it disappear into the dark. "I have a difficult time understanding how you were once the most desirable man in all the empire."

"Just leave it down there this time," Damian said, his hands shaking. He pointed at the letter that was already gone. "Regina has already said everything there is to say. That is just about easing her guilt."

"I am aware that I have said this before, but being at peace with one's self and able to please one's self is the greatest gift."

"I am not like you, Alexandros. We've been over this. You are made for such an existence. The gods didn't make man that way."

"As a matter of fact, they did. I have shared many pleasurable evenings in the company of such, men and women, who have no interests or needs 'of the flesh,' as you seem so desperate for. What I speak of is possible."

"I wasn't debating that. Yes, it is possible, but not for me. The gods blessed you to be a self-contained being all onto yourself, but forged my nature to long for companionship," Damian said, growling each word.

"Which is why it is mystifying to me as I watch you take actions to deny that nature." Alexandros crossed his arms.

"Because of the risk!"

"But it wasn't such a risk before. You practically snapped and a woman hopped into your bed."

"And we have come full circle." Damian spun on his heel and marched down the slope through the dark, back to his rooms in the Undercourt. Alexandros let him go, much to the forgotten prince's relief. He valued his friend like no other, but the secretary could also be too much and not enough at the same time.

Passing through the doorway to his rooms, the door slammed hard into the jamb with the clang of finality like a prison, or a coffin. Standing there, he surveyed his rooms.

They were comfortable enough and not too unlike what he had when he had lived topside in the sun. Still, now they felt cloying and suffocating as they were empty, not the safe refuge they had been when he had first fled the world.

Passing into his bedroom with slow, plodding steps, his eyes drew once more to his bed. Coming to the end of it, he laid his hand on the coverlet where she had lain. Even if she hadn't been the most beautiful woman he had ever seen, he had been utterly captivated by her. It had been her eyes. It was as if she could see him, even through the mask he wore. Kneeling down at the end of the bed, he slid his fingers along it, desperate to find some trace of her that had been. Disgusted with himself, but unable to do otherwise, he pressed his face to it, searching for a whiff of her scent.

"The gods have really thrown me to the dust. I am a worm crawling on my belly," he said harshly as he spun around to drop onto the ground, pressing his back against his bed.

But he could still see her. She was like everyone he had ever been with. Truly. The same tricks that he did to them worked on her. And she responded beautifully. The sound of her voice had been like music. Even when she talked, he could listen to her speak for hours about nothing...

He chuckled at the memories then shook his head. "No. She simply made me feel human again. Nothing more."

If there had ever been a woman he could have loved, it would have been Regina. He knew he didn't have what it took to go through that again. Loving a woman like that simply wasn't in his nature and never had been.

"But respect. Companionship," he said the words out loud. What more could anyone really even hope for in this world?

Not love. Never love.

"But what if *she* wants that?" he asked, thinking of Beauty. It had been a complication he had dealt with a few times. Regina never cared about the women he bedded, unless the woman in question took her grievances to his fiancée.

But he shook his head at the ridiculousness of a courtesan of the Crimson Court falling in love with a hideous monster like him. "That is too much to expect. There is no possibility of her falling for me that way, so I should not even consider it. How arrogant can I really be?"

He knew a courtesan's job was to make men believe that they were falling in love though. It was the fantasy after all. "I will just have to assure her that she does not need to play such games with me." He would never be so cruel as to ask such of her.

"But the truth. She may show me the truth without repercussions." Again, he wondered if he was wanting too much. The truth was a rare thing in the Imperial Court. To desire it often got one killed. It was insane that he should hunger for it now.

He touched his face again. *Especially when the truth is so very cruel.*

CHAPTER 8

AN OFFER OF ENDOWMENT

It wasn't until a couple of days later that Lydia went to speak to the Queen of Virtues. No one but her maid had greeted her when she returned from her interesting assignation, but a message had been waiting that invited her to join the matron. At Lydia's convenience, of course.

"Well, my dear!" Georgiana exclaimed when Lydia made her appearance. "How *was* your evening?"

"Downright infuriating if I'm honest," Lydia declared and sat on Georgiana's settee as resolutely as any petulant adolescent.

"Really? Not exactly the reaction I was expecting," her madam said, shifting in her own seat toward the tea set beside her. Her maid was already in attendance, preparing a fresh cup to offer her mistress. "I have something stronger, if you prefer?"

"No, tea will suit just fine, thank you," Lydia said, recollecting her manners. "And what reaction did you expect exactly?"

"Well, I guess that depends. *Did* you see his face?" Georgiana asked carefully.

"Yes, though he tried very hard to keep that from me," Lydia declared, accepting her own prepared cup.

"You did?"

"You seemed surprised," the Virtue of Beauty noted.

"Well, if I can be perfectly frank my dear, I had thought that if you had seen his face, you would be in here with tears, and I would be serving you my strongest scotch."

"Have you seen it?" Lydia asked.

"I have," the older woman said, soberly.

"And you did not think to warn me? Or at least explain to me what I was getting myself into."

The Queen pursed her lips together as if she had tasted something sour. "Let us say I had faith in you."

"And yet you expected me to be in tears," Lydia sniffed at that.

The Queen of Virtues gave a little shrug. "I am a realist as well, but I am relieved that I was right about you."

Then, a calculating look crossed the madam's face. "What did you think of him?" she asked carefully.

Lydia thought back to the man draped in shadow. "He is ... intriguing."

Georgiana's eyes went round. "So you laid with him?" she asked, reading between her words.

"Yes!" Lydia declared, quite exasperated. "It was what I was commissioned for after all."

"And ... how was it?"

That question softened the courtesan as she remembered. "It was delightful. He was... is a skilled lover. But honestly, I would have appreciated more warning of who I was serving. I went in there with all the wrong arrows in my quiver!"

"You have gone to a client with less information before, and I would think his circumstances would have made it quite evident why you were not informed further as to his state."

"For fear I would have said 'no' outright? I wouldn't have done that," she said defending her integrity.

"And what did you think of his company?"

"What does that matter?" Lydia demanded, then checked herself. This was not the serenity a courtesan of the Crimson Court should display, but her normally disapproving Queen did not seem to even notice the petulant behavior.

"Indulge me," Georgiana pushed. "Forget about the carnal relations and speak of the man himself."

Lydia blew out a breath. "Well, I can see why he was the Crown Prince once." She eyed the Queen a breath, but there was no reaction to that statement. Georgiana was not surprised that she had guessed, which meant she knew and expected her courtesan to have figured it out on her own. "His conversation is excellent, his charm and intelligence more than evident even in his diminished state. We did not get into particulars such as art, music, or his opinions of the theater, but I find myself interested to know them. I dare say, he probably has more of a grasp of the sciences than the average, and I know he has traveled the world."

"You sound like a girl with a playground mash," Georgiana mused, smiling slyly.

"Please," Lydia scoffed at such a notion. "I am not infatuated with him. I'm simply saying... I enjoyed his conversation, as little of it as there was."

"Do you think you would partake of his bed again? Could you?"

Georgiana did not ask such a loaded question lightly, and Lydia decided straight truth was her best option.

"The answer is yes, if he so wished it. I have no issues with his touch or his bed. Yet, I am sure he will not ask for me again," Lydia said, dourly. "I forgot myself, and it sent him into a rage at the end." She set her teacup to the side, no longer taking comfort in its warmth. "I am sorry, but I did not represent the Crimson Court well. I conducted myself like a balmy wench on her first dalliance."

The Queen of Virtues *hmmm*'d at that. "Well, it is done, and considering the circumstances, I think you are being too hard on yourself. And as for a repeat request for your company, one has already arrived."

The madam gestured with a hand, and her maid brought forth a gorgeous bouquet of flowers. Georgiana plucked the card from the bunch and handed it over to her charge. "This arrived this morning with a generous bag of coins."

Unsure, Lydia took the card and stared at the white envelope. "He sent a purse?" she asked, a bit confused. Considering how she left him, it was the last thing she expected. "I thought everything was paid for in advance?"

"It was," Georgiana said. "It seems you *are* a credit to me." The madam noted Lydia's face before she disciplined the expression away. "Tell me what happened, child. I have heard it all before, you cannot shock me."

"It is just..." Lydia worried at her bottom lip with her teeth.

Georgiana's chin popped up an inch higher. "Did he strike you?"

Lydia blanched at that. "No, nothing like that. I... I only asked to see his face. I had glimpsed it during the course of our coupling, so I wished him to feel at ease with me, especially since I had already experienced the worst of the shock. After what he has lost, I wished to give him some small solace of being completely accepted as he is."

She didn't realize Georgiana was staring at her until she had finished speaking. "You are a wonder, child," the older woman said. "Never in a thousand years will I find another like you."

At that, Lydia blushed. Georgiana's praise was worth more than all the gold in the fallen prince's purse.

"How did you guess he was the former Crown Prince? Did he tell you?" Georgiana asked.

"Of course not. Please grant me some credit," Lydia said, setting the card in her lap. "Every man, woman, and child knows the story of the cursed Crown Prince Regulus."

The Queen laughed dryly. "Truly, most have already forgotten about him as nothing more than a footnote to his brother's ascension."

"My memory is not so short. Even if I bought the official explanation, the fact that his name disappeared from everyone's lips..." She licked her own. "Well, now I understand why. The rumors are closer to the truth than that official statement was."

"Thus is the nature of most Imperial statements," Georgiana said dismissively.

"So *what* is the whole truth?" Lydia asked. "How did this ... curse for lack of a better word, happen?"

Georgiana shook her head. "An old witch must keep her secrets, child. Especially dangerous ones like that. You are better off not knowing, especially if you continue to associate with him."

"Has he really requested my company again?" Lydia asked.

"Yes, in no uncertain terms, though I expect this meeting will be more business than pleasure. I believe he intends to offer you a Mistress Endowment."

Lydia's eyebrows shot up, though some part of her was not entirely surprised. "I will admit the thought had occurred to me that this might be where it was leading, but still, to hear it stated as fact..."

"Please, child, it is not fact yet, but if it does not come to pass, I will be truly shocked and shall retire from this profession entirely," the Queen declared, passing her cup back to her maid to be refilled. "In another respect, this is a sad and proud day for me. I will be sorry to lose my Beauty, but I could not be happier for you. I see you as I would my own daughter and it's such an accomplishment at such a relatively young age."

"Am I to negotiate terms myself?" Lydia asked.

"No, of course not! What kind of Queen would I be if I did not intervene in this matter? Believe me, child, we are going to take him for all he's worth," she said with a chuckle nearer to a cackle of impish delight.

Still, Lydia could not partake in her Queen's delight. Her insides had filled with butterflies, and she accepted another cup of tea, taking a long sip, letting the warm brew fortify her stomach. "Well, I am glad to have served as I have. It was an interesting experience all the same."

Lydia's mind's eye filled with the memory of the death-shrouded former prince in his opulent tomb of stone. It was something right out of a storybook or a cheap penny dreadful.

"Are you having second thoughts, my child?" Georgiana asked. "You will be saddled with him during the terms of your endowment and—"

"The darkness of men is not in their faces," Lydia said, with the weight of previous knowledge. "It's their darkness of soul that reviles me. I saw only sadness in his."

"Ha, there is no member of the Imperial Household who survives long without stains on their souls," Georgiana warned.

"And I am a whore made good. Like my soul is any cleaner," Lydia dismissed. She opened his note, reading the short contents within.

I will grant your request.

"If he will have me, I will not refuse his offer."

"I will send your reply immediately."

Chapter 9

NEGOTIATIONS

Lydia felt strange sitting next to Georgiana as the carriage drove them to the meeting. For one thing, she was more properly dressed than her usual assignation wear. Instead of her lovely scarlet gown with its tricks for quick removal or any number of similar gowns, she wore a soft rose pink with all the proper petticoats beneath it. It was the color traditionally worn by a future Mistress, symbolizing her transition from the Crimson District. Her corset cinched to the proper tightness, she felt contained by her clothing, more like armor than a dress. She even had on ankle boots instead of the usual easily discarded slippers, and a proper bonnet.

Georgiana wore something similar, only in a soft buttercup yellow with a bonnet that covered her steel-colored hair. To anyone else on the outside, they would have looked like a mother and daughter on their way to pay a visit to an old friend.

"Please stop fiddling my dear, you look well," Georgiana said, covering Lydia's kid-gloved hands with her own so that she would stop undoing and redoing the button there. "You're like a bride on her wedding day."

Lydia made a face at the turn of phrase, but this was probably as close as she would ever get to matrimony. It all seemed rather fast to her, but such an offer was not one to sleep on.

"Do you think we should stop and get you a bouquet?" Georgiana asked, suddenly.

"You can't be serious?" Lydia exclaimed.

"I think it would be a nice touch," the older woman defended.

"Why not an apple in my mouth while we're at it?"

The Queen of Virtues huffed a disappointed sigh. "Too late to make the stop anyway," she declared, and that, thankfully, was the end of it. "My dear, I wish to ask, what do you know of the Undercourt?"

Lydia blinked at the question. "It is a collection of spies and whispers at the service to the Imperial Court and is as much rumor as it is fact?"

Georgiana made a small sound in her throat but said nothing more as she kept her eyes straight ahead just as the carriage disappeared into its stone tunnel. Though the curtains were drawn again, Lydia only became aware of it when the sound shifted outside.

The younger woman went back to fiddling with her button, holding her breath as they traveled through. At last, they pulled into the cavern and up to the single door. Torches were burning merrily, and the butler from before waited, still wearing his domino mask. Like the previous night, the footman opened the door and pulled out the step, but Georgiana disembarked first, taking everything in stride with an easy aplomb Lydia wished she could imitate.

As Georgiana approached the butler, he bowed formally to her, and she curtsied in return. They said nothing to each other, but it felt as if true sentiments had been exchanged nonetheless. When Lydia approached beside her, he bowed to her as well, and she very well couldn't refrain from curtsying if her Queen had.

Then the butler opened the door to allow the two women inside.

The room had not changed much, though the table was reset and the bed remade.

Her patron stood at the far end of the table as they entered.

Instead of the full body cape, he too had dressed for the occasion. Still in black, his swallowtail coat matched his black breeches tucked into knee-high boots. He stood as he had the night before with his hands tucked behind his back as he waited, pulling on the coat, showing that the waistcoat underneath was in fact a fine iron gray, embroidered simply, yet the declaration of money reflected all the same. Yet, his appearance was still queer as he had a cowl over his head, which allowed the cloth cover to obscure his face once more.

Georgiana went to him immediately, extending her hand for him to take. He gallantly did, his hand gloved, and made the motion of kissing it even if he couldn't actually extend the contact.

"Wonderful to see you so well, Your Highness," she said, curtsying to him.

"Please, you are the Queen here, and I am your humble servant," he said so smoothly Lydia was most impressed.

"Your Highness," she said and bobbed. She kept her eyes averted to the ground and waited for permission to rise since he had the higher rank.

"Damian," he said, a catch in his voice.

Now she looked up, a bit confused.

He cleared it again and replaced his hands behind his back. "I am Damian to you, lady."

She blinked at that and straightened. "Lydia," she offered.

"Lydia," he said, tasting her name. Somehow when he said it, it sounded musical. He cleared his voice again. "I apologize for my behavior the other night," he added, and this time he bowed his head in apology.

"It is understood. I asked too much—"

"No!" he barked in urgency instead of anger, then corrected. "I was a beast, and it was uncalled for."

She nodded graciously. "Then I accept your apology."

He let out a breath of relief.

"Now that is settled, let us begin the negotiations," Georgiana said, pleasantly.

"Yes," he agreed and gestured toward the table. The butler moved to help Georgiana into the chair at the foot, but the prince... Damian came to set Lydia in hers. Once the butler had seated his master, a fourth man appeared, entering through the "secret" door.

"This is my personal assistant Alexandros. He is also my cousin and will document what is agreed upon today," Damian said matter-of-factly.

The personal assistant bowed to the ladies, his face blushing red as he stuttered a greeting and then took his seat to the right hand of the prince. He opened a leather folder and pulled out a neatly written parchment, which he set on the table and turned to slide over toward Georgiana. She plucked it up immediately with Lydia leaning in to look over it.

"This is our opening offer," he said smartly, apparently finding more confidence in his assigned task. "It is of course subject to change, but we hope that you will find it most generous."

Lydia nearly gasped unseemingly. She looked up at Georgiana to be sure she read the top item correctly, but the Queen of Virtues was still reading, mouthing the words as she went through the whole parchment. Once at the bottom, her eyes shot back up to the top.

"The county of Summerbourne along with the title and style of Countess of the Imperial Order?" Georgiana read out loud before looking up over the paper at Damian.

He had sat back in his chair, one leg over the other in the comfortable form of a prince, one hand resting on the table's surface as he waited for her to read. "It is one of my own estates, and I am free to bestow it how I will," he responded. "It will be granted to her in perpetuity upon her completion of five years of service. To her and to any descendants she may have, according to her own will and dictates."

"A countess?" Lydia said out loud, as if that might make it even more real. "He is going to make me a countess?"

"After five years, yes, it would appear so," Georgiana said under her breath, though she did not seem very enthused by the idea. "Is Summerbourne not the traditional estate given to the wife of the crown prince?" she asked, louder than their host.

"If it is available, but it is not. It was granted to me and remains mine to do with as I please," Damian said. "Another estate is already being prepared for my brother's future wife, and none will gainsay my choice."

"None wants it now that it's associated with a cursed prince, more like," Georgiana muttered just loud enough for Lydia to hear.

"Why after only five years?" Lydia asked, her head swimming. "I... I will not..."

"Five years is a typical term of service for an endowed mistress. Is there an option to renegotiate to extend at the end of service, if both parties wish it?" Georgiana asked.

"Of course!" the secretary said as if offended.

Lydia skimmed down the rest of the document. Servants, horses, carriages, and a yearly annuity were also on offer in exchange for her exclusive attention. Everything she could ever want: comfort and security. Choices. Most of all choices. To own something that was solely hers that no one could take away.

She barely heard any of the further words from the wheeling and dealing on minor points as her ears filled up and her breathing came quickly. For a frightening moment, she thought her vision had blanked away and she would pass out, but she sat back and forced herself to breathe slowly. Shutting her eyes before they were shut for her, she simply focused on inhaling, then exhaling, then inhaling again. How could this not be a dream? An impossible, wonderful dream.

"Are you well, my lady?" Damian's warm voice cut through the ringing in her ears.

"I am just... I am..." Lydia tried to speak, but no words came to her. At least no appropriate words. What she wanted to say was *All this for one night's fuck?* But Georgiana would murder her on the spot if she voiced that, and Lydia wouldn't blame her.

"Can we have some water?" he asked, gesturing for his butler, who had already acted to pour her a glass and bring it to her on a tray.

"Thank you," she said and took a sip. It was cold, another surprising luxury, and it did much to cut through the rising bile in her stomach.

"Will this suit?" Damian asked her directly. "Is there anything else you want?"

"I..." she looked up and then at Georgiana. Her Queen gave her a small nod to go ahead.

"May I have a word with you alone?" she asked before adding. "Damian."

Chapter 10

FURTHER NEGOTIATIONS

"Of course," Damian said and gestured toward his secretary.

A bit discombobulated, Alexandros jumped to his feet and then turned to Georgiana. "Uh, m-m-m-may I take you for a-a-a-a constitutional, madam... I mean lady... I mean—"

"Yes, you may," Georgiana said graciously, offering her hand to be helped up from her seat.

"Take her to the Undergarden," Damian said, standing as she rose, giving the Queen of Virtues a small bow as she exited.

Once they were alone, the butler retreated with his own bow and followed behind out the same door. It shut with a grim finality and only then did Lydia look up at her partner in this endeavor.

He had remained standing, the tips of his fingers giving away his anxiety as he fidgeted like a youth at his first festival dance.

"Please, sit," she invited. "I promise I will not devour you whole."

He let out a breath that evolved into a laugh as the tension between them bled away. "I hope these proceedings have not upset you. I had wanted to make an impression, but I fear I may have given the wrong one."

She looked to the offer on the table and set her fingers upon this. "Do not get me wrong, this is incredibly generous. More than I could have ever hoped to have in a lifetime."

"But it is not enough," he said darkly.

"My Lord?" she asked.

He gestured violently at his face. "To get over this. To get beyond the destruction of my face."

She set her hand on his fist. "I have not seen your face. Nor would it make a difference if I had."

He stilled, then lowered his fist to his knee, and she returned her own to her lap. "Then what is the apprehension? Is it the speed with which these proceedings are taking place?"

Again she shook her head. "No, I do not think it is that. After all, do not marriages between you nobles occur with this level of alacrity?"

His head tilted up. "Ah, I see. 'You nobles.'"

I can't believe he caught that, she thought.

"You get my meaning, Lord?" she asked.

"You are concerned about the distance of our births," he said rather than asked, as if he were certain of the answer, and she had to concede, he was right.

"I am as low as it gets. The bastard child of gods know who, found in the gutter of this Imperial City. I am nobody and nothing but what I have made of myself, and that is more by luck than skill," she insisted.

"Which is why I am raising you up into the heavens where you belong," he said. "You are a woman more worthy than your circumstances."

"My Lord, let me be frank?" she asked.

"Please."

"What do you intend to do with me?" she asked matter-of-factly.

His head shifted down, his shoulders posturing embarrassment. "No more than you performed last night."

"Let me clarify. The only reason I can think of that someone like you would attempt to purchase someone like me is because you intend to do things to me that you cannot do to someone of more consequence, someone who is not as easily thrown away. I would know what they are."

"I... I do not take your meaning. I do not intend on keeping you in chains—"

"Do you wish to take me anally?" she asked, her words a straight arrow into his body. He literally flinched as if struck.

"My lady—"

"Do you intend to hit me or bruise me for pleasure? Do you wish to whip me? You have said no to chains, but are you going to bind me to the bed with ropes and feed me by hand like a bird? Are you going to ask other men to come in and take me while you watch?"

"Good Lord!" he cried, standing sharply and stepping from the table.

"This is the subject we are discussing, My Lord. You are purchasing my body as yours. Do you expect me to call you 'master,' and will you refer to me only by derogatory epitaphs?"

"Have men done these things to you before?" he asked, his hands going behind his back as if she were the one keeping him prisoner.

"And women, yes. I have done all that and more. I have no fear of such things, but I would ask that all be discussed before we begin." She eyed him a moment longer. "I apologize if my straightforward speech has shocked you."

"I am not a green boy," he snapped and proceeded to pace the room. "I have done some of those things of which you speak."

"Then I am perplexed by your distress," she countered. "I understand having desires that one is reluctant to actually speak of, but these are our negotiations. I must know what your desires entail before I find myself in a situation where my limbs or my very life could be in jeopardy. Do you intend to hit me?"

"No!" he barked. "I have never laid hands on a woman," then he hitched, "who had not set her hands or sword to me first."

He paced a few more steps, then stopped, straightening.

"I understand. You are only caring for your well-being."

"I am a whore, and you are granting me a title. I would not have been a long-lived one if I did not recognize when I'm being overpaid, when the deal is too sweet. I know you feel desperate, but surely there must be someone more worthy of an Imperial Prince!"

"You are wrong. There are no women I have found who are willing to tolerate the simple torture of my face long enough. I have hired plenty of your profession, and they all refused in the end or performed but with twisted faces and never consented to return. But to find a woman who..."

"Who will what?" she pressed.

"Talk to me. Like the man I once was," he said softly. "I wish only your companionship," he shrugged, "and bed company, if we must be direct. Anything else that we may do together will only be done by *our* mutual consent. I will not hit you." He said the last with deadly seriousness. "I will not call you names other than endearments at your pleasure. I wish us to be friends."

A small smile pressed her lips. "I admit, I like those sentiments, but again, I would be a poor whore if I could put my faith in simple words."

"If I should do any of those things to harm your person, by my own hand and my own volition without your consent, I will immediately forfeit the contract in your favor. You will receive your full compensation with no questions, and you will be free to leave." He gestured to the contract. "I will have it set in writing."

Lydia regarded the contract, thinking it over. "Agreed. Then there is just one last issue that we must face together."

His manner became guarded once more. "Which is?"

"You must show me your face." She didn't flinch or look away but held herself straight on, even as he stilled. "This needs to be if we are to be companions for five years. Better we face this trial together. Now."

His head dropped to his chest, slowly as a fallen flower, the cloth over his face hanging long. "I can't," he whispered. "I have not the strength."

So she came to him. Taking the edges of his mask in her hands, she lifted it carefully, like a groom raising the veil of a bride. He kept his face angled down, unable to lift it, but he did nothing to stop her. She laid the cloth up over his head then slid the cowl back from his hair.

He was as she remembered him and more. A Death's Head remained the best comparison to what she saw, as if the god of Death stood before her. His eye sockets were sunken, and the skin blackened. The rest of his skin was pasty, like soured milk... or bleached bone. A scar cut across one half of his face, a feature she couldn't see before. It started at his nose, which had partially melted into his cheek on both sides, then it continued up that same cheek until it reached his hairline. And his hair was a thick wave of dark brunette, except for a long slash across his skull of bright white, as if something of magic had clawed his head with a single, large, horrible talon, marking him forever. Blackened lips finished the gruesome visage.

Still, he did not look up, allowing her all the time in the world to take it all in. Gently, she touched his cheek with her thumb, brushing it along the soft barrier where the blackened skin met the paler skin. It felt the same despite the color shifts. He flinched at her touch, blinking his eyes open as he became aware of her fingers. He did not pull away, and she touched it again, running her thumb gently along the skin, unsure if it would hurt him for her to do so.

"It is not grease paint," she said softly. "Your skin really is darkened like that?"

At last, he looked up, and then she gasped. His eyes, which she had not been able to gaze into before, were the most beautiful crystal blue. At the sound of her gasp, he looked down to the side with a mournful growl, as if her reaction pained him, but she cupped his cheeks in both hands and forced him to look up at her. Under her hands, his skin felt cool, but she could feel the energy of him, the energy that only a living body had.

She kissed him, full on the mouth.

He whimpered, but she didn't let him pull away, renewing it, massaging her lips into his, begging him to accept her acceptance. The whimper turned to a growl, and he grabbed her harder, pulling her close with one hand, while his other cupped the back of her head. His lips devoured hers, and she closed her eyes to ride the experience. When at last they broke, breathless and shaking, she pressed her forehead into his and let their gasping breaths mingle.

"I think we can be friends," she said.

"Then we are in agreement," he whispered. "Though, I think the Queen would like to hammer out a few more of the finer points."

"Yes, I imagine she will."

CHAPTER 11

THE UNDERCOURT

There were in fact many smaller points the Queen of Virtues wanted to negotiate, including a sort of "bride price" for the loss of one of her vaunted Virtues. Damian agreed to all of it, and Georgiana left with Lydia, a very happy woman. Once secured at last in the fine carriage, Lydia tried to lean back but found her properly laced corset unfit for slouching the spine.

"I suppose I will need to get used to more of this," she said, resettling her skirts, "Dressing properly and sitting upright, watching my manners and such."

"You should always watch your manners, street rat, but I have done what I could," Georgiana said with affection and much faux sighing. "You have done remarkably well for yourself," she said.

"And yet, I will never measure up to you," Lydia countered, "since you are the woman who conquered an Emperor."

"I was one of hundreds my dear. I'm not saying I didn't hold a place amongst them, but you shall most likely be the only woman in his life now."

Lydia snorted, unladylike. "I doubt that highly. He will more likely tire of me one day and replace me when another would suit him better, when he is not as sad and mournful for what he has lost."

"Lydia," Georgiana chided.

"I only speak the truth. Even with a cursed face, he is still wealthy and powerful enough for someone to wish to look past all of it, and he may then take a proper wife. And I will be a distant memory. Hopefully a fond one, but still distant. And then I will console myself with my lonely estate," she said. Pulling on the cord for the curtain, she opened the window and looked out on the late afternoon twilight. The lamplighters were already out and about, lighting the streetlamps with their long poles.

Georgiana kept her own counsel about that sentiment, and that suited Lydia just fine, both women lapsing into their own thinking silence.

Her life had entirely changed in such a short amount of time.

There were more tears than she expected when she packed up what few things she truly wanted to take with her. The other Virtues hadn't been like sisters by any stretch of the imagination, but the way several of them carried on, one would think they had been. She remained gracious with each of them. After all, it was not seemly to fart as one exited the house, as her street mother would have said.

She had a passing thought for the old ugly crone as she watched the footman, her new footman, load up her trunk onto the back of her new carriage.

I wonder what the old bat would think of me now? Her street mother had been kind enough, but not outwardly affectionate. Because what could it have been other than kindness that pushed her to make sure the little girl she had taken on had been fed and clothed? However, she had also said she would not amount to anything of worth and would die disease-ridden on the street somewhere.

"We're all ready to go, your ladyship," the footman said, interrupting her thoughts.

Your ladyship. That is who I am now.

Yet, she felt that any moment, her street mother would appear out of nowhere and drag her away, back to the gutter where she truly belonged. Like she was simply an actress playing the part of a noble.

Yet the footman offered her his hand, and escorted her to the door as if he thought it the most natural thing in the world. Having said all her goodbyes inside, Lydia mounted the steps without a backward glance at the place that had been her home for the last three years.

She honestly hoped to never see it again.

Instead, she looked forward to her new future as the carriage lurched into motion. Like before, she kept the curtains drawn against the day and let herself be carried to her new home, at least for the next five years.

Soon enough, they passed through into the tunnel and pulled up before the door in the wall. Like every other time, the butler waited for her at the door, this time though, he had shed the mask.

Once she alighted, he bowed to her at the waist. "If I may introduce myself, lady, I am Mr. Walter Kinley."

She bobbed in greeting. "Mr. Kinley, it is nice to hear your voice," she said, since they both pretended he hadn't already spoken to her once. She took in his uncovered face; the gray at his temples and the crow's feet at his eyes marked his age as much older. *A fatherly countenance,* she thought.

"If I may be so bold, ma'am," Kinley said, hesitating. "On behalf of myself, thank you for doing this for him. He has been alone for a long time and..." He cleared his throat and ended it there.

"Is he inside?" she asked, giving the butler an out.

"Yes, ma'am, please, this way," he said and opened the door for her. Warmth greeted her face as she entered, the space much as it had been on her two previous visits. Like before, a feast waited for them on the table and her new lover stood by the large fireplace, his back to her. Like before, he wore black trousers and a black coat as well as the black cowl over his head.

"Greetings, Damian," she called to him as the door shut behind her.

His shoulders twitched, and she swore he sighed as if bracing himself and then turned to face her. To her surprise, his face was uncovered. His eyes searched hers warily, looking for any excuse to draw the cover back down, but she, much to her own relief, did not give him one.

Instead, she smiled warmly. "I'm here."

"Yes. Yes, you are," he said, clearly relieved.

Just then the door opened again, her trunks being carried in by the footman and butler. She moved to the side, and Damian lifted his hood back up over his head, turning away while the men worked.

She retreated to his side. "May I ask, where are we? As in, where is this place exactly? I know we went through a tunnel to get here, but I haven't quite worked the rest out."

Leaning up on the fireplace's mantle, he lowered his head below it and cheated his face toward it. "The Undercourt."

That gave her pause. "The Undercourt? But... I thought that was just a myth."

"You know the stories?"

The footman banged another trunk, making it difficult to talk. Both of them shot annoyed glances at the chaos before Damian offered her his hand. "Come with me, let me show you," he whispered, and she took it willingly, noting that he had chosen to not wear gloves this time.

Like before, his skin felt cooler in her hand. She also noted its strength and the roughness of earned callouses, as well the muscle memory of how to hold and guide a lady's hand. They went to the door behind the tapestry, and he led her through into another room.

Glancing about the new room, this space looked to be some sort of office. Against the far wall, a fireplace dominated this room too, though its fire had burned down considerably. Two chairs sat in front of that one as well, less cushy and more like someone would find in a gentleman's club. A large desk sat to one side made of rich mahogany and carved with scrolling and reliefs across the front, not that she had had much time to study it. There were shelves lined with books and another table nearby that seemed to have plans and maps laid out upon it. A space had been cleared on the wall behind that, with pages of paper listed out, some with strings tying them together. Like his bedroom, tapestries and curtains hung in the blank spaces, making the room feel full and cozy.

"Curious," she said, noting it all.

"This is my office," he explained. "Where I do my work."

"Work?" One of her eyebrows curled up, a bit surprised to hear that word come from a noble, even a forgotten disgraced one.

"Yes," he said.

"Are you going to make me ask what it is you do? Is this a game of questions?" she asked, amused.

"I deal with things in the empire that the Emperor or the officials of the court cannot."

"Ah," Lydia said, putting a few pieces together as she looked over the lists on the walls. "You are the court's spymaster?"

"I ... wouldn't go that far," he said, but he looked over his handiwork as if seeing it with new eyes. "But what I do, it is necessary."

She had no intention of saying otherwise. "So your whole residence is under the ground?"

He crossed to one of the curtains beside the desk and pulled it back to reveal a balcony beyond. Strangely, light did not stream through the window despite the blowing. Damian exited onto the balcony, leaving her to decide to join him.

Chapter 12

TRIALS OF A WATER NYMPH

Passing through the curtain, Lydia gasped.

"It's enormous!" she said, and her voice echoed out into the vast cavern. Gazing from the balcony, in the scant light streaming down from above, stood an underground city. Many of the buildings were crushed and cracked from the weight of the cavern above, but in places, she could see broken paths or streets moving through the ruins.

"*This* is the Undercourt," Damian said, leaning on the balcony with both his elbows. "When the first Emperor of Arcadium made his impossible choice, allowing his entire kingdom to sink into the earth as a sacrifice to the gods below..."

"In order to save all the children and therefore the future, yes I know the story. So it really happened? This is where it is?" Lydia set her hands on the cool stone of the balcony as if touching it made the legend more real.

"I don't know if it's true, but much of this runs beneath the Imperial Grounds. I would caution you to not wander off through it though. There are many dangers out there," he said, nodding toward the ruins. "Things hiding in the dark. Like me."

"Then why do you stay here, and are those things going to come and eat us while we sleep?"

Damian chuckled. "No, we are safe here. This used to be the Imperial Palace, and its fortifications are strong. I checked them all."

Lydia nodded at that, accepting his assurances. "Is it just these two rooms then?"

"No, there is more to show you, if you would like?"

"Yes, please. I am very curious about my new home," she said. Then her ear caught a soft rumbling sound coming from far away. "A waterfall?"

Again, her new lover offered her his hand, and she took it. Leading her back into his office, he opened a third door, revealing a long-contained hall. Several doorways branched from that hall, though the two on the left were filled with rubble and dirt. Someone had clearly swept what they could so that the hallway was otherwise clear and walkable.

On the right were three doorways, and Damian opened them in turn. "This is a washroom, feel free to use it as you need. This one is a storage closet, as you see supplies. And this third one…" Opening the door, the rumbling she had heard outside grew louder. Humidity kissed her cheeks as he drew her down a short set of steps. At the bottom stood a larger, circular room.

"A bath!" she declared, amazed at the pool of water greeting her with its dark waves created by a small waterfall pouring in from a hole at the far end. Only a single lantern glowed next to the door, and Damian pulled out a thin lighting taper from the jar next to that, which he lit on the open flame. Walking around the ledge that ringed the perimeter of the pool, he lit similar lamps resting on ledges every five feet or so.

"The water that pours in here is hot. It is believed that there is a natural hot spring nearby." He crushed the lit taper in his fingers once he reached another small cabinet that held towels on top. Opening the doors of the cabinet, she saw jars with soaps and brushes. "This is available to you at any time you wish," he said.

"Wonderful." Lydia plucked at the clasps at her shoulder.

"What are you doing?" Damian asked, freezing.

"You know very well what I am doing," she teased, pulling away at her outer dress, letting it fall around her ankles. Confidently, she turned to present her back to him. "Would you help me out of this corset?"

She waited for what felt like an age before finally the brush of fingers tickled her back. A shiver slid over her skin as one by one, the strings holding her loosened, letting her breathe freely, letting her breasts drop to their natural place. Once it had loosened enough, she shimmied it over her hips instead of waiting for the strings to be completely pulled from their eyelets. She did not have the patience to wait for that. Then, she shimmied her hips further to free herself from the open drawers, kicking them away with her slippers. Paying her attender no mind, she lifted the hem of her chemise, hiking it up so she could access the garters holding up her stockings. Making quick work of those, she freed her legs from both, rolling them down to reveal her flesh, and she heard Damian's sharp intake of breath as she flashed an ankle.

Once she was out of everything but her chemise, she stepped to the water's edge. Steps had been cut into the pool, the edges rounded for safety and convenience. She hissed a breath in as the heat penetrated her cooler skin. They were underground after all, and her toes had gone number than she realized. Now they blazed back to life as the hot water embraced her form, molding her chemise around her generous hips and equally generous bosom.

The water went up to her mid-chest, and she pushed away from the side, floating a stroke's length from the middle before ducking under. Her long hair pulled up, she realized too late she should have pulled the pins before she had entered the pool. Standing up once more, she flung her hair, throwing pins that she doubted she'd ever find again, letting her hair fall somewhat free. Opening her eyes, she pinpointed where Damian stood, still watching with his crystal blue eyes wide, though they had lost most of their color in the dimmer light.

"Will you join me, My Lord?" she asked, as her fingers sought out the rest of the pins holding strong in her hair, floating to the side so she could deposit them into a little pile on the edge.

"You look like a water nymph," he said softly.

She laughed and let herself fall back to float, her hair and chemise wafting around her. With her ears under the water, she enjoyed the feeling of buoyancy. It had been so long since she had gone for a swim. She had to have been a mere slip of a girl then. Floating there, she let her mind empty of all the things that preoccupied it: the last few days, the last few years. She simply allowed herself to exist, and for one glorious heartbeat, she achieved that moment of peace.

But thoughts intrude eventually.

Opening one eye, then the other, she scanned for Damian, having expected him to join her in the water by now. But she floated alone, not just in the pool, but she was alone in the room too.

"My Lord?" she called out surprised, letting her feet drop so she could stand. Spinning in a circle yielded no dark shadowy figure either.

What did I do wrong? she thought, alarmed, moving quickly to the edge of the pool to pull herself out. The romantic mystery of her chemise completely evaporated as she tried to pull herself, it, and at least ten liters of water out. Even with the help of the stairs, she stumbled awkwardly, like a drunken duck instead of an elegant swan. *Not that they got out of the water any more gracefully,* she thought bitterly.

Wringing the chemise out solved a lot of problems, but lifting her arms triggered the sharp pang in her chest, and she hissed against it, tucking her elbow automatically. After three breaths, it released, and she lifted her arm and pulled her right breast aside to look down at the ugly scar. The bane of her existence: deep, twisted, and ugly. The scar only dug from that rib space to about two inches from her breast. Still, every so often, it would twinge like that, spitting out needle sharpness that pierced between her ribs and fired down the side of the breast flesh all the way to her nipple. It used to bring her to tears, and she'd relive that night all over again, but she had become skilled at punching those memories back down, where they couldn't hurt her.

She had become even more skilled at hiding the disfigurement, the marring of her beauty, with artfully partial undress. Most men didn't notice; they were too eager for the taking to care.

But everything is different now. How long until he wants to see me naked? Is this already a problem?

She regretted now, not disclosing the flaw in the beauty he had purchased. Would he be angry when he found out? *Why didn't I think about it at the time?* She had just gotten so used to hiding it.

Her heart pounded as she grabbed a towel and unwound it to wrap around her shoulders. Dashing up the stairs of the bathing room, she hoped he wouldn't have gotten far. She intended to do whatever he wanted to make this right.

She found him outside the door.

Chapter 13

A SLAVE TO TIME

"My Lord!" she cried, surprised, stopping herself barely inches before she crashed into him. He stood with his back against the stone wall beside the door and at the sound of her voice, he turned even more away, hiding his face.

"I'm sorry. I—" he said, struggling. His hands shook, and he tucked them under his armpits. "Dammit to the seven hells!"

"What is it?" she asked softly, her own panic subsiding at the sight of his. She tried to step in closer to him, but he turned even further away, skipping a step to create some distance.

"My lady..." he held out his hand as if to ward her off. "You must pardon me. It has been so long..."

"No, not at all. It's fine," she said gently.

A shiver skittered up Lydia's spine, the towel she had draped around her shoulders doing little to hold back the chill of the Undercourt.

"You're freezing."

"Yes, well, I did just kick off all my clothes and jump into a pool of water," she said jovially.

She took his hand. "Come, let us go back."

He nodded and let her lead him.

The warmth of his office was an immediate relief against the shivering chill of the hallway. Taking baths on the regular was going to need more forethought, but for now, she needed to earn her keep and fix this situation that she had created by her overeagerness.

She guided him over to the door back to the bedroom, only to hesitate a moment, listening for sounds of the other men unloading her things.

"Would you be so kind as to..."

But Damian had already moved, opening the door and passing through, shutting it behind him to guard her immodest appearance.

Another shiver tore through her, but she gritted her teeth to keep them from chattering. She had endured worse before. She could now hear low voices muttering. Then there was nothing. After another heartbeat, the door reopened. Taking her hand, this time Damian led her in.

Her trunks were stacked at the end of the bed, but otherwise, the men were all gone. This fire roared, significantly warmer, and he led her to one of the overstuffed chairs. He sat her, then left for a moment, only to come back and drop something heavy onto her shoulders.

"What is this?" she asked.

"Sheepskin, finely worked. It should warm you up," he said. He then went to the fire, grabbing up a poker to stab at the logs before adding two more to its already merry blaze.

"Not exactly an auspicious start," she said.

"I have dreamed of nothing but having you here. And now you are here, and I conduct myself like a green boy at his first festival," Damian said derisively.

Lydia saw her opening. "What would you like to do with me?" she asked, adding sultriness to her voice.

He stared into the flames. "I am the fool. Trying to recapture the man I once was by forcing a woman like you to be with me."

"No one has forced me to be here. I thought we had a mutual agreement," Lydia said, alarmed. Had she already failed? The promising future after five years of her service, and she was already being cast aside?

"My Lord, please sit and talk with me," she invited. "Tell me what troubles you, and I will do whatever I can to remedy it."

At first, she thought he wouldn't move, but then he complied, dropping into the other chair as heavily as if his body had been weighed down with stones. Then he planted his feet, setting his hands on either armrest of the chair, and lifted his awful head to stare her down; a prince of death sitting upon a throne.

She almost laughed as she realized she had forgotten. She wasn't dealing with a poor destroyed creature, not really. The man before her had once been the Crown Prince of her realm, who would have one day been her Emperor. Their paths may not have ever crossed if he had not been struck down. His loneliness was apparent, and his pain, the damage to his pride, his body twisted into something even he didn't recognize. Even now, when he could have his will and way with her, he was dressed from wrist to ankle, even wearing boots like it was armor. Despite their having come together once already, he had not truly let her in.

And it *was* frankly too fast. Her disrobing so easily must have shamed him, and she—what a fool—hadn't realized that he had not felt comfortable or safe to do the same. She had forced him to bare his face, but the rest of him? What other terrors lay beneath his clothing?

Suddenly, her way forward stood clear.

"Does this please you, lady?" he asked, his voice emerging low and heavy with a challenge from the skeletal face, having failed to withstand her scrutiny.

"It... it surprises me actually," she responded, speaking softly.

The ridges that would have been his eyebrows pinched together, and she realized he did have eyebrows, but they were completely white and blended into his skin.

"What surprises you exactly?" he asked.

"You do not seem ... as I would think the Imperial Princes to be."

He tensed, but she waited, knowing she had struck the right nail, she needed to only have faith in him. "I am not as grand and handsome—"

"You're kind," she said, interrupting him. "You're respectful. You don't carry yourself with the arrogance of your class. You seem used to being served but do not see yourself as greater. You haven't fallen on me like a dog in heat; you have been gallant."

Her words were having their desired effect. Words associated with a prince. Words that no one had spoken to him, she was sure, for a few years now.

"I... I did not wish to disappoint you, lady," he offered, a small crack into his world. She was on the right track.

"I wish the same. I know you said you wished to be friends, but we are still very much strangers to each other, aren't we?" Now she felt embarrassed. "I am used to being a slave to time."

He cocked his head at that. "A slave to time?"

"Yes, while it is my company I share, it is my time that is purchased, so I must be judicious with it. But time doesn't have the same meaning for us now, does it?" she mused. "I mean, there is a time *limit*. Five years."

"But it has just occurred to you that the next client isn't coming," he supplied.

She tilted her head. "No, they aren't are they. Hmm." She regarded him again. "And that does not bother you, does it? That I have been with other men."

"I would be an idiot to let such a fact that I knew very well before bother me now," he said with the certainty and conviction of a prince. She appreciated it.

"But why? I've known man to be a very jealous creature."

He snorted. "I have known that to be true of woman as well, and *I* have bedded my fair share. Does that invoke jealousy in your bosom?"

She had to smile. "I would not be a competent woman of my profession if it did," she conceded. "Then I think we are best just accepting each other as we are."

The fireplace crackled and a log split open.

"You are not a... a whore anymore. I want you to know that," he said, shifting in his seat as much as a prince would dare. "I do not see nor expect you to act that way."

She shifted herself in her damp garments, tugging the warm blanket tighter around her, grateful her wetness wasn't making the wool smell. "I suppose I did not comport myself well, stripping wantonly and throwing myself into a pool like that."

"No!" he said, too loudly, too urgently. He swallowed and amended. "Do not shame yourself, please. You looked..." he struggled a moment, then closed his eyes, as if that made speaking easier. "You were a water nymph, beautiful and sweet. I wanted to join you, but I found I could not." He couldn't have made a braver face in his confession than if he had been a ten-year-old boy.

"Why not?" she asked gently.

He looked at the fire for an answer. "Do you study philosophers?" he asked.

Her eyebrows popped up higher at the change of direction. "I can't say I have," she conceded. "I imagine a prince must though."

"I have sought much solace in them since this," he gestured to his face, "happened to me. Seeking answers no priest nor doctor has been able to give me."

"And was solace found?"

"I do not know, but certain questions have been posed that have changed the way I see this world and the people within it. People like you," he gestured.

"What is the question?" she asked, truly intrigued.

"What makes a human?"

CHAPTER 14

TAKING A PRINCE

"A human? Not a man?" she asked, surprised by his choice of words.

He snorted. "Do you know there are such people who are both? Male and female entwined in various ways and called freaks for it. The common knowledge would have us believe that they are less than human, something else entirely, but I think that is a comforting lie that we have told ourselves. I have seen the most physically ideal of our species do the most heinous, animal acts, and the common knowledge would want me to believe *them* human."

"I have seen such things myself. Demons wearing men's faces," Lydia agreed.

"I do not believe you are any more human for your beauty than I am less for my monstrosity," he said. "We all arose from nature, how can any of us be unnatural? Am I still a man within this body, though it is scarred as it is? Are you any less a being of mind and soul because it rests inside a lovely shell such as yours? The more I sought answers to these differences, the more I found the similarities. I have come to a tentative conclusion that we are not superior or inferior to the other, only different in this form."

Then he stopped, his next words dying on his lips. He made to stand up, she realized to run away, but he forced himself to stay and face her, planting his shaking hands on his knees. "And then I watched you float in the water, beautiful and free with such a look of peace on your face, and all I could see was what a monster I really am. I trapped you here with me, and it is expected of you to offer yourself with a warm inviting smile as a sacrifice to me." He squeezed so hard on his knees, his pale fingers turned pink. "I am the demon with a demon face."

Sliding forward in her seat, she let the blanket drop to the floor. Her partially dry chemise billowed around her as she hit her knees before him.

"What are you doing?" he asked, straightening as she touched his own knees, spreading them apart to make room for her.

"I think that must be obvious, My Lord," she said softly, smiling wickedly at him. "We are bound now for the foreseeable future, and since you claim that all parts of you are corrupted and demonic, I think it only right to see for myself."

She took his hands in hers, his dark fingernails lining up in a neat row for her examination. "You speak of my innocence and yet have forgotten entirely where I come from." She sucked up one of his fingers, only to pull it from her mouth in a long, slow drag. "Did you ever consider that I may like the demons?"

She sucked another into her mouth. Rolling it around with her tongue, she felt the calloused skin of his pointer finger. They were hands that had seen work and weapons. Reveling in the feeling of the finger in her mouth, she closed her eyes and savored the pleasurable sensations.

This close, she could smell his musk, calling to her own body, demanding arousal and her plan fully formed in her mind as to what she was about to do.

Letting the finger slip from her mouth, she opened her eyes to see those crystal blue eyes staring at her hungrily. "Yes, you taste like a man." She let go of his hands and pressed forward, seeking out the contours of his manhood. He had trapped himself in the chair, and while she felt him pull away, she had no intention of letting him escape.

Sweet and pliant wasn't what he needed right now. What he needed was a wanton whore.

Her ministrations worked, and he groaned in response as she hardened him through the cloth. "You sound like a man. I may be almost ready to form a conclusion soon," she said.

"Lydia..." he moaned breathily, but she didn't wait to let him finish any thoughts that might follow on the heels of it. Quickly, she found the buttons of his trousers and sprang them free. The same work was done with the folds of his undergarments, and his noble organ sprang eagerly up as well.

She purred in her throat, running her fingers over it. It was normally formed, the same colors as the rest of his skin with a slight curve that she knew how to make the most of. Perfectly straight men were so boring. As she touched it though, it turned pink like his fingers, the blood filling within to give it color.

"You do not..." he tried again, grasping her shoulders in his large hands, but he didn't have the will to push her away. Her will was not as weakened. She slapped her hand in the middle of his chest and pressed him back.

He complied, allowing himself to be as exposed and vulnerable.

She leaned forward then and kissed the crown of his shaft gently.

He sucked in a sharp breath. His member had brightened to a brilliant dark red.

She slid her hands along it, feeling its warmth and stiffness. When she was ready, she took him further into her mouth, savoring the sensations it elicited there. She actually liked doing this on men. Not when they pounded down into her throat as if she didn't need to swallow or breathe of course, that was always unpleasant if endurable, but this, where she got to use her mouth and tongue as she desired, to tease not only her patron but also herself, this was exquisite.

Her tongue explored him, pulling back his foreskin to reveal the corona of the head. She slipped the tip of her tongue into the tiny holes, lapping in a spritz of salt, cognizant of her partner's hands finally engaging themselves as they brushed back her hair and slid down to feel her back through the damp cloth.

She took him in deeper.

Now she ran her tongue down the underside of the shaft, feeling the line of flesh until it met his balls. Those too had contracted tight, and she slipped the fingers of her other hand into his pants to gather them.

He cried out, and he bucked back, bracing on the chair, but she ignored his actions as she took him fully into her mouth to the back of her throat, at her pace so she could control her gag reflex.

"Aah, ahh! Lydia!" Damian groaned, and she was starting to have a real affection for the way he said her name.

With each stroke of her mouth, a possessive thought passed through her mind. *Mine, mine, mine.*

She knew such thoughts were foolish, but she couldn't help it, such a thing had never been possible to even dream of before, to have only one man, one that belonged to her, but for now, he did. He was broken and sad and fragile, but he was hers, and she aimed to keep him.

The swelling heat in her own nether demanded her attention at that thought, and she lifted up her head to gasp for a fresher breath of air. Her hand kept up its work, using the slickness she left behind to rub up and down.

"Lydia," he breathed, brushing back her hair again, freeing a strand that had caught at the edge of her mouth. She kissed his thumb then climbed up onto his lap. Sensibly, he supported her from behind to help pull her close. All his objections were lost, only his willing compliance remained. They had both come too far to stop it now.

Crying out, she surprised herself by not only finding his cockhead immediately but sliding on so perfectly that they were fully sheathed to the hilt in one breathless second. He filled her tightly, and she hadn't been entirely ready for it, but the whole idea of it made her even hotter.

Mine, her traitorous mind intoned as her muscles clenched around him in response. *He's mine.*

"God, Lydia."

"Damian," she purred and closed her eyes as she rocked, lifting herself up and down, filling and refilling herself with him.

I am consummating this new union, she thought again, and the sensations grew more acute. Dammit, she wanted this, saying all the things in her mind that she never dared to say out loud ever, or even wanted to. He could cast her aside tomorrow and take another woman to his bed, there was nothing to stop him but his own fear, and yet, that word continued to chant in her mind.

Mine, mine, mine.

It built along with her crescendo, rising higher and higher, hungry for more. She wanted him, she possessed him, she took him. After so many years of being taken, this was completely in her control.

Mine!

The ecstatic pleasure burst all around them. Wetness gushed forth from her loins, and he added his own. She became conscious of his hands on her back, having cupped around her torso to help her lift and fall onto him. Now he spasmed as he held her. They crumbled into each other like two buildings who needed each other for support.

He dropped his head forward, hiding it again but seeking comfort more than running from shame, as he pressed it against her breasts. His arms came around her tighter while they rode the remaining tremors of their still existing connection, their bodies fully joined as one. She dipped her head and rested her own cheek against the dampness of his hair, her hands cupping around his cheek. Soon she caught her own breath, letting her fingers seek out trails in his hair, playing with the softness of the white and dark brown.

He sighed contentedly and snuggled, his shortcomings at last completely forgotten.

"You are just a man to me, Damian," she said, speaking before she even knew she would. *I won't let you cast me aside!* she thought.

Chapter 15

HIS WORK

Lydia woke up feeling delicious. Her feet and face were warm despite wearing very little. Slipping out from the covers of the bed, she found herself waking up alone.

"Damian?" she called out, but scanning around the room yielded no sign of her lover. She also had no idea what time it was without windows or a clock present to inform her. There were no other sounds of a busy house shuffling out clients who had overstayed their welcome, or the various women going about their late morning business or afternoon errands before the next round of patrons joined them for the evening.

In truth, Lydia could not remember a time when she had been truly alone.

Slipping from the bed, she took up the sheepskin blanket Damian had given her and wrapped the soft pillowlike material around her shoulders. Her trunks remained still packed and untouched, and she figured she would be preoccupied with unpacking them soon enough. The fire had been banked down for the night, though she had no memory of doing it, so the air had taken on a cooler tang that kissed her cheeks. At least her chemise had dried.

"Oh, my slippers," she whispered, remembering that she had left them by the pool along with her stockings. Carpet had been laid on the floor, but in the places between the various rectangles, cold stone iced through her bare feet, so she took care to only walk where it was covered.

She went to the dining table, noting that most of the food that had been laid out there had been taken away. Instead, a single covered plate sat at the head of the table. When she lifted it up, a warm savory smell of crispy bacon, soft-boiled eggs, and two scones with jam and cream greeted her nose.

Her stomach gurgled in a very unladylike fashion. But still, it was too unsettling to be alone to eat. She needed to know where Damian had gone. Still, she selected one of the scones and hurriedly cut it open so she could slip some jam and cream inside. Sticking it into her mouth, she readjusted her blanket around her shoulders and went to the door leading into the office.

"Damian?" she asked, retrieving the scone from her mouth.

Her lover jumped and turned in his seat at the ornate desk. "Lydia!" he said and automatically started to lift his hood up over his head, before catching himself and awkwardly letting it fall back again. "I'm sorry. I ... forgot you were here."

"My, and here I thought I had made quite the impression," she came the rest of the way into the office.

"Did I wake you?" he asked, setting sheaves of paper into a leather folder on the desk.

"No. But I would like to know what drew you away from our bed," she said suggestively. His pale cheeks actually pinked which meant he must be blushing fiercely. Then he gestured to the wall of papers with their strings of connections. "What do you think?" he invited.

Intrigued, Lydia regarded the wall and took a bite from her scone.

In fact, the wall had been covered in branching and dividing lists of names. All leading up to the top, to Emperor Magnus. Below him were several crests all in the center of their own clusters of names.

"These are all the Houses of the Imperium," she noted, drawing a finger across the crest of House Laon, a very particular patron.

"Correct," Damian said, leaning back against his desk and crossing his legs and arms.

"I suppose it is important in running an Empire to keep track of all within it?" she ventured. "So this is a list of allies, and this is a list of possible enemies?"

"More like a list of those whose fortunes are tied to the imperial crown: those with something to lose and those who haven't decided yet whether what they have to lose is worth risking for what they could gain," Damian said, coming up beside her.

"And what about this House here?" she gestured to the list with the heading "House Laon."

"House Laon is a long-term ally, yes, but the loss of the connection to the throne has made them questionable," Damian's voice nearly growled.

Lydia's eyebrows puckered at that. "Has something happened?"

He paused, then looked from her to the papers in his hand to the ones on the wall. Just then the door opened, and the secretary, Alexandros, entered carrying more papers while sweating profusely.

"Sir, I have the report from Captain Adma—" only then did he come up short to see Lydia standing there in her chemise and the sheepskin blanket. "Oh, my dear lords!" He startled so rabbit-like that the papers he had been carrying went flying everywhere as if this whole situation had been a play and he was the comic relief.

With more cries of distress, Alexandros dove for the papers, gathering them up in a rough pile. "I am so sorry, My Lord, er, my lady. I-I-I-I..."

Lydia giggled amused and had the inclination to crouch down and help gather up the papers, but then her blanket would slip and scandalize the poor secretary more. Once he had regained his feet, Alexandros stepped sideways, struggling to figure out where to put his eyes and thrust the papers at Damian. "And the Emperor ... would like a report as soon as possible," he tried to whisper, but it was a pathetic one.

"Of course he would," Damian said dryly, taking the papers to set on the desk, where he began to sort out the mess of them.

"Does... does she know what's happened?"

"No, she does not," Lydia spoke for herself. Alexandros blanched again.

Damian huffed through his nose, looking very put out.

"What has happened?" she asked again.

"Someone is trying to assassinate the Emperor," her lover said.

Her eyes widening to dinner plates, Lydia looked back at the wall. "Oh," she said dumbly. "Well, that is a concern."

"It is a constant concern," he said, then he turned to Alexandros. "You may go now. And don't come back until I summon you."

"Uh, yes, apologies, Your Highness," the secretary said, and he scurried away.

"I do say I may have scared him," Lydia joked.

"He is efficient and effective, but a mouse would frighten him," Damian agreed.

Yet, all the humor aside did not change or even soften the words now ringing in her mind. *Someone is trying to assassinate the Emperor.* Her usual defenses were deteriorating fast.

"Are we safe?" she abruptly asked.

"From Alexandros? I trust him implicitly..."

"No, no. The Emperor. You said someone was trying to kill the Emperor." She tugged the blanket tighter around her shoulders. "Are... are we safe?"

"We are safe here," he assured, realizing what she said. "Even if they were coming for me, only a handful of people know the

Undercourt even exists and less than that know I'm here, let alone still alive."

Lydia tried to find that reassuring, but she knew she wouldn't until she asked Georgiana.

"Besides, it's not me they want. It is the Emperor."

"How can you be so cavalier about this?" she demanded. "Someone could be invading us. Someone could be preparing for war. Or... or..." she glanced at the wall of Houses. "Or it could mean civil war. People will die."

"Yes," Damian agreed calmly. "It could be all of those."

"And this doesn't *concern* you?"

Damian plucked up one of the sheets that Alexandros brought him and looked at it, reading it quickly, then threw it back. "I have lost three brothers and a sister to that concern. At least two uncles, and a few cousins. All of the Houses eating each other, scrabbling for power and fortune and accomplishing very little for all the trouble."

"They... they were all assassinated?" she asked.

"Not all at the same time. Or even by the same person. There have been plots for coups aplenty since the beginning of empire. This is just the latest," he said. "I cannot do anything about those, but I intend to do something about this. Otherwise, what the hell am I still doing alive."

It was then that Lydia recalled, Damian had spent most of his life preparing to be Emperor. A child when his older brother and sister, both the Crown Prince and then the Crown Princess respectively, had died, the mothers and families of each responsible for the other's deaths. The other siblings, Lydia was fairly sure, were never in line for the throne, having not been born to either the Empress or the official Imperial Consorts. There had only been talk about such possibilities as putting them forward for the crown with some legal shenanigans to legitimize them by ambitious backers. It had resulted in their own apparently questionable ends anyway. That time had been the closest the Empire had come to civil war in a hundred years. She remembered patrons debating about it, thinking their talk went over her head, about whether a rekindling of civil war would break out between the Crown Prince Regulus and his younger brother the now Emperor Magnus. She wondered if his current affliction was the only reason such things had not come to pass.

As she watched him now, Damian, once the Crown Prince Regulus, plucked up a small knife from his desk and spun it thoughtlessly in his fingers while he read from the report Alexandros had brought. The blade was barely longer than one of his own fingers. With incredible dexterity, he flipped it finger over finger, and just when she thought he would drop it, he seemed to scoop it out of the air into his palm and back over to the other side to start the process again.

"Dammit," he muttered in the midst of his flipping, then took two steps toward his wall and stabbed the report into it with the knife.

What world had Lydia been sold into?

CHAPTER 16

A FEAR OF TIGHT SPACES

"I apologize, I think I'm upsetting you," Damian said, snapping Lydia's attention back to him. He plucked up another of the small knives from the desk along with a fresh report. This one he proceeded to cut in twain with the knife along a crease he made in the paper.

Lydia shook her head. "I think after all the fantasy of the last few days, being slapped with reality has been as surprising as if you had slapped me with a fish."

Damian snorted. "Like I said, I will not let anything happen to you."

"Well, I appreciate that," she nodded politely, not believing it for a second. "If you excuse me, I will leave you to your work." She bobbed politely and made to go back to the bedroom.

"Do you have breeches?"

The question stopped her in her tracks. "Breeches?"

"Yes, if you do not, I can provide you some," he said and tacked the now two pieces of paper on the wall beside each other, using pins this time. "I had thought that I would show you more of the Undercourt, so you do not feel so confined and trapped here, with your monster of a paramour."

"I thought you said not to go wandering off into the Undercourt? That it was dangerous?" she pointed out.

"Wandering around in the Undercourt is, but there are safer routes, much like the rest of the Imperial City. I would rather show you the dangers and how to avoid them than let you find out the hard way," he said. "If it pleases you?"

Lydia mulled that over a moment. "I do have something that would suit," she conceded. "But won't I be pulling you away from your work?"

"This work will never be done, and at the moment, I believe the Emperor is safe as long as he stays in his court where he belongs." Something about that statement made Lydia wonder if *that* was a constant problem.

"I will dress and be with you shortly," she said and went back into the bedroom—their bedroom—straight to her trunks.

What she sought turned out to be in the first trunk, which was on top of the second, and she thanked the Lady of Households that was true because she did not relish the idea of needing to shift the heavy thing. Pawing through the different dresses, more costumes than anything, she found what she sought. Pulling out breeches, long socks, and a blouse, she topped the whole ensemble with a cap, once she had twisted up her long hair underneath. While she dressed, she snatched bites of the rest of her breakfast, excited about the new adventure. Within a few moments, she reappeared a very different being than when she had left.

In her new ensemble, she leaned on the door like a street urchin, crossing her arms and ankles to affect a cavalier attitude of toughness. She even tilted her head so the cap hid her eyes. The reaction she got was well worth it.

"Dear lord!" Damian barked. He had been so focused on his reports that he had startled when he finally looked up.

She raised the cap and smirked a wicked half-smile at him. "I'm ready when you are," she said, effecting the harsher tone of the streets.

"What on earth would you need an outfit like that for?" he asked, staring at her. It was strange to see a skull face look so innocently shocked.

"Use your imagination, sir. I think you can draw several conclusions," she teased and sauntered the rest of the way into the room. She didn't sense Damian studying her until she stood next to him, a merriment reflected there. "What?"

"Is that your real voice?" he asked, amused.

"Excuse me?" she protested too much, hearing herself give away the truth by her overreaction. Instead of denying it, she closed her eyes.

"It's cute," he said.

She snapped her eyes open. "It is uncouth," she sneered.

"No, it's like ... watching a kitten hiss at you," Damian said.

Her eyes flared wide. "I... I... I'm not ... a kitten!" she yowled, which did not help her case against the comparison.

Her paramour struggled not to laugh and covered it by gallantly sweeping up her hand to kiss the back, which he managed to do before she snatched it away, unwilling to give an inch, even though she was already losing.

Still amused, Damian went to the door to the hall. "Come, this way," he said.

Annoyed but unable to fume, she muttered some underbreath promises of teaching him some manners after she stuck something uncomfortable up his backside and followed.

They passed through the hall, her leather ankle boots as silent on the stone as Damian's own. This time he led her down to the end of the hall, opening the door there. It was a heavier door, and newer than the others. She noticed too that it had fittings for two bars to be braced across, made with cleaner metal. The bars themselves sat to the side of the door.

"Should we expect a siege?" She nodded at the bars.

"If we are, we'll be prepared," he replied and pulled the door open to reveal another set of stairs leading up. He stood to the side, letting her go first.

"Don't we need lights?" she asked, nodding up the dark cracked steps lit only by the dirty gas lamp installed by the door.

"If someone is not there, it's difficult to maintain the lights when they're not needed on these well-worn routes. All throughout though, especially in the tighter spaces, you have to be careful of deadly gasses. You won't be able to smell them, but a flame near them can be deadly."

He shut their door behind them and locked it with a key, then he held the key out to her on a long leather cord. "Slip this over your neck; keep it with you always."

"You're trusting me with a key to your sanctum?" she asked, touched.

"I'm trusting you with more than that. I've let you into my life. If you are going to betray me, at least you will not have to wrestle with the door," he said, walking up the stairs.

Lydia followed, taking her cap off and slipping the cord over her head. "That was almost poetic," she said.

"I did not prepare some words for when I presented you with the key. Should have known better. Ceremonies with keys, I've always been the one to make the speech," he said.

"I am very honored," she said, hop-skipping to catch up with him as they ascended. Soon enough as the gas lamp's light was swallowed by the dark, they crested onto some sort of slanted landing.

"Now if you continue forward from these stairs and up, you will reach the sub-basement below the kitchens, but that is not where I wish to bring you just yet. That is just for you to know. All our food comes from there, and it's pretty much a straight shot up and down. Only the Kinleys and Alexandros have access, however, through the other door at the top. Your key will open that one as well."

"Noted," she said, picking out another gaslight above them. It had to be two stories up.

"This way," he said as he turned on the landing, plunging into a truly black tunnel.

Lydia hesitated.

"Do you fear tight spaces, lady?" he asked, his voice echoing back to her from the dark.

"Not usually, but this does make one pause."

A slapping sound echoed at her. "As long as you keep a hand on the left side of this wall you will be perfectly fine. This tunnel takes us a ways into the Imperial City."

"Where are we going exactly?"

He hesitated. "I wish it to be a surprise if you can wait?"

She took a fortifying breath. "I trust you," she replied with a lie, setting her hand against the tunnel wall. They continued on in silence for as long as she could stand.

"Do you mind if I ask you more about your brother, the Emperor?" she asked, wishing she could take his hand in the dark but feeling very awkward about it. She assumed wherever he was leading her, they could find other people, and she had no idea how Damian would feel about being seen holding the hand of a comely youth in that place.

"Half-brother," Damian corrected. "I was born by the First Empress, Xander by the second."

"Xander?" She scrunched her nose.

"Emperor Magnus IV, his family name is Xander." Abruptly, he stopped, a fact she only learned when she bumped into his back. Reaching behind him, his fingers found hers, and he pulled her forward. "Walk in front of me, so I know where you are."

She complied with that willingly, but kept their spare hands linked so *she* knew where *he* was. He did not seem to object. "So that means Damian is your family name. I thought you were just giving me an alias when we met, instead of calling you Crown Prince Regulus."

He grunted at the sound of his official name.

Okay, that's a trigger, she thought and decided that she needed to keep talking to see if she could smooth it over. She *needed* him to keep talking, to make all this seem normal. "I know you princes have a dozen names, what else are you called?"

"Regulus Dominicus Damian Justinian."

She waited a count of three. "Is that all?" she mused.

"The second."

"But your family name, the name your intimates call you, is Damian?"

"Yes," he nodded. "You understand it perfectly well. My father's family name was Bertie, but he was known as Regnus VI."

She laughed. "You called your father 'Bertie?' That's sweet."

"I called him 'father' or 'sir,'" he growled. "My father was a cold, heartless, selfish man, who used his children as chess pieces and anyone else who came under his influence. The Empire is a better place with him gone. Even now, there are threads of his actions still pulling us all to dance for his amusement. That is who my father was."

Lydia withdrew her fingers from his hand, preferring to be alone in the dark now. "Well at least you knew who he was," she mumbled dryly. A heavy silence stretched between them.

Finally, he said softly, "I will not lose another brother."

CHAPTER 17

A BAKER'S SECRET

"Do you smell that?" Lydia asked, pausing. They had been walking for what felt like an eternity, having passed through two tunnels and up another slope through a series of broken disconnected rooms before reaching a sort of dry sewer with paved ground and dirt walls. She would have thought the tunnels would smell awful considering the refuse created from above by humanity and their animals, yet these tunnels only reminded her of dry earth and musty petrichor. Not the most pleasant of smells, but comfortably tolerable and easy to dismiss after a while. That was why the sweet smell of fresh bread danced so sharply in her nose.

"We are near one of my favorite places," he whispered, pitching his voice down into her ear. The buzz of his lips so close to her neck made her shiver.

He took the lead then, stepping up to a ladder, or rather a series of wooden planks driven into the hard-packed earth. They emerged through a hole into a very tight space, stone on one side and wood planks on the other. Dim light filtered in through the wall where the slats met.

"Where are we? In a wall?" Lydia asked as the smell of baked goods became stronger.

"Shhh," he hissed at her. "Yes." And started sliding along. The space was so tight, his chest and his back scraped against both sides of the walls, but he didn't seem to mind. On the other side of the wooden wall, Lydia could hear the clanging and banging of a working kitchen as well as voices talking amicably or laughing.

At last, he reached a section of the wall that seemed to have a cupboard installed into it. From a pocket of his coat, he pulled out a small cloth pouch that clinked. Opening it, he withdrew a small stack of coins and set them on a little dish inside. Then he knocked on the cupboard door.

"Back!" he whispered, and they slid back the way they came.

Lydia held her breath, wondering what was about to happen. The talking on the other side of the wall stopped.

Then a single voice said, "Never you mind, go up front and see how the croquettes are faring. We may need to do two more batches before the day is done."

A moment later, the doors on the cupboard opened, and a hand appeared to swipe up the coins. "What would be your pleasure today, My Lord?" the voice asked softly.

"We'll take two peasant pies and two treacles along with a jug of anything cold you have on hand," Damian stated.

"We have cold tea available, just got some fresh ice from the ice house," the woman's warm voice offered.

"You are a gem. That would be perfect," he agreed.

"Will be a moment, the mid-day rush has started." Then the doors on the cabinet shut promptly.

"So there are other people who know your secret?" Lydia whispered. He turned his head back to her in the tight space, leaning in so that their noses were inches apart so he could hear her.

"Not exactly. This is one of the many royal secrets we all share. I've been slipping down here since I was a kid," he said. Then his eyelids drooped as their breaths mingled. Another tingle passed through Lydia as she felt a draw toward him. She was so certain he would lean in to claim a kiss.

Then a pan banged, and he used that as an excuse to pull back, breaking the tension.

What the hell? Lydia thought as he looked away toward the cupboard door. Not liking the dismissal, her eyes landed on the spot on his neck under his ear, the skin stretching over the corded muscle there, a vulnerable spot full of sensations.

Lifting up on her toes, she pressed herself into his shoulder, hooking her hand under his turned-away chin to pull him in. Before he could react, she planted her mouth on that spot.

A strangled sound twisted from his throat.

Just as quickly as she had attacked, she retreated, supremely satisfied.

He looked affronted.

"Is everything alright, sir?" the warm voice asked, as the cabinet opened.

"Yes, Margaret, apologies. I..." he shot Lydia a look, "swallowed a bug."

A paper bag appeared in the cabinet. "Apologies, My Lord."

"No need. You didn't make the bugs. Though, I do believe you may secretly be the Goddess of Baking," he said, taking the bag.

The voice chuckled. "May she keep my stove hot and my back strong," she said invoking the Hearth Goddess's prayer. Then she shut the cupboard.

"And you, my lady, are the Goddess of Mischief," Damian growled.

Lydia moved back along the wall toward the hole, smiling smugly. She went through first and caught the paper bag before Damian joined her.

"Now where?" she asked, already completely lost even though he gave her instructions the whole way there.

He didn't answer, but bodily slammed into her, forcing her back several steps until she hit the dirt wall. His lips pressed into hers, devouring her mouth. Her arms came up around his neck, as much to hold on as to pull him closer. She had no idea what happened to their bag of lunch, nor did she really care at that moment.

This behavior was far more familiar and expected. She felt more comfortable with it, as he tore his lips away to then attack her neck in the same place she had conquered his.

Just when she wondered if things would go further, he pulled himself away. "We don't have time for this, we're going to be late," he murmured.

"Late for what?" she asked dreamily, still riding the sensations of their kisses.

"Where did the pies go?" he asked, holding her at arm's length as if she intended to attack him again, all the while scanning the ground.

The pies did not drop far and were intact when retrieved. Taking Lydia's hand firmly, Damian led her down another series of tunnels, not too terribly far from the bakery. This time, he had brought her to a new ladder, the metal rungs clean, driven into first stone, then wood, leading straight up a narrow shaft.

"What is this?" she asked, eyeing the rungs.

"A surprise for you," he said, "I prepared this myself so it would be easier to climb." Then he hesitated, looking at the ladder. "I... I realize you may not be the sort of lady who likes to... exert herself like this... I should have asked—"

"No, I am," she assured. "I do not mind physical effort of any sort." She looked up. "There just haven't been many reasons for it in the last few years. Not of this nature anyway."

Damian curled up one of his white eyebrows. "I wish to hear more of your exertions of this nature?"

She glanced at him with a sniff and pulled herself up onto the ladder. "There is not much to tell. I started life as a street urchin. And when food becomes scarce, one does what one must, and often that involves a chase afterward."

"You stole food?" he asked, before climbing up the ladder behind her.

"I did what I had to," she repeated.

"But... why did you not stay at one of the city-provided orphanages?" he asked, his words floating up to her as if he had something in his mouth.

She snorted hard at that. "One must imagine that things have to be pretty bad at such places, if living wild on the streets is preferrable."

Immediately, she regretted saying too much. One does not tell truths to someone such as Damian, it is often not something they wish to hear or even think about.

Dammit. My job is to please him, not upset him, she thought. Never had she spent so much time with a patron. The longer this went, the more opportunities presented themselves for her to trip up. *I must be more careful.*

"This sort of thing has a thrill of adventure, does it not?" she asked cheerfully. "The climbing, I mean, and sneaking around through secret passages. It is all quite thrilling."

"I am glad this pleases you," he answered, and she grinned to herself as she climbed.

She had gotten things back on the right track.

By the time they reached the top of the ladder, however, her arms ached fiercely. Winded, she pulled herself into the crawl space and sat on the wood boards, trying to not allow herself to flop back entirely as she fought for breath. It would be unseemly.

"Was that too much, lady?" her paramour asked as he joined her, taking the paper bag with their lunch out of his mouth.

"It has just..." she chuckled at herself. "It has been longer than I thought since I have made such a climb."

He offered her his hand to help her up to her feet, the space they stood in just tall enough for such a thing. "We only have a little further to go," he assured. He kept her fingers in his own, despite the amount of sweating she was doing, and led her through the slats and braces in the crawl space.

"Oh, my word!" she breathed in awe as they emerged onto an open balcony.

CHAPTER 18

TO THE OPERA HOUSE

"Where are we?" she asked as she leaned over the balcony formed by the uppermost edge of a sort of catwalk that circled the enormous room. Finely carved statues lined the length of it, disguising the plain wood and space that supported the structure.

"The Imperial Opera House," Damian said, going to two cushioned chairs that sat waiting nearby on a piece of carpet. A small table had been set up between them, and on that, he set their lunch.

Boldly, Lydia leaned out to look down below into the space. She could see the stage where people, props, and enormous set pieces were moving. Everyone seemed to be working toward preparing for something. Before the stage in its own pit were people tuning their instruments, the notes cutting through the low-level murmur of voices.

"Are we allowed to be up here?" she asked.

"No one can see us from down there, no one comes up here, and even if they were inclined to, they couldn't. The door is mostly forgotten and properly locked." He nodded at her.

"Let me guess," she fished out the leather cord he had given her, "And this is the key?"

"Indeed," he agreed, settling himself in one of the chairs, pulling it closer to the edge. "Join me. This is their full dress rehearsal. It should be a stirring performance."

"How did you know I love opera?" she asked, drawing her own chair up beside his.

"I didn't," he admitted. "But I hoped." He presented her with a napkin from the paper bag, followed by a small pie wrapped in paper.

She took it, still feeling the warmth bleeding through, and ate a small bite. The crust flaked into her mouth, and the first taste of the chicken gravy warmed her.

"Oh my," she sighed as the savory flavors hit. Along with chicken, the pie had bits of peas, carrots, and potatoes stuffed inside. "Oh, this is wonderful."

"One of my favorites," he agreed, biting into his own.

Down below the musicians seemed to finish tuning. From their vantage point, Lydia could see most of the stage below, just not the frontmost edge of the orchestra pit, but all seemed ready. A sharp tapping sound brought all attention to focus and the curtains were drawn closed.

"Which opera is this?" Lydia asked, leaning in to whisper, though who would hear her she had no idea.

"*The Coming of the Dawn*. It is supposed to be a retelling of the first Emperor's story," he answered softly.

A dramatic chord pierced the air, followed by a striking silence. Then a single horn blew a powerful series of notes, slow and grand, epic and sad, full of strength and nobility. Soon, the rest of the orchestra swam up to meet the horn as the orchestra played the prelude. And yet, no matter how stormy or overwhelming the music swelled, that single horn was never drowned out, continuing in defiance.

Soon the curtain opened, just as Lydia ate the last of her pie. She leaned forward to rest her arms on the edge of their private balcony. A woman in an elaborate dress glided onto the stage. At first, Lydia did not think much of her costume as it was dramatically out of date, something from ancient times with a headdress dripping in gold coins and jewels. Then the woman sang out a single pure note, echoing the horn.

And that was it, Lydia forgot all else as she allowed herself to be swept away into the music and the story of the First Emperor and the Empire that almost wasn't. Some small cynical part of her mind knew that this story was most likely all fabrication, sophisticated political propaganda, but it was so well written!

By the time they reached intermission, the former courtesan had tears flowing freely from her eyes.

"They will break for fifteen minutes and start again," Damian said.

"Oh, yes," she said, wiping at her face.

Gently he offered her the treacle, also wrapped in paper. "Are you enjoying it?" he asked.

"Oh yes, very much. I haven't been here in over a year. I'm just now realizing." But then she remembered why that was and stopped her mouth with a syrupy bit of the treacle. This one had walnuts in it!

"You became too busy?" her paramour unfortunately asked.

"I ... didn't have the access I had before," she said then sighed. "The patron I had at the time had a box and would bring me. I couldn't really afford to come otherwise."

"So I'm not the first to share this with you," Damian said, though she couldn't tell by his voice if that disappointed him or not.

She took a cautious side-eye glance at him, and he side-eyed her back with amusement. "I told you before, I am not unaware that you shared your charms with other men. I am not offended if you wish to speak about them. It will not make me jealous."

"Yes, but why? Why wouldn't it make you jealous?" she asked, setting her treacle on the napkin in her lap, to lick her sticky fingers.

"Because I wish to know you, and your past is a part of you," he said, moving to take a bite of his own dessert, only to pause as something in his mind stopped him. "I... I haven't been here since I last came with Regina."

That name sent a thrill through Lydia, like he spoke of a character from another fairy story.

The Crown Prince Regulus's fiancée, the Lady Regina of the House of Laon, daughter of the Duke of Laon. Lydia remembered sitting with the other Virtues and Lesser Virtues chatting and gossiping about the dramas of the noble classes, as reported in the various society papers. She had read the whole story in print, from the proposal and engagement to Regulus's tragedy, which had been rife with more rumors than fact, she now realized. The stories varied wildly, but she didn't care too much because, after all, they were only stories and she had her own life to contend with.

Now those stories are *my life,* she thought.

"What was she like?" Lydia asked gently, ready to take it back and smooth such a question over, but so curious now.

Damian chewed his treacle slowly, his eyes staring into the long distance of memory. Then he swallowed. "She was magnificent and cold. She was my ally." He broke the long stare and adjusted himself on his seat. "Regina and I always knew we would be together. It had been intended for a long time, and our union made a lot of sense. She was from a powerful house that wanted closer ties to the Imperial family. And I got on with her. She allowed me to get on with my life, do what I wanted with whomever I wanted as long as she got to be Empress. She had her share of lovers as well, but we always knew we were for each other." Another pause as emotions rolled over his face, bitterness, anger, grief, resentment, and worst of all, understanding. "Except it was all bullshit, wasn't it? We were never *meant* to be. No one is meant to be anything."

He lapsed into silence, taking a large bite of his treacle, chewing it like he could swallow away his pain.

"She rejected you, once she saw what you became?" Lydia asked softly, unable to stop herself.

"The worst part of it all was she tried," he said, setting the remains of his dessert onto its paper and shoving it roughly onto the small table. "She tried to look past it. Even went to bed with me to prove she could. But then, when it had been decided to remove me from the succession in favor of Xander, *that* she couldn't abide."

He made to stand up, but maybe he realized there was nowhere else to go. "I'm sorry," he said roughly.

"No, this is fine. I want to know," Lydia said, meaning it. "Did she like opera too?"

"What does that—" His voice hitched, and he cleared his throat.

"I just thought that maybe you are just," she gestured with a finger to the opera house and the food, "trying to recapture a piece of what you had lost, you see, by bringing me here."

A haunted gaze met hers.

"It is alright if that is so," she said.

"You must think me such a fool," he disparaged.

"I cannot fathom what it must like to be you," she said, shaking her head. "Even if someone burned me with poisons and destroyed everything I am, I could not begin to understand what you lost."

"And why is that?"

"I've never been a princess," she pointed out.

Down below the orchestra returned, preparing for the next act.

Mindfully, the courtesan slipped her fingers into her paramour's colder ones. "Thank you for sharing this with me. I really do love the opera. And I look forward to coming more often again."

"Right. You were telling me about him, this beau of yours who would bring you here."

She chuckled. "There is not much to tell. He found it more important to see and be seen. I was simply paid to be there to make him look good. It worked out for me amicably. I've never seen this one before. I wonder what's going to happen next, now that the Emperor is in danger."

Chapter 19

AN UNEXPECTED RESCUE

"And how the Emperor blended into the dancers all while spinning with that sword!" Lydia cried.

"It was an excellent performance of skill," Damian agreed.

"Have you seen him before? What is his name?"

"Cyril Pensleeve. I supported him when he was a chorus lad, two years ago. I am glad to see his dedication is paying dividends."

"Can you introduce us?" she asked excitedly.

Damian laughed. "I suppose I can see what I can do—"

He stopped, going deadly still.

Lydia did the same in reaction.

They had traversed the way back to Damian's hideaway, entering the darker tunnels. Lydia had been so excited by the performance, she hadn't felt at all intimidated by the darkness nor concerned by the noise she made. All of that changed now, every nerve standing on end as she strained to sense in the darkness whatever it was that had made Damian stop.

Gently, he laid his hand on her shoulder and walked her back against the wall. She grasped his hand, reassuring herself that he was there.

A sharp shout echoed down the tunnel, and immediately, both of them ducked down. There was such scant light, and her night-vision eyes strained to see anything.

Then at the end of their tunnel, a man appeared. He paused, panting heavily. She felt Damian's hand tense and heard the soft *ting* of his knife being drawn. The man at the end seemed to hear it too because he held his breath, listening.

More shouts from a distance.

Urgently, the man tried to move, but something hit him, pitching him forward onto the ground.

They're hunting him! Lydia thought.

"The royal bastard's here!" a rough-voiced man shouted, throwing light down on the felled man. The light felt almost too bright for a moment for Lydia's light-starved eyes. She saw Damian's profile and the wink of the blade in his hand as he pulled up his hood over his hair, drawing the black curtain over his face, tucking the end into his shirt.

Taking her own initiative, Lydia sank to the ground to lie as flat as possible, using her cap to hide any reflections her face might give.

The hunted man tried to scramble to his feet, but a second rushed in, landing a kick into the man's body. He gasped out, falling to his side, and his attacker landed two more kicks as a third man appeared, this one bearing the lamp.

"There, you got 'em!" lamp man crowed proudly, directing the lantern at their prey.

Damian sucked in a sharp breath. All Lydia saw was a fawn-colored coat as the victim raised his arms in a poor form of defense, the first attacker laughing as he kept kicking at him. The second attacker tried to get in on the fun, but his antics made the lantern swing wildly, throwing light in erratic patterns.

That was when Damian moved. In the disorienting light, Lydia saw him as a disjointed shadow, flashing forward. The attackers didn't see him at all until the first one turned toward the motion in time for his throat to be slashed wetly. While all he could do was grab for his fatal wound uselessly, fall to his knees and proceed to die, the other attacker panicked.

Crying out in terror, he tried to direct the light onto Damian. "Defenders of Light!" he swore at the black monstrous shadow before he too found his chest stabbed repeatedly. The lantern fell from his fingers, dropping to the ground and rolling. The light ended down the tunnel, just as three more men with their own lanterns caught up.

"What in the seven hells is that?!" one of the newcomers shouted.

Damian whirled toward them, his knife forward.

The second newcomer standing next to the first made the sign against evil.

The man on the ground chose that moment to moan pitiably.

"The Emperor's right there!" one of them shouted as he pointed at their victim.

"Are you insane?"

"There's three of us! It's our hides if we let him live!"

That decided things, and all three rushed toward Damian, the emperor's protector, in unison.

The Emperor, Lydia thought, her eyes picking out the man on the ground amidst the chaos. *Someone is trying to kill the Emperor.*

Making one of the strangest decisions in her life, Lydia crawled toward the form on the ground. She barely looked up to see Damian fighting, praying he could really take three at once, but from what little she could make out in all the flashing light, he seemed to be focused on defending the body on the ground.

If I can get him out of here and to safety... As far as split-second plans went, it was all she had.

As she came up to his side, the man on the ground immediately reacted, flailing his hands to ward her off. "Your majesty!" she hissed, desperate not to draw attention to them.

The shadow falling on her was the only warning she got as one of the men rushed at her. Standing up, she placed herself as a barrier before the Emperor.

"Get away from him boy!" the man shouted, the light behind him casting his face into shadow, like Damian's. He swung with a fist, and only Lydia's instincts to duck saved her. With a deep-seated ruthlessness she forgot she had, she drove her fingers into the gooey softness of the man's eyes. He bellowed as they sank in, his weight suddenly bearing down on her. She tried to slide a foot back to brace, only to trip over the body on the ground.

Falling, she panicked before the wind was knocked from her upon slamming to the ground. Everything in front of her seemed to slow to a near crawl. She saw the man she blinded grabbing for his face, screaming wretchedly. The lights behind him had finally stilled, outlining a shadow that brought down an arm, chopping toward the final attacker's back. The blinded man arched against the knife killing him, dropping to his knees, his cry cut short as his lungs lost their ability to hold breath. He flopped with a strangled noise to his side just as the knife was ripped free.

All that remained standing amongst the bodies was the dark shadow. He wavered on his feet, clearly exhausted from the fight. For a heartbeat, Lydia thought he might fall over, but then he stumbled toward her and the Emperor she more or less shielded.

"No! No, no!" the Emperor gasped out, staring up at the dark figure in horror. He tried to roll but Lydia's legs still tangled him, slowing him enough that the dark man reached him.

"Shut up!" Damian roared, freezing everything from the Emperor's antics to the blood in Lydia's veins.

"Damian?" the Emperor finally said, with utter bewilderment. Pulling at the cloth over his face, Damian slid the whole thing back, revealing his ghostly demonic visage in the lantern light.

At last, the Emperor collapsed with relief. "Oh, thank the gods!"

"What the hell are you doing here?!" Damian continued to shout, dropping back to sit, still panting for his own breath.

"Trying to reach you." The Emperor sat up, pushing at Lydia's legs. "It looks like you got them all."

She tried to sit up, curling her freed legs beside her, which startled the man who thought she was a corpse. "Oh, gods! You missed one!" he shouted.

"No!" Damian said, laying a hand on his brother before he swung a fist at Lydia's exposed face. "She's with me."

"Oh."

"Are... are you alright?" she asked, scrambling to her own feet to scoop up the first dropped lantern.

Immediately, she could see how not alright Damian was. His pale skin was drenched with red, the stream of which covered one closed eye.

"Oh, gods!" she cried and went to his side.

A handkerchief appeared as she knelt down, and she took it to press against her lover's face, realizing a second later it was the Emperor who handed it to her.

"Don't worry about me, focus on him," her liege insisted, not that she intended to do any different now that the danger had passed, but the permission cleared up any issues of priority.

"I'll be alright," Damian insisted, letting her swipe enough to clear his eyes so he could open them. "It looks worse than it is. We need to get out of here."

"Take me to your place. I will tell you everything," the Emperor insisted.

Together the two brothers helped each other to their feet.

"Extinguish the lanterns. It's too dangerous," Damian said, looping his brother's arm over his shoulders, the second man having a harder time standing as he groaned and grabbed at his sides where he had been kicked.

"I got it," Lydia said and killed the one in her hand before retrieving the two others, dousing them. Immediately, they were plunged back into inky darkness, and she froze feeling lost in that yawning abyss.

"Lydia, I'm here," Damian said, his voice close. She stretched out into that darkness, and they found each other instantly.

"Lydia? That's a lovely name," the Emperor commented, moaning.

"Introductions later. Let's move," Damian insisted, but his brother was not inclined to listen.

"My name is Xander, by the way."

Chapter 20

MEETING THE EMPEROR

Lydia felt so relieved to see the gaslight of Damian's door. Once it was in sight and she knew where she was going, she hurried ahead to open the way, fumbling her new key into the lock. Gratefully, it opened smoothly by the time the two men approached.

As they helped each other pass over the threshold, she pulled it shut behind, locking it again, then threw the double bars over it for good measure. Secured, she padded down the hall after the men as they headed into Damian's office. Depositing his brother in one of the armchairs, Damian immediately tossed logs on to build up the fire from the banked coals waiting there. Lydia went straight for a decanter of spirits waiting on a sideboard by the ornate desk and poured three glasses with shaking fingers. She downed the first one herself, letting the bite fortify her, before taking the other two over.

"Here, My Lord," she said, though she knew it wasn't quite the right address to the head of her nation.

He didn't thank her, just took the glass with shaking, bloodstained fingers, and she got her first good look at the Imperial monarch as the fire flared beside them. In the warmth of its light, she breathed in how beautiful he was. Blond hair crowned his head with small ringlets framing his face. His bone structure was very similar to Damian's, and in those features, she could make out the man Damian had once been. He was lither where Damian was bulkier, but by no means was he frail or too skinny. Though damaged, he seemed to have attempted to dress down, with a simple fawn coat over soft tan breeches with little of the ornamentation she'd expect the Emperor to wear.

Lydia also realized that when they had encountered him, the Emperor had been running through the Undercourt *toward* the Imperial palace grounds, not away.

"What the hell are you doing out of your guard?" Damian asked at the same time she made that realization.

A pained look crossed the Emperor's comely face as he clutched his glass in both his hands. "I went for a walk," he said tersely.

"You went for a walk?" Damian growled. She tried to bring him his glass of liquor, but he waved it away, like she was a servant, while his eyes remained focused on his younger brother.

"I couldn't stand it anymore; I needed to get away."

"There are those coming for your life, and you decided you wanted to play hooky? You're not a child anymore, Xander!"

"Gods, I wish I were!" the Emperor shouted, leaning back to cross his legs sullenly. It was easier to remember in that moment how young their current head of state really was.

"The danger you have put yourself in—"

"Danger!" The Emperor sneered. "I know those tunnels as well as you. I knew exactly where I was going. And they didn't find me in the tunnels. They followed me in."

"And that somehow makes it better?!"

"Damian," Lydia finally said, cutting through the increasingly louder argument. "You're bleeding everywhere." It helped that the statement was true.

Frustrated, her paramour swiped at his eyes, clearing the blood away, which did nothing to staunch it. "I'm fine," he snarled, but she came up beside him with the handkerchief they had used before, turning it over to a cleaner side. She brushed at the source of the bleeding, and he leaned in to allow her. What she found, instead of a horrible gash, was in fact a fairly small cut near his hair line that had dyed the white hairs red.

"How can such a small thing be so dramatic," she said.

The hot wind blew out of both brothers, all focus on her now, which was preferred to their shouting.

"Come and sit, I'll get some water," she said, taking his hand to replace hers in keeping pressure on the wound. Damian meekly complied and sat down in the other armchair, allowing her to go to the sideboard where a pitcher of water waited inside an ewer. She found some simple washcloths stacked nearby, and she swiped a couple as she poured out the water and brought the ewer over to her patient. Setting it on the floor at his feet, she wrung out a cloth and proceeded to carefully wash the blood from Damian's eyes.

All the while, the Emperor observed them, seeing Lydia for the first time.

"Brother, who is this gorgeous creature," he asked as if she couldn't hear him. It was only then that Lydia realized she had lost her cap at some point in the scuffle, and the majority of her long wavy hair had fallen free of the bun it had been up in.

"This... this is Lydia," Damian admitted reluctantly.

"Yes, but who is she?" the Emperor insisted, his eyes still devouring her.

Lydia straightened and curtsied formally, which didn't have its usual effect since she still wore breeches instead of a skirt. "Your humble servant, Your Imperial Majesty," she said, finally remembering the proper address.

"Servant?"

"She's my endowed mistress," Damian stated roughly.

The Emperor's fine eyebrows popped up like a Punch doll's. "Mistress?" He seemed almost disgusted by the idea, but his instilled manners prevented him from fully expressing it. Though which thing—her being a woman paid for services or the fact that his brother had such a creature—upset him more, Lydia was not sure.

"Yes," Damian growled, pulling the handkerchief away from his face to look at it his blood angrily. "Is it still bleeding?" he asked Lydia.

"Not really," she had to admit reluctantly.

"Good, I can finish dealing with it later," he said, standing up, tossing the reddened cloth into the fire. "I will be right back."

He moved to the door and was nearly through it before Lydia could react. "Wait, where are you going?" she asked, barely managing to pitch her voice down.

"I must deal with those bodies and see if anyone else is looking for him," Damian growled, but then he paused, softening. "I will be right back, you will both be safe here. I'm also going to send a message to Kinley. The upper court must be going out of its mind trying to find him while also trying to keep it quiet that the Emperor is missing."

"I'm sorry, but I do not understand how an Emperor could simply slip away at all?" Lydia whispered, finding herself equally distressed by the idea. "Isn't he watched day and night?"

Damian hesitated. "There are ways," he hedged.

He glanced up at his brother, a complicated look on his face, then took her hand and led her into the hallway. "I am sorry to put you in this position, but try to keep him here. He can be compliant most of the time, just every so often this rebellious streak comes out of nowhere. Stay here and do not open the door for anyone who does not knock twice, then three times, then once." He demonstrated for her on the door, instilling the pattern in her mind.

"The national anthem," she said, recognizing the pattern of the intro.

Damian paused, his knuckles on the door, looking down at them as if they had done something strange. "I suppose it is," he said, clearly having not realized it.

"I will remember," she assured.

Damian opened the door, setting the boards by it, but just before he disappeared through, Lydia grabbed his shirt. The cloth beneath her hands had stiffened with stickiness, but she paid it no mind as she pulled him to her.

"Please do not be too long," she whispered, revealing that she was more shaken than she let on. He squeezed her back.

And then he was gone.

She shut the door and reset the bars across the door, but it didn't really make her feel any safer now that Damian had gone. The little girl inside her longed to go home, go back to the Crimson District. It wasn't that those streets and alleys were any safer or the people there any less dangerous, but they were dangers she knew how to handle. This... this was something else entirely.

Now she had to deal with an Emperor, someone whom she should never have crossed paths with even as a Virtue of the Crimson District. Cruelly, her street mother's twisted voice came back to her again. *It's a death sentence to go anywhere near those nobles. They all smell good and have pretty clothes, but they think nothing about chewing up little girls like you for fun. And they only want you if you have something to give them.*

Squaring her shoulders, she turned her back on the door. "There is no going back now," she said to herself out loud.

He is just a man. No matter how powerful they are, they are all just men. Deal with him as a man, Georgiana's voice whispered to her, giving her spine the steel it needed as her words always had.

"He is just a man."

Chapter 21

MEETING XANDER

The Emperor looked very much like a beaten man by the time Lydia returned to the office. He sat in the armchair leaning forward, his head dropped into his hands.

"May I get you anything, Your Imperial Highness?" she asked, shutting the office door to keep the heat in.

At the sound of her voice, the Emperor sat up sharply, hiding his vulnerable moment, though she thought he had to have known she was coming back, so she wondered if the dejected image was more for show. She had used such manipulations before, and it put her on her guard.

"Where did my brother go?" he asked.

"He went to go get Kinley," she said, though again, she was sure he had heard his brother well enough to already know that.

"Ah, good. Good," her liege said, as he stared off again, the weight of the world sitting on his shoulders.

"Your majesty—"

"Xander, please," he interrupted, chuckling dryly. "You are like... like my sister-in-law aren't you?"

She blinked rapidly at that. "I suppose that is a perspective," she conceded. She *was* dedicated solely to Damian for the duration. "If I'm honest, it all seems quite like a dream to think I could be... related in any way to the Imperial Family."

"I would offer you my condolences," the Emp... Xander said too soberly for it to really be a jest.

She came up to him, and he gazed up at her with the despairing eyes of a child, highlighting again how young he really was, barely past the mark of his majority. Taking up his emptied glass from the table beside him, she went back to the sideboard to refill it.

"Do not worry, Damian will take care of things," she said, hoping it sounded as comforting as she intended it.

"Have you known him long?" Xander asked. "I had no idea you existed."

"Not long, no. This arrangement is very new," she conceded, pulling the stopper on the decanter a little too forcefully so it made a deep thrum. Maybe it was the roughness of her clothing, but she *felt* rough in that moment.

She could sense the Emperor's eyes on her, studying her every movement, and she wished she was dressed as she usually was. It would have been better armor than the breeches.

He doesn't need a soft docile woman right now, looking to him for answers. He needs a nanny, she thought.

Crossing the room, she thrust the glass out. "Drink this," she ordered. "You'll be alright."

He twitched at the order, and Lydia held her breath and her nerve.

Then he obeyed, taking the glass to toss its contents back.

She set down her glass on the other side table and retrieved the ewer from the floor, bringing it now to Xander's side table. Rewetting the cloth, she presented it to him. "Clean yourself up. You will feel better."

He balked at the cloth. "Excuse me?" he exclaimed.

"Fine, would you prefer me to do it for you?" she asked sternly.

"No, no, I can do it myself, I'm not a child," he pouted, which did not help his argument, but he took the cloth and ran it over his face. Upon his first pass, he sighed into the cloth, enjoying the cooler water on his sweat-soaked face. A few more passes, with Lydia refreshing the cloth over his face and hands, and he seemed to feel more restored.

"How are your ribs?" she asked.

"Fucking hurt," he said, then checked himself for his vulgarity. "Apologies, lady."

"No need. I'm not so gentle of ears," she assured. "This has all been one incredibly epic fucking mess."

Xander burst out laughing. "How did my brother find a woman like you?"

"He had to pay for it," she said, laughing along with him.

"Pay for it? What do you mean?"

"I am from the Crimson District," she said, with a hint of pride to stave off any shame he might try to make her feel for it.

His eyes went wide. "Really? Truly?" he asked, as excited as a boy who has just been told she was a pirate queen, his voice in awe with the longing for adventure and delightful wickedness.

She curtsied again. "I am, or was, the Virtue of Beauty."

He nodded, his eyes wide. "I would agree with that. But then... how did such as you end up with such as my brother?"

"He is a prince of the blood and still quite wealthy. Much can be overlooked in such cases," she said.

"Yes, but how can you stand it?"

She paused, unsure of the question. He had asked it so innocently, yet truthfully it was inappropriate.

The Emperor didn't seem to notice. "Letting him touch you," Xander asked, gesturing at her body with a grasping motion of his fingers as if he were imagining his brother's doing the same. "How can you stand to fuck him when he looks as he does?"

She took up her abandoned brandy and took a sip, sitting down in the armchair opposite, and equal with him as deliberately as a queen assuming a throne. Leveling him with her eyes, she took a slow deliberate sip. He actually squirmed.

Ha, I'm making an Emperor squirm! Do you see that, street mother? she thought, but let none of those thoughts make their way to her face.

Feeling powerful, she set the glass on the tip of her knee. "Any courtesan worth her salt would never imagine to speak of what happens between her and her gentleman."

"Even if commanded to by her Emperor?" His spine stiffened.

"Emperor? You said your name is Xander and we are family," she said.

His cheeks warmed, "You are an intriguing woman," he said.

"Like everyone else, I'm just trying to make it to the next sunrise."

"You may think me a cad, but there is a reason I ask you these things," Xander said, examining his glass. "As you are probably aware, Damian is my last brother. We are all that is left ... of our family. And after everything that he has been through..."

Oh, she thought, realizing what the tenor of his questions could mean. *He is worried for his brother.*

"Xander, let me assure you," she said, "My relationship with your brother is purely a contractual one."

"Contractual?"

"Yes, he has retained my services for five years, no more. I am more than willing to be bound to him for that time as long as he has an interest in me."

"Five years?"

"It is not an uncommon amount of time as an endowed mistress," she said, truthfully.

"I see," he said, lowering his eyes as he thought about it. "And what is it he has offered you?"

"I would prefer not to say," she dodged.

"Please, indulge me. I am finding this all fascinating."

She sighed; despite her act with him, he was her Emperor. Best not to push it. "Summerbourne Castle," she said.

"Oh my!" Xander said, lifting his eyebrows again. "He has offered to make you the Countess of Summerbourne?"

"I do not know about that," she amended, shifting in her seat.

"Summerbourne castle is the head of Summerbourne county, if he grants you the castle, the title must go with it. Do you know who traditionally receives the Summerbourne title?"

"No, I can't say that I do exactly," she hedged, quite unsure about this turn in the conversation. "I remember being told that it was traditionally granted to the wife of the crown prince."

"Yes, more or less," he nodded. "It had been granted to Damian upon his mother's death, as he was to be the next crown prince, to hold in trust until such time as he married. It is then supposed to fall to the next heir when the crown prince and princess become the Emperor and Empress respectively."

Cold ice stabbed into Lydia's heart. "But technically, Damian can no longer be the next heir," she spoke softly.

Had she and Georgiana been tricked?

"And currently there is no heir," Xander continued. "Or at least no official heir. Too many cousins with more or less equal claims and not enough support for any one of them to not start a civil war. So the state of the property is technically in limbo. Until I marry."

As much as she worried for herself, she wondered at this man, whom she had more or less dismissed as too young for his office. Now he sat before her, savvy and confident, showing a deeper understanding of the complicated implications than she had understood.

I took Damian at his word and trusted Georgiana to know better. She felt like a fool.

"Do not concern yourself, Lydia," Xander said. "I will discuss the matter with my brother, and we will see what can be done to sort it out."

"I appreciate that," she said graciously but wasn't going to hold her breath. She might pass out.

"Honestly, I'm sure my brother dealt with you in good faith. Even though we removed him from succession, he retained all his titles and lands. He very may well believe that he had the right to do with Summerbourne as he pleased."

"That is reassuring," she added. Just then her hearing caught the sound of a knock. Very faintly and distantly. "I think I heard the signal from Kinley. If you will excuse me." And she got up to go to the hall and the door, grateful for the timing.

She had way too much to think about now.

CHAPTER 22

WAITING

It was not only Kinley but Alexandros as well. Alexandros made such a fuss over the Emperor's disappearance, it distracted any and all other conversation. Both men had to work together, throwing Xander's arms over each of their shoulders to help him walk up the stairs to the court above.

"You've probably broken a rib too, and that is going to be impossible to explain!" Alexandros's wail echoed all the way to the bottom of the stairs.

Lydia smirked, assured that no matter what, the Emperor was now no longer her problem and she could let her shoulders drop from her ears. Still, a pang of loneliness cut through her as she shut the door and locked it this time. She truly was all alone in this dark place she now called home. This time, she did not affix the double bars over the door, not until Damian had returned home.

Retreating back to the warmth of the office, she decided she was ready to divest herself of her clothing. Moving into the bedroom she found everything where they had left it this morning.

Once she built up the fire, she stripped herself, setting her youth's disguise on top of the trunk until she knew what sort of laundry she would need to deal with. She couldn't imagine that, forgotten prince or not, Damian was one to clean his own clothing. In order to find her robe, she did need to push the top trunk off the bottom one, which made a fantastic bang as it settled. Much to her relief though, she had been wise enough to pack her robe near the top. Fishing out her slippers from the lid, she wrapped herself up and went back down the hall to the bathing chamber.

Immersing herself in the pool felt like bliss, the naturally-heated water penetrating to her bones in a painful burning feeling. Soon it eased, and she swam about lazily, enjoying the sensation of buoyancy. Eventually, when no dark foreboding figure emerged from the dark to join her, she fetched soap from the cabinet and washed her hair and body thoroughly.

When she returned to the bedroom, she found herself still alone. This was unpardonable.

"Where the hell is he?" she called to the silence, but the silence didn't answer back. "I have some very choice things to say to him, and he is not here to say them to."

Again, the desire to go back to the Crimson District thrummed through her.

"No!" she scolded herself. "I have come too far to consign myself to being a woman for hire forever." Needing somewhere to put her frustrated feelings, she decided to attack her trunks. Opening the wardrobe in his room, Lydia found that space had been made for her inside. Hangers waited for a purpose. The majority of her dresses hung nicely within, and she found a small dresser for her unmentionables.

She was partway through the second trunk when she heard a banging. Jumping, her eyes first went toward the back door, but then the bangs repeated, coming from the door leading out to the cavern carriage yard.

Her heart pounded in her chest. Then there was a single bang.

The code.

She rushed to that door, picking up the key out of the inner lid of one of her trunks. It turned smoothly, and she hauled on the slab of wood and metal. It was barely open when a figure burst through.

"Damian!" she cried, but it proved to be an overreaction. At first, she thought he would fall to the ground, but quickly he spun in place to press the door shut, turning her key to relock it.

"Are you alright? Are you hurt? Where have you been? What happened?" she asked. He turned to her and stopped. The cloth over his face masked his appearance, puffing in and out as he breathed. She reached for it, pulling the edges out of his shirt to lift it up over his head and slide back the hood.

The first thing she saw was the cut above his face. Crusted with dry blood and sweat, it did not look terrible, barely the length of half her pinky. Still, she held his face as she examined it, scanning over all of him for any sign of a new wound.

"I'm fine," he breathed, grasping her hands to draw them down his face. "I'm fine."

"You were gone so long," she said, her voice cracking under the strain of her worry.

She wrapped her arms around him then, securing herself to the solid feeling of his chest. His own arms came around her, enveloping her in his male smell, but she didn't mind it, not really. It meant he was alive and well. For a brief moment, all other concerns were forgotten.

This is nice. This is wonderful, she thought. She had never had someone to hold before. *Mine.*

At last, they broke apart. "What did you discover?" she asked again.

"First, is my brother gone?" he asked.

"Yes, Kinley and Alexandros took him a while ago," she said. "What took you so long?"

"I was right, there were others searching for him," Damian said, backpedaling away from her and into the room. He observed the mess she had made of her trunks, with a few items still laid out on the bed, but he said nothing. Instead, he redirected his steps toward the office. "From what I could gather from them, they had tracked him from his little excursion through the market. He thought he was being clever, but he was recognized."

"Do you know who they were?" Lydia asked, following him. He went to his armchair and reclaimed it. She slipped to the sideboard and poured him a fresh brandy.

"Yes, I suspect…" he hesitated.

"Who?" She offered him the glass.

"Are you sure you want to know? I don't mean this in any disparaging sort of way, but the more you know, the more involved you are."

"You do not trust me?" She crossed her arms over herself, telling herself she wasn't hurt by that. Of course, he wouldn't trust her, they barely knew each other.

He eyed her carefully, as if sensing the dangerous ground he had trod upon. "I have not been fair to you," he said. "I'm drawing you into a dangerous world."

"I am far from ignorant of where I am and where I stand," she snapped. "You are a member of the Imperial family. I am not so much a fool. I know that my very survival is dependent on your fortunes. If there is anything I can do to help, then I am here."

"I can keep you away from this," he insisted.

"The fact that you believe that is adorable," she remarked.

He furrowed his brows at her but drank his brandy instead of commenting. "It was House Cathor," he said, at last. "When I returned to the scene of the attack, I was able to look at them closer. They were all in street clothes, but two of them were wearing guard coats with the House Cathor crest on it." He pulled a piece of material out of his pocket and showed it to her.

Taking it, she turned the crest on the material toward the fire. It was of a crow bearing a sword in its beak with a rose clutched in its talons.

"Probably the only coats they had," she noted.

"The mistake cost them. I have an idea who is behind this now," Damian said darkly, his voice promising retribution.

"I do not know much about House Cathor," she said, taking the seat across from the forgotten prince.

"They are a family related to the blood imperial and could make a case for a claim as heirs, but because they backed the Imperial Consort over both the Imperial Empresses during my father's rein, they are not on good terms with our family at the moment."

"Rivals, then?"

"Yes, and a coup of some sort would not be out of their reach considering their wealth and influence. The gamble for them is whether it would be enough to not only claim the throne but also hold it. A civil war would not benefit most, but the Cathors would be quick to try."

"In chaos, comes opportunity," she said.

He nodded. "House Cathor's biggest obstacle is that the current Duke Cathor has been unwell for a long time. His son Lord Dominique has been running things as duke in all but name, but trying to place his father on the Imperial throne would not be a good move. Dammit. It doesn't all make sense, but it is the only lead I've got. If I had some sort of evidence that was what they were planning, we could prepare our countermoves."

"You are sure it is them?"

"It's them," he said. "We both witnessed the attempt."

"Yes, and they did call him 'Highness,' didn't they?"

They both lapsed into silence.

"Where do you think the evidence would be if they had any?" she asked.

"I do not know, but I would love to take a look through his house, especially his office. In case he is as clumsy as his guards and has just left clues everywhere," Damian growled. "Even if I could sneak in, he is in residence in the city. I'd be shot as a monster if caught, which is likely."

"Yes, and we don't want that," she said.

A small smile lifted at the corners of his mouth.

"Let's not think about it further. You need a bath, and we need to probably burn those clothes and then I do not know about you, but I am starving," she declared, standing up.

"Did Kinley not bring you dinner?"

She shook her head. "We can sort it out, but one thing at a time, go bathe."

She pointed for the door, and to her relief, he obeyed.

CHAPTER 23

CONSPIRACY THEORIES

"The bad blood between us and the South has gone on too long, too many lives and families destroyed on both sides," Lydia said, unladylike as she spoke around a full mouth.

Damian stared down into the fire, leaning one arm against the mantel. "Reconciliation was always going to be a challenge, and it seems it has only been made possible by the fortunate demise of both ruling monarchs and the ascension of very marriageable heirs."

That made Lydia's eyebrows jump up. "Oh. I didn't know that was a possibility."

Damian shrugged his strong shoulders. "It was always a possibility. There have been countless diplomatic envoys having hundreds of discussions to end the war and one of the ways, through marriage, had always been at the top of the list. For a while there it had seemed that my older brother Aldon would have been united with the Southern Prince, but then both had to get themselves killed. That was the last chance until now for an end through marriage. It would have taken them out of the succession, being unable to bear heirs of the blood, but it would have brought us peace."

"Were you ever up on that auction block?" Lydia asked, waggling her eyebrows at him.

He turned to glance at her and she brought her feet up onto her chair, tucking them under. "I am only curious. The way you describe it, it seems like courtesans and royalty are not so very different."

"Not so very different at all," he agreed. "And no. Never seriously enough to cause me much concern."

"So, these attacks could be from someone to the South who doesn't want this marriage to take place either?"

Damian sighed again. "Yes, I can't completely discount it, but..."

Then an idea struck. "What about a ball? Are the Cathors hosting any balls any time soon?" Lydia suggested, before taking another bite of savory beef.

Damian blinked at that. "As a matter of fact, they are, but what of it? I still would not be able to attend."

"Ah, but... we were just speaking of the Kingdom to the South. Have you ever heard of the masquerade parties they give there?" she asked, as the brilliant idea came to her. "It's a sort of anonymous party, everyone dresses up in costume with masks; supposedly no one knows who is who until the bell rings at midnight."

"It sounds delightful," he said dryly. "Now if only Lord Dominique had thought of it."

"Well he would have to if his Emperor requested it."

Damian stopped chewing, then he chuckled. "Oh my, Lord of Secrets, that would work. It's brilliant. You should have been born a courtier."

"Then I wouldn't be as brilliant. My mind wouldn't have had the challenges it has faced to hone it into the keen blade it is now." She set down her cutlery so that she could use her hands. "Most masks are formed over the face, but I have seen such that encompass the whole head. You could even wear your black curtain mask, and as long as the rest of you were suitably dressed, no one would think twice about it."

Damian plucked up his wine glass. "I will speak to Xander about it."

Pleased, Lydia ate up the last bites on her plate.

"Do you want some more?" Damian asked, gesturing to the plentiful food still waiting to be served.

"No, I am quite satisfied," she assured. "In fact, I should go finish setting my things to rights if we are to have any bed to sleep in tonight."

She stood up and leaned in to give him a kiss on the cheek, which he reacted to with surprise. Eventually, he would get used to the little niceties she bestowed upon him, but it was still fun to see that expression on his grateful face.

Going back into the bedroom, she sighed at the mess she still had to work through and wondered if it would be too much to ask to get a lady's maid. Considering the paramount requirement of secrecy, she suspected so, but she still wished she could pass this task off to someone else.

"May I be of assistance, lady?" Damian's soft voice asked from behind her ear. The warmth of it made her shiver.

She closed her eyes and leaned back as his strong arms encircled her waist. "I would think, after everything you've done for me, it is only fitting." Gently he kissed her shoulder, and she was keenly aware that she still only wore her robe. She had been so warm and comfortable that she had not really thought about putting anything more on.

Slowly, she seized the ties holding the robe closed and pulled her artful knot free. The robe fell open, but not entirely off, and she turned about to present herself.

His breath caught in his throat as he realized what she had done. The slip of her exposed skin peeked through the robe, tantalizing his senses. "There is something else I would rather you did for me instead," she said.

Bringing her arms up, she drew him down to kiss along her collarbone, sending shivers down her spine. He slid his hands along her midriff, slipping around to her back to pull her up against him while his mouth devoured her. She wrapped her arms around his head and held on as she rode the sensations, letting the robe expose exactly enough.

He smelled like her, clean from the scented soap in his bathing chamber. She ran her fingers through his silky hair, dry already from being so short, while hers was still slightly damp.

"More, more!" she cried out, and unexpectedly, his hands went under her rear. As he lifted her up, she caught on quickly and wrapped her legs around his waist, to hold on as he carried her the rest of the way into the bedroom. She thought he would drop her back on the bed, but instead, he spun before he got there, dropping himself onto the bed so that she settled onto his lap.

They kissed, their tongues merging into one mouth. She drank him like water while he squeezed her buttocks, one in each palm.

Suddenly, he broke from her. "Tell me," he gasped. "Tell me to stop if you don't want this."

She growled in frustration and pounced on him forcing him back onto the bed. It was far too late for him to retreat now, and she was growing tired of his doubt. Clawing at his clothes, she yielded up the part of him she wanted.

"Oh, Lord!" Lydia cried out as she writhed above Damian. Still wearing the robe, though barely, the nakedness of her breasts was emphasized by its continued presence. Once more in the dominant position on top of her lord, she arched her back and pressed into him, clenching her body around his stiffness as she slid him into place. Dropping her hands back, she braced her weight on his thighs, so she could arch even more, get even more sensation in all the right places as she worked her hips back and forth. For his part, Damian held on to her and gasped out his own urgent need with each of her rockings.

"Lydia," he groaned.

"Say my name again!" she ordered, rising higher.

"Lydia."
"Again!"
"Lydia!"

She clenched so hard, screaming full-throatedly, his needs and desires were completely forgotten while she took what she wanted. That idea alone sent her over.

She cried out a final time, and the arch swung forward to bring her the other way. Her whole belly clenched in release, and her eyes squeezed shut as the tremors continued.

Damian sat up then, wrapping his arms around her convulsing body, slipping underneath the robe. With one easy turn, he rolled her over onto her back and continued to drive inside her, as urgently as she had been a breath before.

Somehow the new position refreshed her, and she found herself coming again, a new shockwave powering over her as she seized her knees in her hands to pull them back. The new angle was exquisite, and he bellowed as he came, thrusting in her with a shattering rhythm as she joined him once more, all of her internal muscles clenching with release.

At last, they were both spent, gasping, heaps of human flesh.

A moment later, he rolled off of her, both desperate for air.

Usually, when this part happened, she felt disconnected and used, even if only for a fleeting moment, but before that feeling could come, his hand returned to lie on her belly, fingers wide. Both her own hands went to clasp his, and a new feeling of comfort and ease filled her instead. She wasn't alone and had received as good as she gave.

"Did I please you, My Lady?" he asked.

She broke out laughing.

"What? What is it?" Damian rolled on his side, propping a hand up under his head as he looked down at her. It just made her laugh harder. "That is a very strange reaction to give a man with a face like the dead."

"It's just..." she giggled some more, before shaking her head and hands to ward them off. With a fortifying breath she tried again. "It's just that no one has ever, in my entire life as a woman, ever asked me if 'that pleased me.'"

He brushed a finger along her cheek, casting one of her errant hairs aside. "They should have," he whispered. "They all should have fallen at your feet and done everything in their power to please you."

His soberness infected her, and she grew quiet and still herself. Then she rolled forward into him, curling up like the little girl she never was against his chest. He brought around his free arm and hugged her close, pulling her robe back over her body to keep her warm and safe.

Maybe five years would fly by after all?

"Would you go with me to this ball?" he suddenly asked.

She snorted awake, not realizing she had almost fallen asleep. "I'm sorry what?"

He chuckled. "I asked if you would care to attend the ball as my companion?"

Closing her eyes again, she nodded. "Yes. I would love to, My Lord," she said, drifting back into the safety and peace of sleep. Somewhere far away, she had the sense of someone kissing her forehead tenderly.

I think I may be falling in love with him, she thought, but it was an absurd thing to think.

It's just infatuation. Things never stay nice forever, and he will abandon you one day. All men will, when they're done with you, the cruel words of street mother echoed from the dark corner of her mind where Lydia kept her.

CHAPTER 24

BEFORE THE BALL

To Lydia's surprise, a week passed with relative ease. She became more comfortable in her new home, setting her things up in the rooms she shared with Damian.

The rest of her time was spent sleeping for as long as she desired and eating when food was served. She embraced reading, and twice she managed to get back to the opera house on her own to listen to rehearsals.

"Apparently, they had to elevate a new soprano from the chorus to take over the lead role for the Lady of the Empire, but no one is saying what happened to the previous soprano," she told Damian at breakfast.

"Madame Gisella. Knowing her, she may be pregnant again," Damian said.

"Well that is cold," Lydia scolded.

"I do not mean it coldly, only that it is most likely the truth," he defended

"It still sounds cold to me."

"Do you have plans to go out again?" he asked.

"I may if you abandon me again," she faux chided because she was not really offended. She understood he worked to protect his brother, and she had enjoyed her time of rest and ease.

"You are right, I have abandoned you," he conceded.

"Oh! I did not expect... They do not make men like you, at all."

"I had a very particular nanny. She did her best," he answered.

"Hmm, it can be said that I did too; she did *not* do her best. But never mind, what is it that you wish for me to do with you today?"

"I..." he shifted in his seat. "I have a surprise for you. I have prepared something, and there is someone I would like you to meet."

"You certainly like your surprises," she noted.

"I am difficult to surprise," he said assuredly. "The fact that you manage to do it so often has been the greatest one."

That made her smile. "Well, then I would love to let you try to surprise me in turn."

"This is it," Damian said, pushing open a door. The door gave way, spilling light all around them.

Lydia had to cover her eyes against that light for a moment. When she did, she marveled at what she saw.

"This place looks abandoned," she noted, stepping through the door into a large room. The late afternoon light streamed through tall windows framed with gold-colored curtains. A smell of dust filled the air, and Lydia could see a layer of it highlighted in the light across the beech wood floor. A few pieces of furniture sat in clusters around the space, covered in white sheets against the dust.

A contemplative expression cast over Damian's face, as if he were remembering something in that space, seeing it play out before his eyes. Lydia chose not to ask about it. Not even when her paramour pulled his mask down over his face.

"This way," he said and guided her through into the halls beyond.

At last, he stopped before a pair of doors, the only ones in the whole hall. "In here," he said and stepped to the side.

She hesitated in opening the door, until he nodded. Grasping both handles, she pulled both wide.

Lydia stared in utter shock.

The dress hung on a dress form with layers of darkest red that gradiated into oranges and then yellows, beautiful as a living flame. Two women stood in the room waiting patiently as Lydia walked in. She was so shocked by the dress that she almost forgot that Damian stood with her in front of them.

"Do you like it?" Damian asked when she hadn't said anything.

"It's beautiful," she managed to breathe.

She turned to the two women waiting politely. As if it were a cue, both bobbed in unison to her.

"Lydia, this is the Imperial Housekeeper Edith Kinley," Damian said, introducing her.

"Kinley?" Lydia repeated. She examined the woman again, guessing her to be equal in age to the butler, with warm eyes, even as her face was schooled into proper sternness.

"His wife, ma'am," Edith Kinley said. "I am the housekeeper here at the Rising Sun Palace and have served the prince his entire life."

"I see," Lydia said, glad to at least know the name of this place.

"And this here is my granddaughter," Edith continued, turning to the younger woman beside her, who seemed barely able to contain her delight. "Catherine Kinley, though everyone calls her Kitty,"

Kitty bobbed quickly.

"It is a pleasure to meet you, Kitty," Lydia said dutifully.

"If you are agreeable, ma'am," Edith continued. "Kitty here will serve as your ladies' maid."

Now the younger woman's delight was clearer. Lydia was her ticket to a promotion. "I am more than willing to follow your recommendation, Ms. Kinley," Lydia said diplomatically.

"Yes, milady," Kitty squealed and bobbed again.

"That will do, Kitty," Edith said. Then the housekeeper turned back to Damian. "If you are agreeable, Your Highness, we will get Lady Lydia ready. Walter and Alexandros are waiting for you in the Prince's Quarters."

"I will leave you to it," he said and bowed once to Lydia before leaving.

As soon as the door closed, Kitty giggled.

"That will do," Edith chided gently.

"If you will come this way, milady," Kitty invited, "I will help you change."

Lydia complied, coming to a bench set up to assist in the change. Unlike the rest of the palace, these rooms were clean and inviting. "May I ask you a question?"

"Yes, of course," Kitty chirped.

"If ... *Prince* Damian has gone to the Prince's Quarters, which quarters are these?"

"Why, the Princess's Quarters of course," the younger woman said.

"Of course," Lydia said.

A carriage pulled up to the front of the small palace. Stepping outside in full costume, Lydia could see it was indeed a small palace, tucked into the furthest corner of the grounds. The carriage was the same one that had transported her before, and Damian stood there speaking with the footman. Together they turned toward her as she exited. She could not see her lover's expression, but the footman stated his thoughts plainly. His jaw sat on the ground.

"Will I suit, My Lord?" she asked sweetly, adjusting the feathery mask of red, orange, and yellow feathers. The same feathers were worked into her hair, creating a beautiful crest over her head.

"I dare say it will," her prince said breathily and offered her his hand.

Where she stood bright as fire, he was black as night. Like his other clothes, these were dyed black but were of much higher quality. Everything had been edged with silver threads, even the black cloth covering his face. Black feathers with a green sheen like a raven's were placed skillfully at his neck, shoulders, and the edges of his coat and sleeves.

Taking his hand, she let him guide her to the carriage, his other hand tucked gallantly behind him, his every movement the perfection of a prince.

The footman still stood so dumbstruck he almost forgot to open the carriage door.

Lydia felt quite pleased and excited as the carriage rolled through the grounds. There were several other carriages assembling into a line to leave the grounds and head to the nobilities' housing district nearby. On a regular day, Lydia could walk that distance without breaking a sweat, but in full ball garb, she was glad she didn't have to.

"Oh gods," a soft breathy curse pleaded.

Tearing her eyes away from the scenery outside, she noticed Damian's hands shaking. He gripped them into fists, trying to control them. His shoulders heaved up and down as his breath pulled on his mask. Quickly, Lydia laid her hands over his shaking ones.

"You are alright," she said firmly. "You are safe."

"I don't know if I can do this," he admitted. "How can I go in there and face any of them?"

"They won't know it's you," she said, but she realized there was nothing she could say that would reach him, not with him alone in the dark like he was. Urgently, she pulled up on his mask, bringing his face back into the light.

"No!" he cried, clawing to pull it back down, but her will was stronger.

"Damian, look at me!" she ordered.

He stilled and let her pull the mask free of his face. Slips of his hair, already sticky with sweat stuck to his forehead, entwined black and white. She brushed them back with a kind hand.

"I'm here. You can do this," she assured.

His eyes flitted back and forth, searching for the lie that wasn't there. "What if they recognize me?"

"So what?"

"So what?!"

"This is a masquerade ball, they wouldn't dare cross the Emperor's brother, even if they did guess. But I bet none will." Everything she said was logical, but would it be enough?

At last, he took a shuddering, but deeper breath in. "You will stay with me all night?"

"Yes," she replied, and she laced her fingers between his gloved ones so he could feel the truth of that answer.

"Thank you," he whispered.

They lapsed into silence, the carriage barely moving in the line out of the Imperial Grounds gates. Somewhere outside in the other carriages, merry laughing and singing could be heard from the excited partygoers.

"I thought it would be so simple," Damian said after a moment. "Just for one night."

"Sometimes when the fear won't go away, you are just going to have to do it afraid."

He lifted her fingers and kissed them gently, then pulled the mask back over his face.

"You think I'm terrified now, wait until you ask me to dance with you."

Chapter 25

THE IMPERIAL PHOENIX

"Beautiful," Lydia breathed as she walked into the venue on Damian's arm. The building was a mansion, one of many on the street, well-appointed with crenellations and parapets like a mini castle. The partygoers streamed up the walk to the front door. Music and flowers were everywhere with footmen in fine livery sporting the black and gray colors of the House Cathor.

Once they had alighted from the carriage, Damian had seemed steady, offering his hand to help her out before tucking her own into his arm. He even bowed automatically to any man who crossed his path, each of them doing the same as the ladies curtsied.

He led her along with the throng into a golden-lit ballroom full of the murmur of talking. Couples were already dancing with everyone around them commenting. In an adjoining room, a banquet had been laid out allowing attendees to dine before or after joining the dancing. And just as predicted, no one questioned Damian's full mask. In fact, there were several other men who sported them as well, including a ghostly knight and someone trying to affect a headless scarecrow. There was such a myriad of costumes that Lydia wondered if she had inadvertently started a trend in parties for the next few years.

Unlike most balls in the Imperial City, there wasn't a herald announcing the arrivals as everyone was meant to be anonymous. But everyone knew when the Emperor arrived.

An anticipatory hush rolled over the crowd, and the dancers stopped as the music found a more or less natural end, before switching to the empire's national theme. Those gathered parted back against the wall, creating an alley for the Emperor.

"Interesting," Damian muttered.

"What?" she asked, leaning into him.

"It is just, I've never seen this from the outside before."

Now a herald did appear, dressed in gold and white with a white domino mask over his eyes.

"Announcing: the Imperial Phoenix!"

The room erupted in applause as an elegant man entered. Dressed in more gold with highlights of white and jewels of blue, he emitted a calming radiance. Behind him, instead of coat tails, was a train of real white peacock feathers. He entered alone with no escort, a sure signal to all the room that he was still a bachelor.

The Emperor made a circuit around the space, appreciating the applause, making an Imperial wave back to his subjects. Lydia applauded with the rest of the room and noticed that Damian did not. Instead, he kept his hands firmly behind his back, the shadow to his brother's light.

"Strike up, fiddlers! Let's have the first dance!" the Emperor declared to a room full of cheers.

Lydia flipped out a fan in front of herself. "And of course no one comments on how there has been dancing this whole time before he arrived," she said to Damian.

"Of course, the party doesn't begin until the Emperor arrives," he said, turning about to survey the room.

"I don't think you're joking," she said.

"I'm not."

Not knowing what to do with that, Lydia did her own sweep of the room, only to realize suddenly that the whole room was looking back at her.

She stopped the fluttering of her fan, suddenly struck with terror as she realized it. Even Damian had taken a step back from her with everyone else. Then she realized why.

The Imperial Phoenix had approached her.

With a gallant bow straight out of a fairytale, he held out his hand to her. "May I have this dance, lady phoenix?" he asked. The room was so quiet that the gasps could be heard as loudly as screams.

Reaching out with one of her red gloves, she didn't dare glance at Damian, despite every fiber in her being demanding she do so. Instead, she met the Emperor's—Xander's—eyes twinkling merrily at her through his white and gold mask. The second their hands touched, the music started up. Everyone else in the room stayed back as the pair of phoenixes took to the floor. Trying to ignore all of them, Lydia focused on the music intro, trying to figure out which dance they were starting with.

"The Madrigeze Waltz," Xander whispered to her as if reading her mind, and thankfully, it was one she knew.

They assumed the starting pose, and in the next breath, Lydia swooped into it. As they spun about the room, her skirts whirled with flashes of bright color, chasing or being chased by the white feathers.

"You are an excellent dancer," her partner noted.

She was too breathless to respond.

About halfway through, others joined the dancing on some unknown cue or protocol she didn't know. Soon they were one of an eclectic menagerie, dancing and laughing with the steps.

"Thank you for taking my hand," Xander said as he brought her about to the center.

"It wasn't like I had much of a choice," she noted. "I can practically feel all the daggers being thrown at my back. Besides that, I am your *brother's* mistress." She scanned the crowd as best she could while spinning, searching for Damian's visage, but it was impossible.

"That is part of what made you the perfect choice," Xander said, grasping her hand to dip her in sync with everyone else on the floor. "My first choice could set off all kinds of rivalries. Parents floundering over each other to catch my eye while it still can be caught. And here I am dancing with a mysterious woman, untouchable, unknowable. They will focus on that mystery and not on attacking each other. And since I know you have no such designs on me, because you are my brother's endowed mistress, I am completely safe to dance. And I do love to dance."

"Hmmm," she said. "Well I cannot argue with your logic, but how did you know I was even going to be here, or which one was me?"

"Damian told me of course."

A simple answer, but one that surprisingly stung.

Of course, he chose the phoenix *for me, the same as the Imperial Crest,* she thought, feeling stupid. She had thought she was the Personification of Flame and had thought no further than that. She had let herself become complacent.

"If this was some sort of plan between the two of you, I would have appreciated being informed or even asked."

Xander's eyebrow arched high enough to clear his mask. "An Emperor does not ask, but commands," he said.

"Command he may and did, but he cannot order anyone's feelings, and mine are much put out."

"My god," Xander breathed as the dance ended, with a low dip, his face inches from hers. "You are an Empress born."

Her heart leapt, both by the close proximity—what it declared to the room—and his declaration. As before, the room erupted into applause as he straightened them up, ending the dance. To add to the performance, he brought her hand up to his lips to kiss it. "Next time I will ask, my lady phoenix."

Her breath fully taken away, she was not able to say anything before he was swept away into a crowd of eligible women and the parents he so feared. They were already setting up his next few dances, forcing him to make careful political choices.

That left Lydia suddenly very alone in a room full of people.

"Lady Phoenix, may I have the next dance?" a man in a Lion mask asked, bowing as he approached her.

"May I have the next one after that?" a Monkey asked.

"I would like to reserve the next two!" a noble Horse cried. And more and more young men approached her.

"I... I..." Lydia said and pulled out her fan to flutter at herself. "I am so sorry, my lords, I need a moment to catch my breath. I... I can't believe that just happened!"

"Come, there are chairs over here," a Deer with a full rack of antlers said, offering his arm for her to take.

"I will get you some punch!" a Rabbit and a Fox both declared, before running off to race with each other to get it.

She accepted the offer of an arm from the Deer and let him lead her through the small throng of men and a couple of women she had gathered, all seeking to either dance with her or share attention with her. In many ways, it felt no different than at one of Georgiana's soirees when she was searching out new client. It was a situation Lydia knew well.

"What was it like to dance with the Emperor?" a woman wearing a Moon Mask asked. The chairs they occupied were set up under the arches at the far end of the ballroom, their backs to an open hallway that led toward the washrooms and powder rooms.

"He is such a beautiful dancer!" a different woman wearing a Rabbit mask cooed, leaning forward, clearly someone who should forgo the wine in favor of punch.

"I felt so light; it was like I was a feather in his arms," Lydia sighed, affecting as much empty-headed frivolousness as to give these women a run for their money.

"Would you like some more punch, Lady Phoenix?" one of her new menagerie asked.

Before she could answer, however, a woman screamed somewhere in the direction of the privies.

Chapter 26

MEETING THE LADY REGINA

Like everyone else, Lydia stood up and rushed toward the scream. Only a handful of people near that hallway heard it, as the music and the ball had drowned it out, so most of the room continued dancing despite the alarm. The open hall bled into a closed one that turned the corner leading to the ballroom privies.

A small group of people rushed around a woman lying on the ground.

She had pushed herself half up with one hand while the other blocked her face as if she expected someone to attack her from above, the whole time crying and shaking her head back and forth. Three guards were already in attendance. One, a woman herself, had knelt beside the hysterical lady, attempting to soothe her while the other two were running down the hall trying to find the source of her distress. A washroom attendant leaned out of the room and framed two other ladies attempting to leave.

"Chrysanthemum!" one of the noblewomen cried, with equally shrill tones of distress, high pitched enough to make Lydia wince as she pushed her way past the attendant to fall on the ground with her friend. She flung her arms around the victim. Only then did the Lady Chrysanthemum stop her antics, grasping onto her friend.

"Oh Marigold! It was so terrifying! All the Lords of Light! I thought he was going to take me!"

"Who? Who was it?" a third noblewoman asked.

Just then two footmen came up the servants' stairs at the far end of the hall, the tails of their fine coats flying.

"Did anyone go down that way?" one of the guards demanded, and both young men flinched.

"Uh... uh no, no," the taller one said.

"I think he went this way!" the second guard who had gone the other direction shouted.

"You come with me, you go fetch more hands at once, but keep it calm. We do not want to alarm the party if we can help it," the first guard hissed urgently.

The taller footman obeyed, chasing after the guards while the smaller one stuttered in place, his face going pale, and for a brief moment, Lydia wondered if he too would flop over and faint dead away. Then he collected himself to stumble down the stairs, clinging to his orders.

"Please, my lady, you must calm down," the remaining guard said, "Tell us who attacked you."

"It was the God of Death himself!"

The other women gasped. Lydia's heart thumped hard in her chest.

"Oh, for pity's sake. It's a masquerade! She's obviously had too much to drink and is making a fuss over nothing," one of the noblemen that had come rushing declared. This ushered several of the other men back to the ballroom.

"What is all this now?!" a more authoritative voice called out just as the men went to pass into the ballroom. As one they all bowed at the waist to the new woman joining them. Dressed all in purples with winks of reflective baubles all over her skirt, the Night's Sky removed her mask in an effort to see clearer.

"Lady Regina!" the noblewoman holding the sobbing lady on the floor cried out.

Oh crap, Lydia thought, as she regarded the woman who had broken Damian's heart.

But naturally, Lady Regina turned away from Lydia to look down on the scene with an even composure that any queen would envy.

Of course, she would have no idea who I am, and if she did, we're all in masks. Still, Lydia remained guarded. She had made a splash after all as Lady Phoenix.

"What is wrong with her?" Lady Regina asked.

"I do not... I have not..." poor Lady Marigold attempted to speak, but her words were overwhelmed by Lady Chrysanthemum's wailing on the ground. She reached new heights of sound as she had a new audience to perform for.

"It was horrible, Regina!" the younger noblewoman wailed. "Death! A face like a skull, he came toward me. The God of Death came to take me away! I do not want to die!"

"Hush, that is enough," Lady Regina commanded, not harshly but firmly. It had the desired effect as Lady Chrysanthemum forced herself to take a shuddering breath.

The guard who had been trying to get answers from the distraught young woman stood and backed away to give the assembled nobles space.

Lydia's true desire was to seek out the "God of Death," hopefully locating him before the guards did. Yet, with so many witnesses, Lady Phoenix was far from conspicuous.

After a few moments of concerted effort, the lady got herself under control, hiccupping instead of openly weeping.

"I... I apologize, Lady Regina," the young woman said, remembering herself. Her friend continued to pat her shoulder.

Lady Regina's expression softened. "It is quite alright, Chrysanthemum. It is clear you have had quite a shock. This is an exciting time for you."

For a brief moment, it seemed the young woman would start crying again, but her composure held.

"Do you think you could get up off the floor now?" Lady Regina asked, arching an eyebrow at her.

"Yes. Yes," she said, and with the help of a footman leaping forward to assist, she managed it. Now that she had gained her feet, Lydia could see how young she was.

She looks barely sixteen, Lydia mused. Very likely new to court and there to seek a marriage match.

Regina nodded with approval. "Now, can you tell us what happened? What did you see? As calmly as possible."

"I... I was on my way to the powder room when I saw him." Chrysanthemum indicated the stairs. "He had a face like a skull. And it is like they said, I thought at first it was a mask, but then he turned to me and... and I realized it was his face. It looked like a rotting skull!" Those gathered to listen all gasped. "Then he dropped his actual mask over his face, a black sort of cloth, and ran down the servants' exit."

Fearful cries emitted from the gathered crowd, with another noblewoman fainting dead away.

"Well that's a little much," Lydia murmured softly as that woman garnered more attention for her swooning from those around her.

She thought no one had heard her, but then she felt the pressure of someone's eyes on her and noticed Lady Regina looking directly at her.

"I think I know what happened," Lady Regina turned back to the young woman. "A skull-like effect can be achieved with charcoal. Can you be sure it was not one of the younger noblemen having a game at your expense?"

Chrysanthemum wound herself up to protest, only to hesitate as she thought about it. "Oh, the Cartermens."

"I would not doubt it. This sounds like one of their tricks," Lady Regina agreed. Heads all around nodded as well.

Lydia admired the woman's technique. *The Lady Regina would have made a splendid Empress,* she thought. She controlled the crowd so completely.

Obediently, the majority dispersed with much to gossip about and more dances to be had. Lydia took it as her cue to exit from the situation too and out of the scrutiny. Still, she could feel the eyes and sense the whispers as she retreated toward the privies.

"Can I assist you with anything, milady?" the powder room attendant asked as Lydia entered and took a seat on one of the cushioned settees waiting there for the purpose.

"No, I am fine, I just need a moment," Lydia said.

"Are you sure you do not wish me to loosen your stays for you?" the attendant asked.

"No, thank you," she insisted a little more forcefully through a hint of gritted teeth.

The powder room attendant bobbed and made an excuse about getting more something, Lydia hadn't really been paying attention to what, and left, actually giving her a moment alone.

Lydia waited, counting and listening for when she thought she may be able to sneak away to find where Damian had gone.

Fortune was not with her, however, as the door opened again a few moments later.

"Hello?" a voice called from her main sitting room, stopping her in her tracks.

"Oh, for heaven's sake!" Lydia whispered and opened her fan to block most of her face, a clear indication that she wished for privacy.

"Ah, Lady Phoenix," the woman who entered said.

"Lady Regina," Lydia responded. *Now this is interesting.*

"Oh, I do apologize," Lady Regina said as she spotted Lydia's fan signal. "I did not mean to disturb you. I had hoped to speak with you about the incident." The lady indicated a finger toward the hall. "You seemed quite level-headed all things considered, and I wondered if you saw something that would be of use?"

"I saw nothing," Lydia said, shaking her head. "I arrived with everyone else when I heard the screams."

Lady Regina's eyes measured her a moment longer. Then she took a step into the room to try to put her purple mask back on. "You know, don't you?" she asked softly, toying with the words on her tongue.

Chapter 27

A Risky Undertaking

Breathing heavily, Damian pressed his back against the wall. Tearing the mask from his face, he gulped down larger gasps of air. It had been worse than he had imagined, and the poor little noblewoman hadn't even seen his face!

All he could do was focus on the next breath until his hands stopped shaking. He had retreated down into a sub-basement of the house. The servants were all too busy with their work to pay him any mind as he had descended down into the depths. Yet their voices frightened him, and just as two wine boys came down the sub-basement stairs, laughing loudly, he turned around and squatted down in a corner beside some barrels. His black clothing hid him well as they came and went without being any the wiser to his presence. Pressing his sweating forehead into the cold stone, Damian counted to thirty before standing, getting his panic attack under control.

"I am sorry, Lydia," he whispered, remembering that he had abandoned her at the ball. Feeling like a fool for making her promise to stay by his side, he shook his head and refocused on what he had come there to do.

The only light in the room came from the old-fashioned oil lamp hanging by the stairs, so Damian relied on his memory of the place as he worked his way around the casks into a second room connected by a narrow doorway to the first. In this room were dozens and dozens of shelves with their diamond-shaped cupboards holding just as many bottles of wine in each. It had been a few years since he had hidden here with his then compatriots, stealing from Duke Cathor's stock with all the giddy youth such an adventure could bring, but he remembered where Dominique had showed him the cellar's greatest secret.

And it was still there. Hanging against the back wall, in a darkness the majority of the world wouldn't see stood a heavy wooden door. Making his way to it, Damian's shoulders unknotted in relief. The door itself was split into a top half and a bottom half, both with their own locks and handles. And both were locked.

"Never simple," he muttered and slid his fingers along the edges of the door frame. Sure enough, a nail had been driven into the wood on the right side where a black iron key hung flush against the jamb. Unless someone knew it was there or knew the workings of human nature, they would not have seen it.

The key turned smoothly in the well-oiled locks, but Damian chose to only unlock the bottom half of the door, in case any wine boy got sent into the room looking for a particular vintage. Stairs were revealed behind leading up in a tight spiral.

Just then voices echoed in from the main room.

Ducking down below the top half of the door, Damian squeezed himself through and pulled it closed behind him, just in time for the voices to come into the very room where he had been hiding. He held very quiet, palming out the stiletto he kept in a sheath on his forearm. He did not wish to use it, but he would if he must. The wine boys didn't seem to notice anything amiss, and he heard the clink of several glass bottles as they were fetched.

He did not have time to linger. Carefully, he stood up and made his way up the stairs by feel in the utter dark. They wound about a few times, but since he had no idea how many steps there were, he just focused on the next one before him, while holding his hand out searching for the end of the line.

When his palm hit the corresponding door, it rattled loudly in its jamb.

Hissing, he pulled his fingers back and held still, listening for anyone alerted by his error.

Off in the distance, he could hear the lively orchestra playing and the murmur of hundreds of voices talking all at once. In his mind's eye, he saw Lydia dancing with every man, bird, and fish the Imperial Court had to offer. She had been a brilliant dancer, the gown he had made for her flashing as potently as real fire. Every eye had seen his beautiful woman, and every tongue had been set in motion by her mysterious appearance.

At least I could give her this, he thought. *Maybe I should have at least danced once with her.*

Pushing that intrusive thought away, he refocused on the task at hand. Gently, he re-laid his fingers on the door, skimming over it until he found the edge then down to the handle. Carefully and quietly, he pressed on the curlicue handle, but the door did not yield. After more probing, he found the keyhole beneath. Sucking a deep breath in, he knelt on the steps and fingered the key into the hole. Then he pressed his ear against the door and listened, but heard nothing more past the thick wood. He would simply have to take his chances. He turned the key until he met the moment of resistance, took another breath and clicked it over. The door popped away a half inch from the jamb, letting in a slice of light from the room beyond.

Still no reaction from anyone inside, so he lined his eye up to peer through.

He had remembered correctly. The stairs had taken him directly up to the Duke's office. Dominique's office now.

The room stood empty, though a pair of gaslights were down to the lowest setting, giving the room a calming twilight. The scent of cigar was thick in the air, and he spied the smokey remains in an ashtray on the desk. Someone had been there not too long ago, and if Damian were to guess, Lord Dominique must have been in residence taking a break from the party. As charismatic as his old "friend" could be, he had a proclivity to become overwhelmed at such events.

Damian emerged from the door, closing it behind him. Nothing else in the well-appointed room moved. From the inner side of the door, he could see that someone had cleverly fashioned it to match the wooden panels of the wall, blending it away when he closed it.

"Let's see what other secrets you have in this room, Dom," he breathed, pulling his mask back over his face as he went straight to the most obvious place for keeping secrets: the standing safe behind the desk. While the box was made of heavy black iron, the safe had been decorated with golden touches at the feet and edged with filigree. The dial in the middle sported elegantly painted numbers, looking impressive and impenetrable.

If you didn't know the combination.

Turning the dial with a gloved hand, Damian blessed his handy secretary's ingenuity in acquiring the combination for him. The handle clicked satisfactorily. Inside, Damian rifled through the papers within, flipping through to find something, anything. Most of what was contained within were accounting books and an ornate box holding jewels, but wedged between the pages of one of the books, there was a torn scrap of paper.

"I see," Damian whispered to his find. He had a brief thought of sticking the paper in his pocket, but he remembered an old saying from his father. *What is better than getting information about your enemy, is getting the information without them knowing.* Quickly, he went to Dominique's desk and seized the quill sitting in the well there. Borrowing a sheaf of expensive paper, since that was all the nobleman had on hand, he scribbled quickly, copying everything over from the scrap.

He had almost finished when he heard the sound of the main door click open.

He froze just as a guard entered, who froze in turn.

"What are you doing here, My Lord?" the guard asked cautiously.

Damian straightened, grateful for the mask over his face. Striking a noble pose, he looked the man up and down. "I could ask you the same thing."

A guilty look passed over the man's face, and Damian noticed that the guard's unshaven chin. Not at all in line with the uniform of the Cathor household.

"I..." the intruder said, licking his lips. "I heard a noise; I came to investigate."

Damian flipped closed the inkwell and picked up his list as if the man in front of him were the least of his concerns, despite the tattooing of the man in black's heart. "I am here awaiting Lord Dominique's pleasure. You had best scurry off and inform him that he has kept me waiting for a good half an hour."

"Uh, yes, My Lord," the guard said, only for the door to open to let in another equally rough-seeming guard. His eyes went wide at the sight of the faceless figure before them, and he swore once more crossing himself. The first guard whispered to him, and the second nodded and added a "Yeah, alright."

Then he was gone.

During this exchange, Damian slipped the intel he had stolen back into the book and placed it in the safe, pushing it to shut, but he was unable to finish the action as the second guard regarded him with suspicious eyes.

"You say you're waiting for Lord Dominique?"

"I must say, your speech betrays you," Damian said, moving away from the safe, toward the more open space of the office. "I didn't think House Cathor was doing so poorly they needed to find their hires near the port?"

The guard's eyes narrowed to razor edges. Without another word, he pulled a knife, proving Damian's suspicions correct. He palmed his own but kept his hand at his side so as not to give it away.

"Come on then."

CHAPTER 28

DANGEROUS ENCOUNTERS

Lydia's eyebrows shot up.

"You *know*, don't you?" Lady Regina repeated when Lydia didn't answer immediately.

She did.

She knew exactly what had happened out in the hall, or very close to it.

When she didn't answer immediately, the true noblewoman held out the black ribbon from her mask.

"The attendant seems absent, would you mind tying this up for me," Lady Regina asked.

Sensing the trap, Lydia stood. Taking the ribbons in her fingers, she carefully slid them through the layers of Lady Regina's dressed hair, careful not to catch an errant strand.

"You play the game quite admirably. If I didn't know better, I would think you have been at court for quite a while. But I do know better," Lady Regina said.

"Yes, well there are more courts than one in this city, are there not?" Lydia said, confirming what she felt Lady Regina had implied.

"Ah, I see," Lady Regina cooed. "And you wear the Imperial Phoenix well."

"I am a loyal servant of my Emperor," Lydia said simply. "But it is not the Emperor I serve."

Lady Regina's eyebrows drew together. "If it is not the Emperor you serve then…"

Their eyes met in the mirror. The tension between them rose.

"I am only here to serve in the Imperial Court. I have no intention of causing any trouble or stepping on any toes," Lydia assured her.

"And… how is he?" Lady Regina asked.

A thrum ran through Lydia. "I apologize, who?"

"Damian. How is he?"

Lady Regina whirled then, seizing Lydia's hands in both of her own. "This is not a question of a rival but of one who still cares for his well-being. How *is* he?"

"He is well," Lydia assured. She had hoped those words would be reassuring, but instead, tears beaded at the bottom of the noblewoman's eyes.

"He is well," she repeated bitterly. "How can he be well? Such a thing is not possible in this world." She turned away to lean on the vanity as she struggled to remaster herself. "Do you know of our story?"

Lydia folded her hands demurely before herself, taking the pose of an innocent nun. "I know of what is said, but no, I do not know the entirety of your story."

"Then what do you know?!" Lady Regina hissed, her pain sharpening her words.

Lydia sighed. "You could not bear to look at what had happened to him, and so he let you go," she said, carefully picking her words.

Lady Regina raised her eyes, sardonically smiling. "He was perfect, you know. He would have been the greatest Emperor our nation has ever seen. He had a vision and the intelligence and the savvy to see it happen. I would have been his perfect partner."

The bitterness faded back to sadness, and she regarded Lydia. "How can you stand to be near him?" she whispered, her voice as haunted as her eyes.

A spike of ire shot through Lydia's heart. She gripped it tight. It would neither benefit her nor Damian to be cruel to his former fiancée. Damian had so few allies as it was. "I have seen darker things than him. All that is dark about him is his face."

Lady Regina's lip curled. "What are you? Some sort of saint?"

"I'm just a whore," Lydia replied simply. "Ripped from the streets of hell."

A heavy pause waited between them.

"You have an interesting turn of phrase," Lady Regina said, reasserting her noblewoman airs. "Is there anything I can do to help you?"

"No, not at this time. If you'll excuse me," Lydia said, and she moved to leave.

"I may be harsh, my feelings are still raw, but... I am grateful," Lady Regina called out just as she reached the door. "Truly. I am grateful that there is someone, somewhere, who can give him a moment of peace."

And what about my peace? Lydia thought bitterly.

But she said nothing as she finally escaped.

"I truly am sorry, but I must find my escort," Lydia said, refusing yet another invitation to dance. She had threaded the whole ballroom over the last hour, trying and failing to be inconspicuous. Everywhere she went, people tried to engage her in conversation and when she asked if anyone had seen a Lord Raven she had been directed to three facsimiles, but none of them were Damian.

Leaving the last invitation to dance from a snake of some sort looking spitting mad, she turned into the dining hall. She did not see Damian in there either.

"Lady Phoenix!"

Groaning, Lydia curtsied toward the Imperial Phoenix, who had been feasting at one of the tables. Granted, if she hadn't been so focused on her search, she should have noted him as he was the center of the rest of the room's attention.

Standing, Xander gestured for her to come to his side. Plastering her most serene smile on her face, she glided over and bobbed deeply before him.

"Lady Phoenix, let me introduce you to our host this evening," Xander said, pulling closer another man who had stood up with him. Like his Emperor, this man had dressed as a silver bird of some kind, a fantastical version.

The silver bird went for her hand before she had a chance to offer it, in order to kiss the back.

"It is wonderful to meet you, Lady Phoenix," he purred, the voice sounding familiar. Their host? *Lord Dominique,* she remembered.

"It is a pleasure to meet you as well, Lord..." she hesitated, hoping he would fill in his creatures.

"Silver Crow," he said, naming the fictional bird.

"Ah, the Prince of Murder," she said, recounting the fairy tale.

"You know it, Lady Phoenix?" he asked.

"I have a great passion for the old stories," she said truthfully.

"Well, I suppose things such as books and tales have not come up in our *previous* encounters," he said, smiling wickedly. Where Lady Regina had spiked her with heat, this Lord Silver Crow spiked her heart with ice.

He knows me. He knows who I am! Lydia tried and failed not to swallow. His grin sharpened even more as he watched her quiet signs of panic.

"You two know each other?" Xander asked, his own eyes suddenly becoming wary, his hand rising to rest protectively on Lydia's shoulder.

The move did not go unnoticed.

"I think so, Lord Phoenix, but I cannot be sure. The masquerade has quite got me confused about who is whom. You look very much like someone I used to know and spent much pleasant time with," he said, gentrifying his tone, removing any of the implications he had earlier.

"I cannot be sure until midnight if we have met before or not, but it is a pleasure to meet you now," Lydia said graciously, finally placing where she had heard his voice before.

I suppose it was inevitable that I would run into one of my former patrons, she thought. More than anything, she wished Damian would show up in that moment and save her from this situation. But like all the times in her life before, she had only herself to rely upon.

"Lord Phoenix," she said, turning away from Lord Silver Crow to address the Emperor, "May I ask, have you seen Lord Raven about? I seem to have lost my escort."

"Are you much concerned, lady?" Xander asked.

"Only that it is improper for me to be about without him, even with so many lovely men of the court to fill my dance card," she said, giving a cheeky wink.

"Phoenixes mate for life, do they not?" Lord Silver Crow noted.

She wished she could kill with looks. It would be so efficient.

"Well, until you find him, may I take his place as a chaperone?" the Silver Crow said. "This is my ball, and I would be remiss if you were not having as good a time as possible. Would you care to dance, Lady Phoenix?"

"You may have her after me," the Imperial Phoenix cut in, stealing her hand back possessively. Lydia wanted to groan. Gods knew how this little scene looked to all the eyes watching.

There was nothing for it. The last thing she really wanted was to let this Silver Crow get her alone to ask uncomfortable questions. And the Emperor was the Emperor no matter what mask he wore.

With another of his elegant bows, the Silver Crow backed away, giving her a promising wink, and Xander once more escorted her out to the dance floor.

"The Gallop," Xander called to the room as they took to the floor. A cheer went up, and the musicians reset themselves, the music set off to the races. With the fast pace skips and spins of this dance, there was less opportunity to talk, let alone catch one's breath. Yet, Lydia could not help laughing as she whirled and spun, the liveliness of the music and the joy on Xander's face. At last, they reached promenade section, where the slower movement allowed for some brief conversation.

"The office is on the second floor to left," Xander said quickly.

"Oh" was all she had time to say, and they were off again.

When the dance finally ended, the Silver Crow, applauding along with everyone else, crossed to take his turn with her, but the Emperor charged forward instead.

"You were telling me of a new Victrola that you just purchased?" he declared, spinning the Duke around and forcing him to walk with him. This time, instead of standing there stunned, Lydia faded back into the crowd before she too could get waylaid by enterprising young men eager to dance with the Emperor's apparent mysterious favorite.

Chapter 29

DANGEROUS DISCOVERY

*Trigger warning - depictions of attempted sexual assault

Slipping out of the ballroom proved easier than earlier. Some partygoers had started to leave and several others had gone to other rooms to rest and talk in a quieter space. No one headed upstairs though, so Lydia went straight to a footman standing at the bottom.

"Excuse me," she said, with hushed urgency, leaning in close enough to flash him the hint of her assets at the top of her dress. "Can I sneak upstairs to use a washroom?"

"There is a washroom over here," he said, starting to gesture toward the ones on the other side of the ballroom, but she intercepted his arm, holding it in both of her hands, which allowed her to squeeze her breasts to make them pucker a little bit.

She had his full attention now, all while seemingly innocent. "The line has been long forever, and I simply cannot wait any longer. Please, I won't tell a soul, I promise."

The footman stared a second too long, so she gave his arm a little shake, restarting his brain. "Uh, yes, alright," he conceded, "but be quick."

"Thank you!" she said with air-headed enthusiasm before running up the stairs. Safe on the second floor, she turned left as instructed down a short hall with a pair of doors on opposite sides. Continuing the theme of left she opened the ornately carved portal. Sure enough, inside was a nobleman's office, complete with a heavy mahogany desk, carved with reliefs of men, money, and memento mori. A few dark shelves held books, and the rest of the space had expensive paintings of dramatic scenes as well as a set of tall curtains. In one corner behind the desk, there stood a large ornate safe, painted with flowers and wheels.

Ducking into the room and shutting the door behind her softly, she went directly to the safe. To her surprise, it was unlocked and slightly ajar. Was Lord Dominique that careless or had someone already opened it?

"Damian," she called out softly to the room. There were very few places for someone to hide within, only the curtains and under the desk made any sense to her. But she could see under the desk and there was nothing. She directed her attention to the curtains, but to her shock, the door to the office suddenly opened.

"Ah, interesting place to find you," the Silver Crow said as he entered, shutting and then locking the door behind him.

Fear seized Lydia's throat, but she turned out to face the nobleman, hiding the door of the safe with her skirt, which naturally pushed it closed so she could spin the lock shut with a hidden hand.

"I could say the same of you," she countered, pulling out her fan with a snap.

"Why? This is my office? You are the intruder here, Lady Phoenix," he said teasing her pseudonym. "So the question now is, who are you working for? The obvious guess would be the Emperor, but I cannot think of a reason why the Emperor would hire one such as you to do such dastardly work."

"You seem to be implying an awful lot while saying very little of substance," Lydia said, wafting the fan in her face, while she tucked her other arm across her chest in an implied defensive gesture. She took a step toward the window, but the movement set the Duke off.

"Not a step closer, Beauty," he growled, using her Crimson District name and, finally, confirming that he knew exactly who she was. Instead, he counter-stepped that direction, effectively blocking off the only form of escape available. With the door locked, she was truly trapped and no good excuse or story would work to talk her out of this situation.

"I have no direct ties to the Emperor," she said, trying to salvage what she could. "No more than you do, sir."

"Sir? You should be calling me my lord. And you should be whipped for even attempting to affect to be one of your betters," he growled, still stepping closer with slow measured treads. "Did you really think I wouldn't remember you? Half the men of the nobility have been in your bed, you whore."

"If you think such claims are going to upset me, you are sorely lacking in ammunition," Lydia said bravely as she continued her own retreat, only to find her back bumping against the furthest wall too soon. There was nowhere left to retreat.

"What were you doing in my office? What were you looking for?" Lord Dominique pressed, moving forward quicker now that she was trapped.

"The washroom," she cried out as he seized her fan arm just as she tried to whap him with it.

His thigh slammed into her hip, and he hurriedly pressed his body against her. She tried to deflect him with her free hand, but it was the one stuck in the corner and didn't do nearly enough before he thrust his elbow into her throat. Then he slapped her hard across the face. The mask took the brunt of the hit, though it tore away as well. He then seized her hair, forcing her head up and back. Lustfully, he licked the side of her face in one possessive, lewd swipe.

"Get off! she commanded, but it did no good.

"I'm going to fuck you good, and then you are going to tell me everything," he promised in her ear.

"Too bad I won't notice with that tiny dick of yours," she spat back defiantly.

He pulled her head away from the wall by her hair and slammed it back. Stars broke out in Lydia's vision, and she took it as a small favor. Maybe she would be too insensate to be aware of what was happening to her.

This isn't right. This isn't fair! her mind screamed as it had so many times before.

Her legs gave out, and she slid down to the floor. Her mind detached from what was happening around her, and she wished she were anywhere else.

I wish Damian was here, she thought.

She remained on the floor, leaning her back against the wall. Something was happening beyond herself, but there was no understanding it.

"Damian," she said weakly. She wanted to be safe in his arms again. She knew such a thing was a lie, no man could actually make her safe, but she had felt it, even if only for a moment.

"Lydia. Lydia!"

The voice pulled her back, and refocused her on the man now squatting in front of her. She wrestled to pull away from him, her last bit of defiance.

"Lydia, it's me!" the voice said with concern, raising his hands so her fists hit his palms without trying to grab or harm her.

That more than anything else broke through to her. This wasn't Lord Dominique.

"Damian?" she asked, and saying his name solidified him in her vision. He knelt before her, a black shadow of a man with his bone-white face, his usually cool blue eyes warm and wet with concern.

"Damian!" she cried, wrapping her arms around his neck. He held her tight, and over his shoulder, she could see Lord Dominique lying on the ground.

"Did you kill him?" she asked.

"No."

"Pity."

"We need to go," Damian urged, standing and lifting her from where she held on to his neck.

"Was it a mistake? Did I make a mistake?" Lydia asked as a wave of nausea rolled through her, threatening to make her lose her feet.

"No, you didn't make a mistake," he assured, but she wasn't sure about that.

"I shouldn't have tried to find you. I led him right to you," she continued.

He didn't contradict her that time. Instead, he brought her arm over his shoulders. "We're leaving," he assured.

"Wait, my mask," she said. "At least it can hide..."

He popped down and retrieved it from the ground. The ribbon was still tied, so Lydia pulled it over her face. It didn't sit perfectly, but it would do to hide the worst of the damage. Damian repositioned himself under her arm, and she pulled down his own mask over his face, tucking it into his collar. With his arm around her waist, she felt steadier, and together they could walk from the office.

When they reached the door, Damian inserted a key. She had no idea where he got it, but that was when she noticed he was missing his gloves and his hands were stained with drops of blood.

"You did kill him," she said.

"No, but if it wasn't for you, he would have caught me with a body," Damian said.

"What? I don't understand." she said, the world wavering again as they moved through the door. Damian leaned out for a second to check the hallway.

"I'll explain later," he said.

"How did he get up here so fast?" she wondered out loud. "He was with the Emperor."

"The man with the Emperor is most likely a decoy," Damian explained, as he turned her to walk down the hallway away from the ball.

"But I recognized his voice..."

"We can sort it out later. We need to hurry. I have the carriage waiting in the alley."

"Okay," she agreed and focused on putting one foot in front of the other. Her head felt better and clearer until they reached the top of the servants' stairs. Immediately, her stomach roiled. "Oh, crap."

"Close your eyes," Damian advised. "Trust me."

Despite the risk of getting caught, no one appeared as they made their way to the ground floor. And then they were out the side door into the blessed dark.

"Are you alright, milord?" the footman asked, as they reached the side of the carriage.

"I have her, get the door," Damian said urgently. Lydia didn't care, she just focused on trying to get through the door while the world insisted on spinning.

Once inside, her notorious companion slid in beside her, wrapping his arm around her shoulders. She fell into him and kept her eyes closed the rest of the journey away.

CHAPTER 30

WHAT WAS DISCOVERED

"You're going to be alright," Kinley assured Lydia back at the Undercourt. He patted her hand reassuringly, giving her a gentle smile. "You took a bump to the head, but ice will solve it, and I would like you to keep awake for a few more hours if you can."

"Thank you," she said, smiling as she readjusted the pack of ice at the back of her head, trying to not think about how expensive such a remedy was. *Damian can afford it,* she thought indignantly. "I've had worse before, I can assure you. I will be fine. I would know if something were really wrong with my head."

Kinley *hmm*'d at that, but he didn't contradict her.

She gestured at Damian who had been pacing their bedroom the entire time. "Now see to him, please."

Like someone had switched a Janus face, Kinley turned to his master dropping the kindly, solicitous demeanor entirely.

"My Lord," he said through his teeth, pointing at the chair pulled up by the bedside. It was definitely an order, not a request.

"Here, milady," Edith said, holding out a bowl to her filled with a steaming brown liquid.

"What is it?" Lydia asked, taking it in both her hands.

"Medicinal tea from my home village. It will help with the pain and clear your eyes," Edith said.

"I told you, I'm fine," Damian protested to Kinley. Then Edith shot him a look with her eyes that would have set nations ablaze. He closed his mouth and sat down obediently in the chair. He even held his hands out to Kinley to look over.

"These will swell," Kinley noted as he pulled up the stool he had been using. From one of the bowls on the tray by the bed, he selected several chips of ice, which he placed into what looked like a small rubber bag, adding a little water from a pitcher for good measure. Sealing the bag, he slapped it roughly onto Damian's right knuckles.

"I hope all of this was worth it," Edith said as she turned back to her tray on the other side where she had brought some soup.

"I'm so glad you brought all this; I forgot to eat at the ball," Lydia said.

"Drink the tea first, and then if it stays down, you can have soup," Edith ordered.

"Yes, ma'am," Lydia said, not to be cheeky. *Maybe this is what it is to have a mother who cares about you,* a rebellious small voice in her head said before she could quash it.

"I hope this was all worth it," Kinley repeated his wife's comment as he looked at a small cut at the corner of Damian's mouth, before opening that mouth to check his teeth.

"I've suffered worse in battle," Damian derided round Kinley's fingers, but then he noticed Lydia watching him, and a look of guilt washed his features. "I am sorry for getting you into this, my lady."

"*Was* it worth it?" Lydia asked, sipping another mouthful of Edith's earthy tea. It didn't taste amazing, but it was palatable, and the heat warmed inside her chest. She did imagine her head getting clearer.

Damian paused Kinley's ministrations to pull a tattered piece of paper from inside his shirt. It had blood on the outside and had been folded in haste. He handed it to her. "I was able to copy this before I was discovered," he said.

Edith took the bowl from Lydia so she could receive the paper. Inside were hasty scribbles, but she managed to make them out. "What is this?" she asked.

"I believe it is a list of the attempted attacks on the Emperor's life," he said. Kinley and Edith froze and exchanged enigmatic looks. Then Edith broke, uttering a one-word prayer as she made the sign against evil across her chest.

Lydia skimmed down the scribbled words, until she saw the last few lines at the bottom. "Guards attacked in the street. Snake in the garden. Poisoning?" she read out.

"It seems incautious to have made a list," Kinley said, holding his hand out to receive it from Lydia, who gave it over gladly.

"It seems insane," Lydia said, picking up the bowl of medicinal tea to take down the last swallow.

"I'm grateful for his arrogance," Damian said. "At least now we have some idea of what he may be trying next."

"Has he done all these things?" she asked, marveling that the list filled the page.

"I will have to compare my own notes, but I know a few of them that, yes, while thwarted, and had never reached the level of Xander's attention, have been attempted as well. Yes."

"Is this enough to bring to the Emperor or formally accuse Lord Dominique?" she asked more importantly.

Damian stood up then, waving Kinley away. The butler allowed it, seemingly satisfied with the care he was able to bestow. He started cleaning up the medical supplies while his lord started pacing.

"Honestly? No. If Lord Dominique were anyone else, on that list combined with my word, we could bury them all, but he is the scion of a rival house, and we would not be able to divorce the politics from the accusation without insurmountable proof,"

Damian said as he paced back and forth so fast he practically ran. "Honestly, my hope had been to not find anything."

She drew more mental lines. "So what kind of evidence will be enough?"

"Short of a body?" Damian sneered.

"My Lord!" Edith scolded.

Damian paused in his pacing to give her a look that said, "I didn't mean it," before he continued. "We would need to capture his conspirators in the act publicly enough to involve the other Houses. Then it would be about finding a culprit to blame and the Imperial House's ability to steer them to the right conclusion."

"And in the meantime, Lord Dominique thinks I've found what he is trying to hide and will be intent on getting rid of me to cover his crimes," Lydia said. "Assaulting a woman such as me would harm his reputation, but it would be me in handcuffs or dead. What I've witnessed would not be enough for what you describe."

"Kinley, send for Alexandros," Damian suddenly said. "We are leaving the city."

"My Lord?" Kinley questioned, sending another glance back toward his wife, but she didn't have any answers.

"Where are we going?" Lydia asked in place of them.

Damian returned to the edge of the bed and sat down. "While I do not believe Lord Dominique will find you here, you need not be trapped down here for your recovery. Would you…" he hesitated, and she could tell he was making the decision right then and there, "What would you think about seeing the place that will one day become your own?"

"Summerbourne?" Edith said. "My Lord, we have minimal staff there, and we would need a week to get it ready for your lordship and the lady."

"It will be fine, Edith," Damian countered. "We will need very little. It is for her recovery. Alexandros can take care of the arrangements. It's what he's paid for."

Lydia laid a hand over Damian's, calming him. "I would like that very much," she agreed in order to keep the peace.

Her words galvanized him. "Excellent, we will leave as soon as things can be arranged."

We? It took her aback, but she realized he said "we." He intended to come with them.

"What of your brother?" she asked carefully.

"I've taken steps to ensure he stays safe now. I've brought my cousin to court, who has sworn to stick with him no matter what. He even has a special dispensation to disobey the Emperor."

Lydia's eyebrows jumped. "There is such a thing?"

"The Emperor's word is not absolute," Damian said. "Any ruler who tries to have absolute power will find themselves absolutely dead, and often sooner than later."

"A fool may speak truth to a king," Kinley said, timing his words as he left the room.

"I think you can have this now," Edith said, trading the empty tea bowl for the stew.

"To Summerbourne, then," Lydia agreed.

Edith also retreated from the room, pulling the door closed, finally leaving the two of them alone.

"You should eat," Lydia said, indicating the other bowl resting on his side, forgotten.

"You didn't make a mistake," he said. "Before ... when you came into the office."

"I get it now," she cut in. "I was intended to be your distraction so you could pull your tricks."

"For all the good it did me," he said, rubbing at his forehead. "Nearly got myself caught. Twice."

"Lady Chrysanthemum?"

"Yes, and then later, when I was discovered by two of his lackeys ... I was able to dispose of one out the window, but he could have found me behind that curtain with the other if you hadn't distracted him. God, I'm a fool."

"What I don't understand is why did you ask me to stay by your side? Earlier in the carriage. And why did Xander tell me where to find you?"

"For the first, I simply misspoke. I realized too late when I slipped away what I had said and how it would be confusing for anyone. As for Xander ... he does not have the stomach for this. And because I was late returning, he probably became worried."

"Yes, he seemed more informed of the plan than me, clearly," she said sourly.

"It had not been my intention to involve you at all."

"Then what did you want me there for?" she asked sharply.

"I ... thought you would enjoy yourself," he answered. "Like I said, I'm a fool."

Any other ire she harbored went out to sea. "I did. It was great fun," she assured. "But next time you better at least dance with me once before you disappear."

"On my honor."

Chapter 31

ESCAPE TO SUMMERBOURNE CASTLE

"*The Lord of Kinsington Place* was a farce, and I think you know it well," Lydia exclaimed.

"Do you say that as a matter of opinion, or are you saying that the format of the play is intended to be one of farce?" Damian countered.

"Do all your answers come in the form of questions? I feel like I haven't discussed anything of import with you, it's just been one long game of—"

"My lady," Damian said, holding up his hand to stop her while his gaze drifted out the window of the carriage. "We are almost there."

She turned to follow his gaze and lost her breath in the next moment. Though the world had turned full dark as the carriage cleared a line of trees, she saw a great estate house filled with light. Stately columns of the rectangular buildings made it look like a temple to her eyes. A sacred place she did not belong to, and she felt so small.

A cool hand took hers.

"Do you like it?" he asked.

Tears beaded her eyes as she tried to look at him, the skeletal face blurring away. "It's beautiful," she said.

"No," Damian shook his head, not accepting her platitude. "Do you *like* it?"

"I... I'm not sure if I dare," she answered softly.

"What do you mean?" he asked, leaning closer to catch her gaze.

She huffed, wishing she had had the courage to bring it up sooner. "Xander told me..." she hesitated. If any other patron had done this to her, she would have demanded an answer immediately before proceeding, but why was she so reluctant?

"What did he tell you?" Damian asked warily.

She sighed again. "He said that Summerbourne is not yours to give to me. That its ownership is in question?"

Sitting up, Damian's brows furrowed together so hard she could clearly see the white hair bristling on his face. "Oh really?" he said, shifting his jaw. "Is that what he's claiming?"

"Yes, that is what he said. Since you cannot be the heir anymore, Summerbourne is traditionally granted to the Crown Princess."

Damian attempted to stand up as if he intended to march back to the capital right up to his brother and fight right then before dropping back into his seat. "I'm going to fix this, Lydia."

"So... he's right?"

"No! He is very much wrong and..." He took a sharp breath in, forcing himself to calm down, even though he still growled at the end of his exhale. "I will clear it up. You have nothing to worry about. I will honor the contract no matter what."

The carriage pulled up in front of the house sooner than Lydia realized, the wheels crunching on the gravel. Through the windows, she could see at least a dozen people lined up the steps leading to the front door. Maids on one side and footmen on the other led up to a pair waiting at the top. As the carriage came to a full stop, two of the footman on the ground stepped forward. One opened the door, while in perfect sync the other pulled the steps.

"My lady," the door footman said courteously, offering her his hand so she could disembark.

Lydia adjusted her bonnet, hoping it did not look too disheveled from the trip, and nervously took the footman's hand. The rain had stopped, but the ground showed damp in the gaslight torches on the opposing sides of the door.

Trying to effect her best, most proper pose, Lydia stood in front of the waiting people, tucking her hands before herself as she waited for her partner to exit the carriage. To her alarm, instead, the carriage pulled away, leaving her standing there alone.

"Oh! I..." she said, looking desperately between the vanishing vehicle and the two people at the top of the stairs who had started to descend. "I'm sorry... I don't..."

"Welcome to Summerbourne, your Ladyship," Kinley said, bowing at the waist after he came down the stairs with Edith to greet her.

"It is a delight to greet you, your ladyship. Welcome to Summerbourne Castle," Edith added.

"If you will come this way, we will introduce you to your household, my Lady." Kinley gestured toward the line of people waiting.

Several of them straightened up even straighter than they were already standing, and Lydia wondered how many of them knew what a fraud she was. They were going to be serving someone who should have been one of them. Surely the smiles they were flashing at her would fall immediately if they all knew the truth.

A flurry of names went by, and Lydia couldn't even hope to hold them all in her head. She smiled and nodded to each introduction, however, and each servant bowed and curtsied in turn. Finally, they reached the top, and the housekeeper turned to one young woman whose dignified smile was threatening to burst at the seams into a full-fledged grin.

"And you remember our granddaughter, Kitty," Edith finally said.

"Hello, milady," Kitty said, bobbing.

"I am sure you are tired from your journey, your Ladyship, but there is an urgent matter that we must discuss with you, and it cannot wait until morning," Edith said, leaning in to speak in a lower tone.

"Oh, then yes," Lydia said, her mind sprinting to several pressing possibilities.

"This way, milady," Kinley said, offering his arm to help her up the stairs and through the doorway.

Warm candlelight made the dark wood panels glow richly. While not a modern castle, the design of the castle spoke more of the weight of its history than its opulence. Old paintings of dignified nobles from other eras lined the large hall in which she stood with plants in enormous pots and a stately grandfather clock ticking away. Two philosopher's columns framed the door as she entered, and a few steps past the foyer, she felt drawn two directions. To her right lay a switching back grand staircase with beautiful stained-glass windows behind it all the way up to the next floor. To her left stood a pair of doors that led into a room filled with books and paintings. The hall extended all the way to the back of the house with what seemed like branches going left and right.

Before she explored further, Edith came up beside her while Kinley continued on down the hall, heading toward the back of the house.

"Your trunks will be delivered to your quarters, milady," Edith continued, "And Kitty will see that they are unpacked by the time you wish to retire. Bath water is being heated for you as well, along with a bite of supper."

"Well then we must see to this issue because I very much wish to partake in all of that," Lydia said with a hungry smile. The housekeeper nodded and gestured for her mistress to head into the room with all the books.

Like the entryway, this room felt ancient. There was a soft scent of old books. Lydia took a deep lungful and detected notes of polish and flowers, which there were several vases of throughout the room as well as a handful of gas lamp sconces on the walls between the shelves. At the far end, she spotted a ladder on wheels to reach the higher shelves. There were several comfortable looking chairs forming reading nooks and a fireplace with a square of couches set up in front of it. She could imagine a family meeting up there to share an evening and a fire. As she stepped further inside, Lydia noted that tucked by a large window set into an alcove, a little back from the direct view, was a large stately desk. It looked set and waiting for a master to come conduct the county's business. She supposed that might soon be her duty, now that she was Summerbourne's mistress, more or less.

"Where should I—?" Lydia asked, turning to Edith for direction on where they expected her to go to tell her of this urgent matter. Edith easily gestured toward the fire.

As Lydia approached and prepared to sit down on one of the sofas there, a pair of maids entered with a tea cart. Sitting down, Edith finally remembered to pull off her bonnet. Edith retrieved the topper and left with it just as one of the maids passed her a welcome cup of tea.

"Is there anything else, Lady?" the other maid asked.

"Uh, no. No, I don't think so," Lydia said, and then both young women bobbed to her in unison and left out the door they had entered in. And just like that, Lydia found herself alone.

Lacking any further direction, she took a sip of the tea and let it drive the chill from her. Left sitting there, she grew concerned for a moment, and when half the tea was gone, she reconciled that she needed to get up and go find out what was wrong. Setting down her teacup, she stood up, turned and then immediately startled.

"Dear Lords! You scared the life out of me!"

CHAPTER 32

THERE IS A PROBLEM

"Dear Lords! You scared the life out of me!" she exclaimed, grabbing for her chest to check that her heart hadn't burst out through it.

"I apologize, lady," Damian said, and he took a few steps further into the room. Behind him one of the bookcases shifted, sliding back into place seamlessly with the rest of the wall. "I did not want the rest of the staff to see me."

"Is that a secret passage?" she asked, truly excited by the prospect.

"Yes, indeed," Damian said. "This castle is chock full of such secrets. I will show them all to you in due time."

Just then Edith and Kinley entered, the butler bearing a stack of correspondence. Yet, Edith did not pull the door closed until Alexandros entered, dressed in an Inverness coat with no hat and apparently no trousers or shoes.

"Alexandros? You are here too?" Lydia asked, her eyebrows shooting to the ceiling.

"He brought the message," Edith explained as if it were perfectly normal. In fact, everyone seemed perfectly at ease with Alexandros's presence and state of dress.

"But how? You were at the Undercourt when we left, how can you have gotten here before us?" She looked to Damian for an explanation as he did not seem nearly as flummoxed as her at Alexandros's appearance.

"Oh no," he said softly, his eyes widening.

Now everyone reacted, their eyes mirroring their master's.

"Alright," Lydia said regarding them all. "There is apparently something here that everyone knows that I don't."

Alexandros himself stepped forward, fidgeting frantically. "Oh, My Lord, we really don't have time for explanations right now!"

Damian's pale lips thinned in his face. "Then you better show her quick."

The secretary huffed, picking at some dry skin on his hands with his nails as he rubbed them so frequently, then he abruptly ... shrank.

Before Lydia's eyes, the figure of the man disappeared into the coat as it dropped down to the ground. For a brief moment, the cloth continued to move and undulate as a form wriggled from within. Then Edith leaned forward to pick up the coat and out spilled a bird with brilliant red, orange, and yellow feathers.

"A phoenix!" Lydia cried, stepping back from the impossible bird. "They still exist?"

The phoenix turned its majestic head toward her, resettling its feathers on its back. And then resettling them again. And again.

"Yes, the Imperial phoenix still exists," Damian said. "And he is bonded to me. You may turn back now," he said the last to the bird who was so unsettled he seemed to be molting underfeathers. Edith dropped the coat back over the bird and a few moments later, Alexandros stood before them.

"This is why you trust him implicitly," Lydia said, barely able to breathe from her amazement. Damian nodded.

"But why do you have him acting as your secretary of all things?" she asked, then amended, speaking directly to Alexandros. "Why are you acting as his secretary of all things?"

"It was one of the few jobs I have yet to do, and honestly, this is not that pressing of a matter!"

"Oh, sorry," Lydia apologized.

Damian held out his hands to placate the bird... man... secretary. "Come and explain. It looks like this situation is going to take a moment to figure out then?" he asked, nodding to the tea set.

"We have a situation, My Lord, that has complicated things," Edith started.

"Your brother is coming!" Alexandros reported through his upper register.

Kinley cleared his throat at the impropriety. "Apparently, his Imperial Majesty is due to arrive the day after tomorrow." And handed over the correspondence.

Lydia's heart leapt at that news. "What? Here?" she asked and looked to Damian. She noted the Imperial Seal while Damian scanned the contents then passed it to her before he pressed his fingers on either side of his temples to rub. "Why?"

"We don't know," Edith said.

Lydia didn't bother to read the contents, just noted the signature at the bottom before tossing it on the coffee table.

"Dammit, I told him to stay in the city," Damian said, irritated. He started his pacing. "And so like him too, to simply show up somewhere with little to no warning."

Alexandros wrung his hands. "That is quite correct, My Lord, I don't know what we are going to do because it sounds like he has his whole court in tow. We have the *room* to accommodate them and their servants of course, but that is over a hundred beds to be prepared, never mind the amount of food that would be required for them all. We need at least two weeks and he's given us a day!"

"I plan on sending word to the village to pull in any and all hands, but we thought it best to wait until your arrival, Your Lordship," Kinley said.

"Can he do that? Can he just arrive at a house that doesn't belong to him?" Lydia said, asking her thoughts out loud.

"He's the Emperor," everyone in the room said together.

"This was not what I had planned," Damian growled. He turned to face Lydia. "I apologize. You were supposed to be safe here, but he's bringing the whole damn problem to you!"

"That brings us to the other issue, the Emperor's message contained orders to make up the master bedroom for his personal use..." Alexandros added, clearly that statement caused him acute distress.

"Absolutely not," Damian said in no uncertain terms. Edith and Kinley exchanged apprehensive glances.

Alexandros nearly fainted. "Sir, the Emperor—"

"Does not own this place ... and never did," he growled and turned to look toward the windows, but they were covered with long curtains, obscuring any outside view of the night.

Lydia looked to her housekeeper and butler, but they cast their eyes to the ground, waiting with worried faces.

"We welcome the Emperor to Summerbourne Castle," she said.

Damian turned to her, saying nothing, his body language telling her little.

"We have little choice at this point, am I correct, My Lord?" she asked, as Edith refilled her cup of tea. "The Emperor cannot be denied, and obviously, there is some bureaucratic oversight that is causing this situation. We can assume that the Emperor believes that this castle is more or less empty?"

"One could presume," Damian said carefully. "I did not apprise him of our plans."

She nodded. "And there we are. So I will prepare to greet our guests. Unless you would rather we leave and let them have the place?" She took a sip of her tea.

He started pacing again. "While I have other estates, I cannot be too far from the capital right now. I had wanted you to get some rest after what happened at Lord Dominique's ball, but my other estates are open to you as well."

"I'm fine, I told you," Lydia insisted, resisting the impulse to touch the place where Lord Dominique had struck her. The mask *had* absorbed most of the blow, and there were no marks really, but the flesh was still a bit tender there. "So is that what we're going to do? Leave?"

Damian growled. "No. If he thinks that he can lay claim to this estate, our quitting it would make such a thing easier for him to do." He regarded Alexandros. "I know you've flown a lot today, but do you think you can return to the capital and inform my brother that the Summerbourne Castle is not available for his spontaneous holiday?"

Alexandros picked harder at his skin a moment. "I can yes," he agreed after a moment.

"I appreciate it—" Damian tried to say, but Alexandros interrupted him.

"I'm not a courier in this life though," he reported snippily.

"I understand. You can refuse if you wish," Damian said, bowing his head to the bird of legend.

"It's fine. It's fine," Alexandros muttered and shifted again into the coat. Lydia longed to see the full transformation without the cover, because her mind just couldn't reconcile how it was done.

Soon the beautiful bird emerged from the coat and shook out his feathers. He then waddled over to the door and Kinley went ahead of him to open the way. Unable to help herself, Lydia stood up and followed to watch as the bird strutted to the door, shook his wings once more and took off into the darker night. Except instead of disappearing into the blackness, light seemed to glow from the creature's feathers. She watched him for as far as she could before he disappeared entirely behind the tall trees.

"Wow," Lydia breathed as Damian stepped up beside her. "He's so ... awesome."

"Yes," he said, matching her pitch.

"And he's yours?" she asked.

"No, not exactly. He's my friend."

"I thought the Imperial phoenix... I thought he could only be bonded to the Emperor?"

Damian shook his head. "Often is, but not exclusively. When he is reborn he bonds to whomever he wishes, and it may not even be the same person it was before his reincarnation. They are reborn every twenty years as long as no harm comes to them."

"That is..." she laughed softly. "All the stories are true? What about unicorns and dragons?"

Damian shrugged. "I've never seen any of those creatures, but Alexandros is real."

Studying his profile as the forgotten prince watched his friend fly away, Lydia laid a hand along his cheek. "Thank you for sharing him with me."

He took her hand and kissed the palm.

"I should have told you about him sooner."

She shook her head. "We are getting to know one another piece by piece. These things will come in their own time."

"I will get this thing sorted, with Summerbourne. I will not break our agreement," he assured.

"I... I believe you."

Chapter 33

THE COUNTESS

Once the plans had been settled, Lydia finally found herself upstairs in the master suite. Standing inside, she marveled, for it was easily twice the size of her bedroom in the Crimson District. The canopied bed stood as the main feature with tassels and curtains waiting to be drawn. The carpet was a rich forest green while the walls were a soft sky blue as if the bedroom were in the center of a meadow. Like all the other rooms, this one had its own fireplace, and a warm fire crackled within already. There were even faux pillars in each corner, echoes of the ones in the main hall. Side tables and a small desk completed the room which had another door that led to a large closet and dressing room that continued through into its own bathing room. Her clothes had already been unpacked and hung up in the closet, and she was surprised to find Kitty had laid out a nightgown and robe for her.

"Your bath is ready, milady!" Kitty chirped with nearly overwhelming enthusiasm.

"For heaven's sake, Kitty," Edith chided. "Her Ladyship can hear you quite well enough, no need to shout it at her!"

The young woman, who may have been about the same age as Lydia, if Lydia were to guess, immediately dimmed herself. "Apologies, Ladyship. I get overly excited sometimes."

"It is alright," Lydia assured and passed into the bathroom. "I am just about as enthusiastic for this bath, if you will help me undress?"

Kitty brightened up and jumped forward. "Yes, milady."

"I will go check on your supper," Edith said and graciously took herself out of the room.

It took no time at all to get out of her travel-worn clothes before Lydia could step into the gracious warm water. The water stirred, scented with lavender mixed with something she couldn't quite place. Placing it would have been more effort than Lydia was willing to expend at that moment, and instead, she sighed, letting herself sink up to her neck.

Kitty had twisted her long hair up and out of the way a moment, but now she returned with another wash basin, which she set at the head of the tub.

"Shall I wash your hair, milady?" the maid asked.

"Yes, please," Lydia agreed.

"I have this very special soap just for this," Kitty said, as she pulled up the stool for her to sit on as she cared for Lydia's tresses. "It smells like roses! I found it in the market the other day when we went shopping for personal effects for your Ladyship. Ms. Kinley thought it a bit too much; I think it's gloriously romantic!" And the maid continued talking like that for the entire time she washed Lydia's hair. The courtesan turned mistress didn't really mind. She simply closed her eyes and listened, picking up some of the stories of this new household she had earned with her trade.

"I'm sorry, milady, am I prattling on too long?" Kitty asked, when she finally took a breath and realized Lydia hadn't said a word the whole time.

"No, no, not at all," Lydia assured as Kitty poured a bowl of warm water over her hair to rinse it of the soap, which Lydia had to agree was romantically nice. "In fact, do you mind if I ask you a question?"

"Not at all, milady!" Kitty said enthusiastically as she started toweling.

"What were you told about me, when you heard I was coming here?"

"Oh." Now that had rendered the maid speechless. "Um... nothing really. Only that Lord Damian would be bringing a new countess to stay and be the lady of our manor. I was so excited to be among the first to meet you when we came to prepare you for the ball."

That sounded correct. "But who do you *think* I am?" she pressed.

"Um... my Lady, Countess of Summerbourne."

Okay, that one was on Lydia.

She turned in the bath to look at her maid, one arm looped over the side of the tub. "But who do you *think* I am? What do you suspect?" she said, giving the maid no room to wiggle out of the conversation.

"I think..." Kitty shut her mouth again, as if determined that would stop what she thought from coming out of her mouth. "It is not my place to say, Lady" was her final, resolute answer.

Lydia supposed that was a good thing; she didn't want a dumb maid who didn't know when to keep her mouth shut. Kitty was clearly not mentally deficient, simply unworldly. She had had no need to grow up too fast in order to survive. Lydia found herself envying the little maid. While the courtesan now found herself almost a countess, how much happier would she have been as a maid, with parents who had obviously loved her and a place she truly belonged without even needing to think or worry about it?

But wishing for another life wouldn't actually make it come to pass. If so, she would have been on her hundredth life by now.

Anxious now, Kitty recapped the sweet-smelling bottles and put them up on the sideboard by the tub when Lydia grabbed one of her hands.

"I apologize, I do not wish to put you on the spot. I just..." Lydia looked down, affecting shyness she didn't feel. "I just want to know... what you all think of me, of all this."

That appealed to Kitty's romantic nature.

"Oh, my Lady," Kitty said, leaning in conspiratorially. "It is all terribly romantic! Like out of a fairy tale. You must have the purest heart to be able to look past Prince Damian's curse to see the man he is inside. It is a pity that you cannot marry him in earnest, being that he is forbidden to marry, but this is the next best thing, is it not? Neither of you will have to be lonely anymore."

"He cannot marry?" Lydia sat up genuinely surprised at that. "You mean he has not married yet."

"No, no, he can't marry anybody. It's part of the curse," Kitty insisted. She stood up and went to fetch Lydia's robe and slippers, leaving her to think about that statement. *He cannot marry?* she thought.

Lydia didn't probe that chestnut any further that night.

Kitty returned holding out the fine robe to her, but as Lydia stood up to slip it on, the little maid gasped.

Instinctively, Lydia's arm tucked against her side along her left breast, not to cover the breast, but to cover the deep puckered scar that she knew the maid had spotted when she stood. Cursing herself, she realized she had let her guard down and let someone else see it, the one major flaw in her otherwise desirable body.

"My Lady, what... who did that to—"

"It is nothing," she snapped and took the robe from her maid to cover herself.

Kitty said nothing more, and the moment passed as she helped her mistress into her slippers. The bath had left Lydia so sleepy, it was a wonder she kept putting one foot in front of the other, let alone two thoughts in the same basket.

Leaving her bathroom, a fine dinner greeted her, set up on a little table before the warm fireplace. The two armchairs waiting there had been pulled up close to it and a shadowy figure sat in one, staring at the fire.

"Damian?" Lydia asked, and Kitty quickly bobbed and scurried out the door with a knowing smile on her face.

He started and turned to her. His face was laid bare to her, though his eyes still told her he remained wary of her judgment. Since only time could secure his trust, she smiled and went to seat herself in the other armchair.

"Did you bathe yourself, My Lord?" she asked.

"Oh," he said, running his hand over his shorter hair. "Yes." He wore only a shirt and loose trousers with braces to hold them up. The top buttons of the shirt were undone, however, allowing her a full view of his neck and collarbones. She had seen many men naked before, yet somehow just the sight of their collarbones made them seem that much more undressed. Lydia figured it must be what men see when they spy a shapely ankle or even knee.

"So what is the plan for the evening after we dine?" she asked, lifting the cover off her plate herself. Beneath the warm aroma of a thick beef stew greeted her nostrils. It may not have been the fanciest meal the noble class would eat, but it was perfect to warm up after a long, cold trip and before a heavy sleep. Crunchy little bread loaves had been served with it, and Lydia knew she was in heaven with the first bite.

"Sleep, I should imagine," Damian said, hesitating before plucking up his own spoon, making himself join her.

She smiled at his action.

"What?" he asked.

"This is pleasant," she said sweetly.

"Oh," he looked down at his spoonful of stew. "I suppose it is." Yet, he still hesitated under the pressure of her gaze. "Will this do? Is there anything more you want?"

Lydia blinked at the questions. "I... I suppose it does," she said truthfully. And for the first time in her entire life, she decided to trust it.

CHAPTER 34

A MISTAKE

Lydia woke up feeling warm and safe. Rolling over, she found herself tucked into a shoulder with an arm that naturally came around her, pulling her into the nook along his body. Breathing in the scent of the man beside her, she slipped her palm over his bare skin, feeling the planes and dips of him, all while her eyes were closed. Slowly, her exploration went lower and lower, over his stomach, finding the dip of his belly button.

His chest rumbled as he stirred.

Mischievously, she slipped her hand lower, following a trail her fingers discovered made of hair as it led from his belly button down through a forest until it encountered the greatest tree.

"Mmmm," she moaned in her own throat as she encircled the tree with her fingers, feeling its soft velvety surface.

"You are playing a dangerous game," Damian said softly, pulling her closer so he could kiss her forehead.

"They are the only games worth playing," she said as she started to pump slowly with her hand. He kissed her nose, then her mouth, and only then did she release him so she could hold onto something more stable as he rocked up above her. The quilt they had been sharing fell away. In the pre-dawn light, she could see his ghost-like skin all the way down from shoulder to buttocks to his feet.

"You exposed yourself," she said, noting it. "I was pretty sure you had a shirt on when we went to sleep last night."

"I became too hot in the night," he murmured as he planted kisses along her collarbone. "I hope it does not disturb you too much.

"Not at all," she said as she arched up to help him in his exploration.

His fingers pulled her nightgown, parting the top so he could get more access. But soon, he became unsatisfied with that, and tugged up on the bottom edge, sliding it up past her hips, then her ribs.

"No," she said catching it in time before it exposed her entirely, pushing his hands back, then going to distract him with a kiss. "I want you. I want you now!" she said against his lips and scooted herself down into position.

Instead, he scooted down himself to kiss her stomach. She allowed it, keeping her hands on his shoulders as his own kisses went lower and lower. She moaned hard as his lips met her lower ones, dancing over nerves as his tongue explored her. Writhing on the bed, she opened her legs to allow him more access, and he cupped her bottom in his hands so he could feast easier. His talents turned her into a puddle, and she forgot everything except the feel of his mouth on her.

She barely noticed when he climbed back up her body, nor when he pulled at her nightgown, once again aiming to disrobe her.

"No!" she cried too sharply to pretend it had been anything else but a denial.

"What's wrong?" Damian asked, startled, the haze of their lovemaking dispelled.

She tugged the nightgown down to her stomach. "Nothing, nothing, I apologize," she tried to amend, and tried to reach for him again, but this time he held his hands up.

"Lydia, why won't you let me undress you?" he asked.

"My Lady! My Lady!" an urgent call came from the other side of her bedroom door, followed by desperate knocking.

"Well, that disturbs the constitution," Lydia noted, using the excuse to roll away and pull down the nightgown safely over herself.

Wordlessly, Damian rose to do the same, retrieving a pair of his trousers hanging over the back of the vanity chair. He disappeared with them into her dressing room while she went to the door.

"My Lady!"

"One moment, Kitty," Lydia called as she grabbed for her robe. Damian exited her dressing room, plucking up his shirt as he went. He padded quickly over to the door that joined the master suite to the mistress's suite, the irony that they had switched proper rooms not at all lost on her. Once he left, she belted the robe closed and went to open it to her maid's frantic face.

"What is it Kitty? I was just about to call for you, though it is still a bit early for me," Lydia said.

"Oh, my Lady! He's here!" Kitty cried, wringing her hands so hard they were bright red.

"He's here?" Lydia's mind searched for who the maid could mean, and only one thought came to mind just as the maid said it.

"The Emperor! He's arriving as we speak!" Kitty squealed.

"But... but he wasn't supposed to come until tomorrow?" Lydia asked. *Did Alexandros not make it to the capital?* she thought.

"We just had word from Peter!" Kitty said as if Lydia would know who that was. "He came over on Matthew's horse just as the Emperor crossed the edge of the estate. They will be here any moment. We must get you dressed!"

Whatever Lydia thought about that was lost as the maid practically tackled her back into the room, rushing her into her dressing room and bathroom.

During the course of dressing and hair, where Lydia barely had a chance to use the chamber pot, Kitty went over the whole story, where the gamekeeper's assistant Peter, had spotted the Emperor arriving on horseback with an entourage of at least a dozen other noblemen and guards. The Emperor had stopped to speak to the gamekeeper, whose name turned out to be Matthew, hence the owner of the horse, giving the assistant a chance to ride up to the estate to give the warning of the Emperor's imminent arrival. Apparently, the house was all in a furious uproar.

"Oh, we're not going to make it!" Kitty said urgently, tearing through the hung dresses, trying to pick one suitable to meet the Emperor.

"That one," Lydia said with confidence, pointing to the rose-pink dress she had worn for her endowment meeting.

"Are you sure?" Kitty asked, taking it down.

"Yes, and these," Lydia said, swiping up a bouquet of white and pink summer flowers from the vase in her dressing room. "Can you weave them into a crown, like the Lady in Maii?"

"Like the summer deity?" Kitty repeated, struggling to comprehend. "I suppose, but..."

"Good, give me the dress, you start weaving. Hurry, hurry," Lydia ordered, taking her pink dress so she could drop it over her head.

Moaning, Kitty went to the bathroom to do as her mistress bid, dumping the vase's water into the now empty tub and picking out the flowers.

Using her clever fingers, Lydia did up the ties on the dress that she could reach on her own and made adjustments to her hair to accommodate her forming idea. Kitty's fingers proved to be just as clever as she wove a summer crown of flowers as quickly as Lydia could fasten her dress. With a wordless synchronicity that should have only been possible with a long acquaintance, they traded the crown and the stays, Lydia lifting the flowers to her head as Kitty finished adjustments to the dress.

"How do I look?" Lydia asked.

Kitty bit her lower lip, her brow pinched in worry. "Are you sure about this, milady?"

The courtesan smiled. "Believe in me."

"My Lady!" Edith called as she crossed the room to the dressing room, only to come up short when she saw the unexpected Countess. "What on earth?" she asked, baldly staring at the woman.

"Slippers," Lydia ordered, and Kitty scurried to grab them up.

"Slippers?" Edith asked, trying to process what she witnessed.

"Yes, Edith, good," Lydia said as she stepped into her shoes as Kitty placed them in front of her feet. "Get all the maids and footmen you can and have them bring every bit of flowers in the house into the foyer."

"What?" Edith exclaimed.

"We don't have time, your Lady gave you an order," Kitty said, showing some steel.

"Please, Edith, trust me," Lydia said, touching the older woman's arm.

The touch seemed to bring the housekeeper back to herself, and she jetted forward to comply with Kitty and Lydia right behind her. Every servant they encountered on the way down to the foyer was pressed into service. Soon Lydia found herself by the front door, directing people as they brought vase after vase of bright flowers, setting them out along the walls and on every available table surface within easy reach. She even had Kitty run back to her bathroom to retrieve the remaining flowers from her crown.

"Edith, where is Lord Damian?" Lydia asked when she was able to grab the housekeeper again.

The older woman leaned in to speak more conspiratorially. "He is staying out of sight," she assured. "None in the court but his Imperial Majesty can see him."

Lydia nodded her understanding, and the woman moved on finishing the last touches as the sound of horses trumpeting cut the preparations short.

"Everyone! Outside, line up for greeting, now. Just set whatever you have down where you are and go!" Lydia called. All at once, the servants rushed out, straightening jackets and fixing apron strings as they assembled on the steps.

Kinley joined his wife at the top of the steps, giving his new mistress a worried look as he pulled the door shut.

And then all was quiet and waiting.

Chapter 35

THE EMPEROR ARRIVES

She did not have to wait long. Softly she could hear the sound of gravel kicking up as horses bellowed objections to being drawn up so short. Men's voices barked and laughed in chorus with it. Holding the loose flowers to her chest, Lydia glanced around at the chaos of her making and selected the best place to position herself. She barely got in place when the door flung open.

Xander entered, laughing. "No, no, don't fret Kinley, we're not going to require much, we're just getting away from the stuffy stuffs of the Capital—"

He stopped sharply as his crystal blue eyes fell on Lydia.

"Oh!" she cried out softly, as if startled by his sudden appearance.

The young man, Emperor Magnus the IV, let go of the door and walked in further. The door never hit the jamb as his fellows piled in, as awestruck as himself at the sight before them.

"Lady Phoenix?" he asked, mystified.

Lydia rose, even though she hadn't been fully bidden to yet. "Welcome, your Imperial Highness. I didn't know you were coming so soon," she glanced around at all of the flowers around her. "We were not prepared just as yet."

He barely noted the flowers as she had him completely entranced. "I could not have received a better reception than if the Goddess of Summer herself had greeted me," he said gallantly. He came forward and offered his hand, which she took. He kissed the back of it with a sweeping elegant bow.

After his warm, lingering kiss on her bare skin, he straightened and clasped that hand to his heart. "You must forgive us, Lady, for arriving on such short notice and barely announced."

"I thought Summerbourne was unoccupied?" a not too subtle whisper cut through from behind the Emperor. A few heads were nodding.

"Apparently, there has been some oversight," the Emperor declared, putting an end to any other comments from the gallery. "We were unaware that Summerbourne Castle was occupied, and for that, we offer you our humblest apologies."

"Think nothing of it, sir. I am but a humble servant ready to serve the crown," she said with another gracious bow. "My home is your home."

"Imperial Highness." Lord Dominique stepped forward out of the crowd of men, and Lydia's heart sped up. "Is this the enchanting creature who took my ball by storm the other night?" he asked, smiling, though his predatory eyes carried a warning. Her performance was not working on him.

Lydia curtsied to him, lowering her eyes demurely so she wouldn't have to keep meeting them. "Welcome, Lord Dominique. Thank you so much for hosting such an entertaining evening. My breath was taken away."

Lord Dominique nodded as courtesy demanded in front of his Emperor. "And these are your holdings?" he questioned. "I was very certain there was no Lady at Summerbourne, nor had there been since the late Emperor's first wife passed."

"Obviously, she is the Countess of Summerbourne, one of my cousins," the Emperor declared boisterously, as if he were certain of the truth, and therefore, it became the truth.

"Obviously," the other man agreed, yielding to his lord with a bow of his head before turning to Lydia. "Forgive me, Lady, I did not recognize you. If I may formally introduce myself, I am Dominique, Scion of House Cathor. It is a pleasure to meet such a Beauty."

Then a third man popped up, throwing his arms around both the Emperor and the Scion of Cathor with a cheerful, informal camaraderie. "Petre, I'm also this rascal's cousin," he piped, shaking the Emperor, much to his Imperialness's delight. "You are related to the Wexon line, are you not? You can tell by the hair. All of the cousins from that line have dark hair."

"Oh yes," the group of men said, all agreeing as one, nodding their heads, except the Emperor of course, who would never agree in consensus as a group like that. That sort of unconscious body language had been trained out of him from a young age.

Instead, he added to this story they were building about her. "That would make you my third cousin through my grandfather, I believe. So the Imperium finally sorted out the inheritance right after the Crown Prince..." He stopped speaking then, his face going still.

"I do not know if things have been settled, in truth, but I was told I could stay here for the duration," she confirmed, offering him cover for his odd pause.

"Then I declare that settled now, Lady Lydia. I formally declare it so. You are now the Countess of Summerbourne, by Imperial decree," the Emperor crowed. There were murmurings from the group of men at this, and Lydia struggled to understand what it all meant.

She was now the Countess of Summerbourne? What did this mean? What did all these noblemen think? What would Damian think?

Is our contract still valid?

All these thoughts sped through her head as Xander took her hand to kiss it gallantly, and all the nobles applauded.

"Well, this is all very interesting, but I'm starved!" one of the other young men declared and charged into her library as if he would find a repast waiting for him there.

"That was the Viscount Louis of Coralus," Scion Petre said, as they all groaned at the rude behavior. "You'll have to excuse him. The only one who can keep him in line is his Imperial Majesty here." Petre slapped at the Emperor's shoulder where it still hung over cordially.

"Xander while here!" the Emperor said, and then redirected his gaze to Lydia, "And I would invite you to join in that as well, my Lady. Call me Xander as if I was just another long acquaintance."

"At least, until the rest of the court arrives," Dominique chimed in.

The Emperor Magnus... Xander, heaved a long exasperated sigh. "Yes, until the rest of the court arrives. We do apologize again for the inconvenience."

"As long as you are willing to bear with us as we get preparations up to par, it is no inconvenience." She looked over the noblemen's shoulders to see Kinley and Edith standing, waiting patiently by the door.

"If we can be of any assistance, please use us as you see fit, Lady," Xander said.

"Lydia," she supplied, meeting him first name to first name.

He grinned and nodded. "Yes, of course. Lydia, then," he said before he turned toward the waiting servants. "And I insist, put us to work. We are a bunch of ne'er do wells who need to earn our keep."

There were mock groans from the bunch, but all in good fun.

Kinley nodded. "Well, if you insist your Imperial—"

"Xander, please. I do insist," the young man stressed.

"But... you're...." Kinley and Edith looked at each other.

"Xander, you are causing the staff distress," Dominique chided, crossing his arms again.

"Let us go into the library and let the servants go about their duties," Lydia said, boldly reaching out to touch the Emperor's arm. He didn't mind or object, though she could feel the eyes of the other noblemen on them both, practically hearing the scrape of slate boards as they ran mental calculations. She ignored them all and focused on the balance of keeping her people safe and these new invaders happy.

Xander seemed to comply with that idea and offered her his arm to escort her through. Still clutching the loose flowers in her other arm, she took it with a gentle smile and let him lead her wherever he wanted to go.

As they entered the library, she saw that a handful of the nobles had gathered about the fire with the rest that had hovered around the Emperor walking that way, though three of them seemed to be poking around the books.

"Okay, you lot!" Xander called out, catching everyone's attention, not that he ever truly lost it. "We need to earn our supper here, so you are going to do anything that this Lady asks of you to get this place ready for us!"

This time, instead of groans, they all stood up like soldiers ready for battle.

"If I could get a few of you to help distribute the flowers in the entryway, that would be of great help," Lydia said. Before she finished, Dominique stepped up beside her.

"Carwell, Sandburg, Karkov, to the hall," he barked, jerking his head at them. He listed off a few more names, and Walter took over their charge, while a few more got assigned to housekeeper Edith.

"Change beds! You can't be serious!?" one of the young men objected, but only got himself cuffed for his rebuff.

"And don't flirt with the maids," Petre added, which of course brought the attention that there were pretty maids involved, changing the young men's tunes. Several of the maids were waiting at the top of the grand stairs to overhear the exchange and giggled as they fled with sheets clutched in their arms.

Soon enough, there were beds enough made up for all the nobles who had appeared and lunch made and served to them out on the lawn near the garden under a pavilion that had been erected for the purpose. The nobles seemed quite jovial about their fun little jaunt into domestic work and wouldn't stop talking about it while they sat to eat. Lydia did not join them, but begged off, insisting she had other preparations to make, which happened to be true.

But even then, she didn't duck into the library to help Edith sort out the rooming assignments.

There was only one person who she needed to talk to right now.

Chapter 36

CONTRACTS BROKEN

"Damian?" she called as soon as she got into the master suite. No one responded, though outside she could hear the calling and bustling of the staff, who were grabbing their lunch in shifts.

Taking a pointless glance into her dressing room and washroom, she spun to go to the door that joined the master suite with the mistress suite. On the other side stood a room that mirrored hers with more earthy tones in the carpet and walls. A bed with burgundy curtains stood empty, the bed made and untouched. The only way she knew anyone occupied this space at all was the fact that Damian's clothing hung in the closet.

"Damian!"

Still no response.

She went back to her room and approached the faux pillar. Sliding her hands over the surface, she tried to find a latch or handle, anything that would open the secret door. Yet, all was smooth. There didn't seem to be a latch or anything, even along the seams. Then the pillar clicked and popped open. She had no idea what she had done to trigger it, but she seized the outer edge to pull it wider, only to come up short as she came face to face with her missing paramour.

He lowered his hand, dropping it to his side as she stood there staring at him, and suddenly, she didn't know what to say to him.

"I'm not going to fight it," he said first instead, his voice so small she barely heard him. He wasn't looking directly at her but rather at a spot over her shoulder.

"Not going to fight what?" she asked, grasping onto the last thought. Too much had happened too fast, so she didn't know what she was going to do or what it all meant or what the right answer would be. "Damian, answer me."

She realized she wanted him to fight. But fight what? Fight how?

He shook his head. "Please don't play with me. You don't have to play these games. I don't blame you. In a choice between being the Emperor's mistress or being mine ... no one would make a different choice." His voice cracked, but he swallowed it down. "Just... if you could do me the courtesy... how long were you planning this? Did you intend to seduce Xander as soon as you could, thinking that it was only a matter of time before you met him, considering my status, or did it just happen and you took advantage when you met him?"

If he had stabbed her with a knife it would have hurt less, and she would have understood it more. "Is that what you think of me?"

"Please give me some credit, and don't use indignity against me to make me question what is perfectly logical. Everyone would have made this choice if given it. I would have made such a choice," he sneered, then closed his eyes. "I just want to understand how long. Was it when I left you together alone? Did you take that vulnerable moment to charm him?"

"He cried, the whole time. I comforted him," she argued, though she also remembered her powerplay at the time. She told herself it was to help Xander get control of himself, to give him what he needed, but was that all it had been? Had she maybe, on some level, wanted him to like her? Wanted him to admire her…?

She backed away from the secret door, shaking her head, retreating from her thoughts as much as from her paramour. Her former paramour. She was no longer his creature now, was she?

I'm officially the Countess of Summerbourne. Now finally realizing exactly what that meant. She had broken the contract and walked away with everything. The courtesan in her applauded how brilliant she had been.

"You think I tried to entice the Emperor to spontaneously grant me a title and lands?" she snapped, surprising herself with how offended she was at the idea. "I did not *know* he was going to do that."

"No," Damian conceded, emerging to go to the fireplace, where the fire from the morning had died down. He grabbed the poker and proceeded to stab at the coals. "No, I don't suppose you would. I think you just got the cards you needed to make the most of the situation, and that with Xander's flare for dramatic gestures came together in a beautiful piece of well-played luck."

"And what?" Lydia spat. "I was simply supposed to refuse and deny his offer?"

"Of course not," Damian said, slapping the poker back in the tool rack with a sharp metallic clack. "I knew what this was with my eyes wide open. I was buying your time and attention. The fact that you had the grace to accept the arrangement, I am grateful."

"You don't sound very grateful!" she flounced to one of the armchairs and sat down, crossing her legs and arms.

"I just thought you would give me some more time!" He whirled on her, and she realized too late her mistake. She had put herself in a vulnerable position as he towered over her.

"I thought I signed an endowment, not a prison sentence," she said roughly and tried to burst up from the chair to escape the trap. He immediately knocked her back down.

Clamping on the arms of the chair with both hands, she turned her head and braced.

But the blow she expected didn't fall.

"You think I'm going to hit you, don't you?"

She opened her eyes a slit to look up at Damian, wondering if his soft voice would prove to be a trap. Noticing, he backed away a step, as if he was just becoming aware of what he had been doing. Becoming aware that she was afraid.

"I... I apologize," he said. His hands shook.

She opened her eyes all the way, confused. Realizing she didn't know what to do, she stood, clasping her hands before herself anxiously. This felt so uncomfortable, now she wished he *would* hit her. Then she at least knew where she stood.

"You... you aren't being fair," she said, wincing as soon as the words left her mouth.

"Explain."

Too late now, she doubled down. "How many times have you stated that I can't possibly care for you because of your appearance, but you act as if the inverse isn't true. You wanted me because of my..." She couldn't call herself a beauty. She never felt like one, never really saw one in the mirror. She always thought it ironic how she had been titled as Beauty when all it had ever been was a lie. People saw what they wanted to see when they looked at her. It was never *her* they saw. "You were pleased by my appearance. That's what you bought and paid for." *Just like everyone else,* she thought, tears beading in her eyes.

He opened his mouth to say something.

She wanted him to deny it, but then he closed it again before conceding, "You are right."

It hurt. It hurt so much she wanted to wail with it. If only she could let herself break.

Damian punched the wall, making her jump. "I wanted... you represented to me everything that I had lost."

"And it won't last," she said, taking herself to the window. "My appeal will fade. I thought you would regret it that you wanted me for a whole five years. My newness, my shine, would tarnish, and you would want to be rid of me for another newer plaything."

"There are no other women who would accept me. I looked for them," he said.

She scoffed. "There are always women desperate enough. It's you who has the high standards. You selected a woman from the Court of Virtues, the highest level of courtesan." Unwanted tears burned in her eyes. "A common whore from the street would serve you just fine." Her words were as thick as her tears.

"Then, I suppose that is my lesson then," he noted, his tone flat. "I will take it to heart, Lady."

He moved to the secret door, then hesitated. "Like I said, I won't fight it, Countess of Summerbourne. I really do wish you all good fortune... for your future..."

She didn't hear him leave until he had closed the pillar.

Stubbornly, she turned her gaze away from the temptation of going after him. Such a thing would be truly foolish.

He's right, she thought. *This is the best for me. As the Emperor's mistress...* But she couldn't finish that thought. She could see it, she truly could, how events had played out to her best advantage. This property was hers now. She had beaten the contract. She was free, with all the comfort and security she could ever want.

Mine. Mine.

Down below in the yard, the Emperor and his small court of men were running around with what looked like pall mall balls having a grand time of it. So many of them handsome and none of them the masters of her. Xander crowed in triumph as his ball smacked hard into the pole and the other men politely clapped and laughed as he skipped about the field, joyful and powerful in his youth and beauty.

There was so much she could do with a young lover like him. Being the Emperor's mistress was a crowning achievement. More wealth and fortune was sure to come her way. A new name, a new reputation. She truly could leave her old life behind.

"I never thought you ugly," she whispered, knowing Damian was gone and couldn't hear her. In the window, she could see her reflection, a ghost in the glass. A ghost with tears in her eyes.

Chapter 37

THE EMPEROR'S MISTRESS

"You summoned me, your Imperial Highness?" Lydia asked as she bobbed before Xander.

"No, no, I told you, please call me Xander. I'm just an ordinary bloke," he insisted.

"My apologies, I forgot," Lydia lied, blushing demurely, more for the benefit of the other men in the library. They were all lounging about on the settees and chairs. Every available sitting place had a body filling it, and there were considerably more chairs in the room than had been originally.

They certainly have made themselves at home, she thought. She had a powerful desire to see them all just go.

Xander, for his part, had taken up residence behind the desk, her desk now, and had been downing a glass of white wine with Lord Dominique and Lord Petre, both perched on opposite sides of the desk. The whole tableau looked like an icon of one of the gods of creation with an angel and demon framing him respectively.

"Well, Xander," she flirted, leaning in conspiratorially, "What can I do for you?"

"I was hoping you would join me for dinner? I desire to eat on my own this evening, and I would love for you to join me if you are willing."

Of course, I would be willing, she thought bitterly. *I don't want to lose my head.*

"I am honored!" she actually said.

Because you would, wouldn't you? You'd be the type who would punish anyone who refused you. Maybe the thoughts were unfair, she really didn't know Xander very well, and what she had seen of him had been under intense circumstances.

He did allow me to speak to him as an equal twice now.

While she debated in her head, the noblemen spoke cordially amongst themselves for a moment, then the Emperor stood up. All at once, the room stood up with him, even the men who hadn't been facing him.

"Shall we, my Lady?" Xander asked, offering her his arm gallantly.

She took it graciously and smiled beatifically for the room as he led her upstairs. Leading them out of the library were Imperial guards. The guards had been around the estate along with the noblemen all day, but she hadn't really noted them otherwise. Now, as two more fell in behind them, she became acutely aware of their presence.

"It can be a little unnerving at first if you're not used to it," Xander said softly as they walked to the guest quarters he was using while visiting.

"What is? Being in your presence?" she quipped.

He chuckled. "The guards. You do not have to worry. They know you have consent to the Imperial Body. They will not keep you from me."

"Oh. I see," she said and imagined several scenarios of the tough looking men and women around her doing terrible things to her in defense of their charge. "Thank you for that."

"We are family now," Xander said as they reached the door. The two guards who had gone ahead of them opened them seamlessly as they approached. Within were two more guards standing by the windows. Kinley and two footmen waited inside next to a dining table fit for an Emperor.

Kinley bowed to them both, not at all surprised to see Lydia. Instead, he gestured toward the table, and the two footmen pulled the chairs for both of them to sit. She waited until the Emperor moved to take his seat first, grateful again for all her training.

"You may serve us, then let us be. We can fend for ourselves, can we not, Countess?"

"You seem to take great pleasure in saying my new title," she noted as she laid her napkin over her lap, watching from her periphery as the footman lifted the lids on their meal, while the Imperial Guards waited by the door for them to leave.

"I think I enjoy saying it as much as you enjoy hearing it," Xander said, as he took a drink from his wineglass.

"Yes, indeed," she genuinely beamed, picking up her own glass. "It still does not seem real yet, that someone such as I could *ever* attain such a title."

"You obviously became misdirected when the gods sent you to Earth. I have never met a nobler creature than you," he said, as the doors shut, truly leaving them alone. "If I had it in my power, I would make you as my Empress."

Carefully, she set her wineglass down. Somehow, hearing such a platitude, even one he would never have to prove, therefore he was free to lavish, made her feel sick, not thrilled.

She laughed. "So does that mean what it seemed to mean when you bestowed this generous gift on me?"

"What do you think it means?" he asked, his eyes twinkling.

"That I am now the Emperor's Mistress," she declared as if the idea excited her.

He was the soul of delight. "I do believe it does, if that is, you agree?"

"Well, I would like to point out one concern it raises for me," she said, picking up her cutlery.

"Yes?" Xander said before sticking a bite into his mouth.

"This situation, it does break my contract with your brother, and I would hate something like this to come between you two."

Xander continued to chew for a moment, an odd look crossing his face. A mix of apprehension and child-like defiance. "I know of your arrangement. I didn't think it was right. To force someone like you to have to please someone like him. I knew I had to save you."

Lydia gripped her cutlery tighter in her fingers. *Who asked you to?* she thought, offended by his arrogance to presume he knew what she would want. *How is he any different? Now I'm compelled to share* his *bed?*

But why does this make you so angry? a more sensible voice asked inside her.

She told that voice to shut up.

"Though I suppose I must warn you, depending on how things go, I may not be allowed to enjoy your company as long as I would otherwise like," Xander said.

Now that made her cock her head to one side. "What do you mean?" she asked innocently.

"I received word before leaving the capital that my envoys have reached an agreement with the Queen to the South. Apparently, she has agreed to our terms for a ceasefire leading to a lasting peace, pending our marriage."

That truly shocked Lydia to the core. "You mean, the war is over?" she asked, letting herself express exactly how she felt, mystified.

Xander sighed. "Yes, I did it. I am the Emperor who ended the war and brought a unified continent under our heel. More or less."

"You do not seem terribly happy about this development?" she noted.

"It has to do with the conditions around this agreement. She will be my wife and Empress, but she will still be the sovereign head of her own country, and it will only pass into the full auspices of the Imperium after it is passed to our joint heir. And at the rate things go around here, we'll need an heir and at least two spares, if not more, just to be safe."

"If I can be so bold, the way you talk about it, you make it sound like you're breeding horses."

"It is like that in a way," he chuckled. "You're very witty, you know?"

"Thank you," Lydia allowed, even while her brain was thinking rapidly.

"I must say, you are taking the news very well," he said.

"How do you mean?" she asked, wary that she might have made a mistake and what *that* could mean.

"Well, I understand that women can get very jealous, knowing that the one they have given their hearts to is bound to be... well bound to another," he said.

She saw the trap for what it was, even if he hadn't meant to set it. The fact that he assumed she had given her heart to him grated. Quickly, she forced a smile, implying she was putting on a brave face. "I cannot lie, I am a little disappointed. But even after you are married, it is not like I won't be able to see you every day. And I can serve you in so many other ways. I'm already so grateful to you." She picked up her napkin and dabbed at her bone-dry eyes.

"Oh, now I've upset you," he bemoaned, clearly touched by her display.

"No, no, I'll be alright," she said, clearing her throat and sniffing prettily. Why men fell for tears like this she had no idea, but it worked every time.

I wonder if Damian would fall for such a trick?, and then she wondered if he could see their little performance. Suddenly, the hairs on the back of her neck stood up on end at the idea of him watching them somewhere in the walls, through a dozen secret spy holes.

She cleared her throat. "More importantly, do you suppose the assassination attempts will stop?"

Now he grew more sober. "I do not know," he admitted. "If it was her people trying to end the war by ending me, it wouldn't serve her now. But if the troubles are coming from within the Imperium, then we need to ferret it out fast before she arrives."

He stared off, an old, weary man looking out a young man's face. Lydia was reminded of what Damian said.

Two brothers and a sister, already dead. He and Damian are all that are left, she thought.

"You will find them," she assured.

Xander remembered himself and lifted his head. "Thank you, you are a great comfort to me," he said. "And who knows, maybe my wife will be amenable to allow me to keep you around once the heirs have been secured?"

The urge to stab him returned.

Also, she understood that he expected to bed her tonight. Probably right after dinner. And she suddenly very much did not want that.

CHAPTER 38

ESCAPE

It was an old trick, but there were reasons the old tricks were old tricks. It worked.

Xander lay in his bed snoring. It had taken several bottles of wine to get him like that, and he had drunk most of them with Lydia sipping a little and acting more drunk than she was.

The tensest moment came when she got him into the bed. Falling backward, she laughed and rolled. He came over her, his breath full of wine. Reaching out her arms welcomingly, he leaned in, and she kissed him.

As far as kisses went, it wasn't terrible, but she also felt it pretty standard. She went through the motions of it anyway, using her tongue in such a way, adjusting her pressure to his. His eyes were closed as he savored, yet hers remained open the whole time. She studied his face, measuring his reactions.

Have I always done this?

She realized she had. She never closed her eyes when she kissed a patron.

Except for...

Unable to push the thought away, she did push the Emperor back, rolling him onto his back so she could slide up alongside him.

"Let me show you," she whispered, brushing her fingers down along his cheek and jawline soothingly, "what a courtesan of the Crimson District can do?"

"Ooooh," Xander sighed. She kept her fingers moving, caressing his skin gently. He had already shed his coat and his shoes, so it was a simple thing to work at his clothing. Freeing a button, caressing his skin, gently laying a peck every so often. All while she worked, he sighed and relaxed. His breathing evened. He drifted. By the time she got the last button of his shirt free... he snored once and rolled onto his side.

Relieved, Lydia lay back, staring up at the dimness in the curtains above. She became more aware of the pressure in her chest and the twist in her guts. It wasn't exactly that she wanted to cry. Maybe she wanted to scream.

She could do neither, but she did slide carefully from the bed. Fetching her slippers, which she had kicked off when they had tumbled into the bed, she tiptoed to the door. Outside, she startled at the sight of the guards framing each side of the door. They, by contrast, did not react to her. If she couldn't see them breathing, she would have thought them statues. Cautiously, she stepped past them and the four others at either end of the Emperor's hallway.

Elsewhere in the castle, it was very quiet. Unlike the Emperor's hall, most of the candle lights had been put out, leaving only moonlight through the windows outside to guide her way back to her rooms. That moonlight called out to her, and she paused at one of the windows. Down below, the dark had swallowed most of the garden, edging everything with a highlight kiss from the sky above. Having lived her entire life in the city, she had no idea what could be hiding out in the wilds of her garden, though she was sure "wilds" was the wrong word for it.

"Maybe it's just the moonlight, that makes it seem more sinister," she said softly to her reflection in the window.

Then she sensed a presence on her other side.

She looked up expecting it to be Damian. Desperate for it to be Damian.

"May I have a word, my lady?"

"Lord Dominique!" she said too loudly in the quiet of the night, abruptly, straightening.

"It is alright, Lady, no need to startle. Let me just be the first to offer you my congratulations." He smirked as he folded his arms to lean against the wall next to the window, a creature made of shadow.

"Congratulations? I don't know if I've done very much to be worthy of that word," she said carefully, narrowing her eyes at him.

She calculated in her head that if she screamed, the Imperial Guards would be close enough to intervene. But Lord Dominique didn't have a clear weapon on him. Like the Emperor, he had divested himself of his coat and cravat, showing off his neck and collarbone to an almost scandalous degree, if she could *be* scandalized. His sleeves were rolled up, and while one hand grasped his opposite bicep, he examined the nails of the other in a show of practiced casualness. It looked insufferably annoying, but it also clearly showed he had no knife.

"Let me try that again. Well done on becoming the Emperor's first mistress. It is quite an achievement, especially for one such as you."

"I don't think you mean that as an insult at all," she mused.

"Certainly not. You, madam, have the most interesting luck. It was only last week when I was summarily informed that the services of the Beauty of the Crimson District would no longer be available to *any* clients. Then, imagine my shock when I found her invading my privacy, uninvited in my own house. And now," he pinned her with a knowing look, "I find you the Countess of Summerbourne."

"And I find myself late for my bed," she said curtly. She bobbed once and tried to step away.

"I would like to apologize," he said quickly.

"There is nothing to apologize for—"

"For attacking you at the ball." He straightened from the wall, putting his hands behind his back in a formal posture. "I made a gross assumption about your presence there. I learned from my guards that it was not you who had invaded my home, but a man."

She hesitated, measuring him for deception, but if he were baiting her in any way, he did not clearly advertise it.

"You struck me across the face, Lord Dominique. A mere apology does not begin to compensate for such a thing," she said, testing her newfound power granted by her position.

"You are right, it does not. But I offer it just the same, as well as my unconditional support."

"Your support?"

"Yes." His stance relaxed again. "You're going to need it in this court. I offer it as my recompense for my actions."

"I do not know if such a thing is wise."

He scoffed. "You will need support, there are many in this court who would work to supplant you as the Emperor's Mistress—"

"No, that is not what I mean," she said, waving her hand. "I agree with the need, but you are asking me to trust you. However, I do not even understand who you thought I was before ... that warranted the need for this grand gesture."

Lord Dominique's smarmy grin dropped from his face. He stamped one foot, looking more akin to a horse needing to run than a man who was the master of his fate. "My guard informed me when interrogated, that you went upstairs to find a washroom."

"That is correct," she conceded.

"So what led you then, dear lady, to my private office?"

"I..." her mind raced for an answer. "I heard a noise."

"What sort of noise?"

"I..." she ran through the things Damian told her about his encounter with one of Dominique's guards. "I'm not sure what it was I heard. It sounded like a... a grunting, or a wounded animal?" She feigned continuing to struggle for words, and he waved her off.

"As I suspected, my Lady. You were innocent in all this, and I jumped to an extremely unfortunate conclusion when I saw you."

"What is this all about, my Lord?" she asked, pressing her advantage, curious as to what Lord Dominique might tell her.

Glancing over his shoulder, he took a cautious step toward her. "What I am about to tell you, you must swear to tell no one, not even the Emperor," he said.

"I swear," she lied.

He searched her face a moment longer, still hesitating.

"I was a courtesan of the Crimson District," she whispered. "I have the discretion of a priest."

He nodded, accepting her statement. "Someone is trying to kill me," he whispered.

Not what she expected to hear.

"Who?"

"I don't know!" Lord Dominique turned away, running an anxious hand through his hair. "There have been three attempts in the last month. The latest at the ball. Someone broke into my house and instead of killing me, killed two of my guards."

Damian, Lydia thought. She schooled her face, but it didn't matter, because now that the damn had been broken, Lord Dominique was talking. *What is it about me that always makes men want to confess their souls?* she wondered, not for the first time.

But she blessed whatever deity granted her such a gift, for it was coming in handy now.

"Previously, I had been poisoned. I almost died. I was barely able to keep it a secret from the court. With my father's ailment, losing the heir to disease would be a disaster for my family's interests."

Instinctively, Lydia laid a hand on Lord Dominique's arm. He calmed, remembering himself.

"I am sorry for what you have suffered," she whispered, reminding him through action to keep his voice down.

He clasped her hand. "You have always been an angel to me. Thank you." He moved to cup her face, and to kiss her!

She bucked her head back, before she even realized what she was doing. "My Lord!" she said, then stumbled to cover the action up. "The Emperor—"

Lord Dominique lifted his hands away and took a step back. "My apologies again, Lady. I have forgotten myself." He chuckled dryly. "Forgotten we are both no longer in the Crimson District." Then he seized her hand so that he could plant his kiss there. "I hope that being parted from me will not break your heart. I know how much you longed for my..." He stopped and blushed, then withdrew from her hand. "I know that I will never forget our time together."

"It stays in my heart, forever," she assured, pressing a hand to the aforementioned spot.

He nodded and started to withdraw only to stop. "Promise me that you won't do our thing with the Emperor. I don't think I could bear it, imagining him doing ... *that* to you."

Oh for gods' sake, what the heck was 'our thing?' she thought.

Instead, she turned her head away dramatically, thickening her voice, "Please, just go. It's too much..." and then she hiccupped a sob. It did the trick, and he withdrew, finally leaving her alone. When she was sure she was alone again, she stopped her soft sobbing, cleared her throat and went back to her room proper.

Damian waited there.

CHAPTER 39

DARK DESIRES

In the light from her fireplace, he slid back his hood. His eyes met hers, glowing in the dark pits of his eyes. The naked hunger there sent a shiver through her. From his skull-like face, she again felt she had been visited by the god of Death, and he wanted to devour her whole.

And she wanted him to.

He moved then, crossing the space so quickly she startled, backing up a few steps. She barely shut the door behind her when he was upon her.

"Ah!" she cried as he lifted her up, tearing at her clothes. Her breast burst forth from her dress before he devoured it with his mouth. His other arm came around her waist, jerking her forward, he offset her balance, pressing his body against hers as her toes left the ground. She had no choice but to wrap her legs around him, the slippers dropping free from her feet. His hardness pressed into the right place and she groaned, heedless of who could hear.

Punish me! she thought but had no ability to say.

He ravished her like a demon, and it only made her hotter and hungrier.

I don't want the Emperor! she thought. *I want you!* She knew she needed to tell him, needed to say it for herself.

Yet, still, she said nothing, only moaned hard against him.

He nibbled her nipples, sparking sharp sensations that never quite crossed over into pain. Not to be outdone, she slipped her hands down the back of his shirt, pulling at anything that yielded. The cloth lifted up, and her hands rolled down his cooler skin, feeling the muscles and ribs undulate underneath.

God, she wanted him now.

She pulled on his shirt, lifting it up higher. It needed to come off. He had to drop her back to the ground so he could surrender his arms, lifting them above his head. She ripped off the cowl he wore and threw it far away, toward the fire for all she cared.

She wanted him inside her. Now.

Making a few feeble tugs at the ties of his trousers proved unsuccessful. Instead, he grabbed her up like he had before, but this time he pivoted to drop her a few steps onto the bed. She bounced, forcing the breath from her.

He stood at the edge of the bed, looking down at her with contempt as he tugged at his trousers, undoing them to free himself entirely. Her gown had ridden up to her waist, exposing herself to him.

It was all so very hot.

She tried to divest herself from her own clothing, but the dress wasn't easily removed while lying down. And he didn't give her the chance to stand up. Instead, he pushed her back and seized her open drawers to rip them off her legs. Fabric tore, but she didn't care. Firmly, he grabbed her knees and split her legs apart with a determination that said he was going to fuck her and there was nothing in the world that was going to stop him.

She didn't care. He could do anything to her, anything he wanted, and she would do nothing to stop him. She wanted it all.

His fists sank into the bed on either side of her body, his knees bumping up against her butt. She tilted her hips up to receive, and he thrust forward. The head met her entrance and resisted only a moment before bursting through all the way to the hilt.

She cried out, unabashedly before his hand came over her mouth, muffling her cries. Wrapping her own arms around his neck, she buried her face into his shoulder and continued to cry full-throatedly as he thrust again and again, all the way out and then all the way back in. The long deliberate strokes caused her to gush wetness. She felt primal, like an ancient woman being taken as sacrifice to one of the Wild Gods. Or a tribute to a barbarian warrior conqueror, with his battle make-up of a skull on his face.

Despite muffling her voice, his own joined in lower, shorter grunts. He adjusted their position, straightening his legs so he could arch back, rising above her and out of her reach. Yet, his eyes stayed on her steadily, devouring her as much as their bodies devoured each other. Despite the intensity, this was not a frantic coupling.

He changed speeds and tempos, going slow and agonizing when he wanted to nibble her flesh some more, below her ear or at the base of her neck. Then he would arch again, and she would cup his face above her while he sank into the depths of her. And when she writhed too much, he punished her by pressing her down and pounding fast and hard and furious.

And she came. Many times.

This had never happened to her before. She had been pleasured before with a patron, yes, but someone who deliberately served her like this, sought out her every nerve ending and *all* the hidden pleasures there, not just one or two; never had such a thing been possible. The heights were reached again and again.

He never seemed to tire.

Never sought out his own satisfaction.

All the time those eyes burned into her, pinning her there as much as his cock pinned down her hips.

She did not think such a thing was human.

And she wanted more.

At last, when she thought she had been completely wrung out, he took two of her fingers in his mouth and licked them hard with his tongue. Soaking with sweat, she writhed. Then he removed the two damp fingers and slid them down, bringing them to her pearl.

She knew what he wanted her to do then. She had done it many times herself. He wanted her to end this. Touching the nerves there shot through her like lightning in a storm. Mustering his strength one last time, he pounded, their skin making slapping noises as they collided again and again. Her finger worked, triggering the final climb up the mountain above the storm clouds.

He closed his own eyes this time, and she knew that when she crested, he would too. His legs straightened on the bed, changing the angle, making the strokes deeper.

She couldn't stop it.

She couldn't breathe.

She didn't want to.

Her whole body clenched down, and her cry strangled in her throat. Her body contracted, and she thought she would end in oblivion, dispersed into a thousand exploding soap bubbles. She thought she had.

He came with her, strangling out his passion himself.

Then he collapsed down onto her, his weight pinning her back into the world. She didn't care. She couldn't move. A small part of her ached, but it was nothing compared to what she had just experienced.

It was like she had been to battle, and they both won and lost the war. Lying there as a fallen soldier, she only focused on breathing and the warm waves of delight that washed over. He finally rolled off and lay beside her as still as she was, waiting for their breaths to return to normal. Nearly falling asleep, she shook awake once more when he pulled her closer against him, bringing her to the nook where his arm met his shoulder before drawing the blankets over them both, safe and warm in their primal cave.

Just a man and woman together. No more. And no less.

And still not a word spoken by either of them.

She wanted to say something. To tell the truth. To tell him that it hurt her feelings, what he had said to her earlier. It had hurt when he said that he wasn't going to fight for her. That it made her feel like he didn't really want her. That all they were was sex and need, and nothing more. She wanted to admit she was afraid of him leaving her behind. She felt afraid of falling in love with him, or succumbing to this vulnerability he brought out in her. That she knew this moment of safety couldn't last.

And yet, not a word passed her lips or his. Vaguely, she became aware of his deeper breathing, the lull of his sleeping breath like an ocean of lapping waves. Softly, she slid her hand over his chest, feeling his own sweat as it cooled. He was *warm*, warmer than any other time she had touched him. Warm and alive and for the moment still hers. She examined his sleeping face. In the dimness, she couldn't see the disfigurement, only the outlines and edges.

No, it isn't the lack of light, she thought. *It's just him. I only see him.*

She had never made lovecraft with a man like that before.

And they had not spoken a word between them the whole time.

Tomorrow, she thought. *I'll talk to him tomorrow. I'll be brave tomorrow.*

Chapter 40

Waking Alone

Lydia woke up alone. Normally, that wouldn't have been a surprise, but after waking and stretching, she remembered what had happened last night. They had made an absolute mess of her bed. She had fallen asleep in her clothing, and her skin ached where the seams had pressed in as she sat up.

"Damian?" she called cautiously, directing the name toward her washroom.

There was no response. Getting up to her feet, she went toward the windows, casting a glance through her dressing room to see that the washroom was in fact empty. Beyond the morning gray hung above, but the damp seemed to have already fallen all around, making the grass below a marshy sort of green. Her view showed her the gardens and the lake beyond them.

Lydia turned away from the windows and went to the door to try to call for Kitty when she noticed a green pull cord beside the bed. It had blended into the color there but popped out to her now that she had a need to call for assistance. She knew she would need a quick bath before dressing and information about the state of the house.

She heard nothing when she pulled it but decided to give her lady's maid a moment before trying again or shouting. Instead, she shed her outer dress, went to the washroom, and took care of her other more pressing needs before Kitty arrived, all while ignoring the hollow feeling inside.

Their timing ended up perfect as she came back into the bedroom just as Kitty rapped twice on the door before opening it.

"Good morning, milady! I'm so sorry. I was about to come to check up on you again when you called. Edith said to let you sleep after the chaos yesterday, and the rest of your guests are still resting themselves anyway," Kitty reported without Lydia needing to say anything.

"That's fine. Is there hot water for bathing? I don't need much, just a basin will do," Lydia asked mechanically.

"Yes, milady, one moment," Kitty said and scurried away, forgetting to shut the door fully behind her. Lydia stepped up to do it herself, then paused a moment as she saw through the crack Lord Dominique speaking to Kitty at the end of the hall.

Now that is curious, she thought and watched them. The interaction only lasted a moment, then Kitty bobbed and hurried off toward the kitchens presumably, while Lord Dominique glanced toward Lydia's door. Despite the instinct to slam the door closed quickly, the sudden movement would attract more attention than the slight crack. So she held still and let her eyes drift to his shoulder so they didn't actually make eye contact. After a breath, he turned and walked away. She opened the door slightly wider to watch him go, his shoulders highlighted with his simple but finely made coat.

Definitely curious, Lydia thought and finally shut the door.

Alone in the oppressive silence in the room she felt her nerves were on fire. "Stop it," she whispered to herself, tamping everything down harder. She couldn't let herself feel. There was too much at stake. Waking up alone was nothing new…

Going to her vanity, she set to work on her hair while she waited for Kitty to return. By the time she had gotten through the tangled post-coital mess, the hot water arrived.

"Kitty, why did Lord Dominique stop you in the hall," Lydia asked as her maid set the pitcher she carried on the stand with the ewer in the washroom.

"He wanted me to inform you that the Emperor has asked you to join him for breakfast. Edith is taking care of it now, and Grandpa... I mean, Kinley will be attending him with two footmen being allowed to serve as well," Kitty said as she moved over to help Lydia out of her remaining clothing without comment.

"Being allowed?" Lydia said, catching up to what Kittie just said.

"Yes, there was some issue earlier about who would serve the Emperor as his other Imperial servants have arrived. The rest of the court will be here in a few hours," Kitty said before leaving with the dress Lydia discarded to hang it up for cleaning in the dressing room.

The Countess of Summerbourne went at herself with the sponge, the warm water dripping down her body onto the towel Kitty had laid out for the purpose. "How can they trust our servants and not their own?" Lydia asked.

"Well... Grandpapa has been an Imperial servant for decades, before I was born anyway. And the two footmen were both born here like me, so they can't possibly be assassins. Christopher can barely make himself kill a chicken for dinner, and Theodore is doggedly loyal to the crown. Do not mistake me, I am a loyal citizen myself, but he is *quite* avid. Even Grandmama finds it a bit much."

Lydia pondered a moment. "So there is a difference then between the regular servants and the Imperial servants?"

"Oh yes, definitely. Imperial servants receive greater training and often come from similar families called Equerry Imperium. Also, Imperial servants, when they retire, are granted the title of Sir or Dame with their pensions. You have it made for life if you become an Imperial servant. You have to be sponsored to even take the tests if you aren't from one of the Equerry families."

A sponge bath had set everything to rights, and soon, Lydia dressed properly and stepped into a dove gray gown embroidered with periwinkles around the cuffs and midway down the skirt. Despite this, she longed for the days, which were only a few short weeks ago, when she could wear something simple and comfortable versus appropriate.

"To be rewarded with an Imperial servant is an honor for the nobles who receive them too. The fact that Kinley serves you is a sign of your prestige!"

"Would you wish to become an Imperial servant?" Lydia asked as she waited for her buttons to be done up in the back.

"Oh, I would give my eyeteeth to be one, milady! But even if I could be sponsored for the tests, I'm nowhere near ready. I only just became a Lady's maid. I still have so much to learn."

"I think you are doing a fine job," Lydia complimented as she sat down to let Kitty at her hair.

"Thank you, milady," the maid said and proceeded to remake the simple style Lydia had put up into something more appropriate to attend the Emperor's breakfast.

"Do you know anything about Lord Damian, this morning?" Lydia asked airily as if she didn't really care but was merely curious.

"He left this morning, set out himself on horseback, even though Grandpapa..." Kitty stamped her foot, "I mean Kinley, tried to send Louis with him." Kitty finished with a final pin set in place. "There, I think that came out fairly good if I do say so myself."

Lydia forced a smile as she looked in the mirror at her reflection. It didn't reach her eyes as her heart sank at the news that she had been left behind without a word as she thought. *There is so much I need to tell him.*

Kitty didn't notice her mistress's distress as she continued to pat and adjust, giving Lydia the time to master herself.

"Certainly better than I could have done," Lydia assured after a moment and stood up. She was starting to feel more like a pet than a person with all the grooming. "Is the Emperor breaking his fast in the dining room or his own quarters?"

"His own quarters."

Armed for battle, Lydia went to attend her new patron.

Once more, when she stepped into the hallway lined with Imperial Guards, it felt more akin to walking through a haunted forest filled with a heavy miasma. Only these trees were armed with swords and unkind eyes. Kitty left Lydia at the end of the hall, watching with her hands clasped in front of her chest as if she were praying for her mistress's safety. It was not reassuring.

When she approached the door, one of the guards stepped forward, and she congratulated herself silently for not flinching. Instead of attacking her, he opened the door to let her pass through wordlessly.

Within, a table had been set up in the Emperor's quarters taking the place of where the armchairs had been the day before. The Emperor sat at the head as was expected, and he remained seated even as Lord Dominique and Lord Petre both stood as she entered.

"Good morning, my lady," Xander said, bouncing once in his seat as if he wanted to jump up, protocol be damned. Instead, he gestured graciously to the seat to his right, the place of honor. "Please join us for breakfast."

She nodded and smiled and walked serenely over to take the chair, Kinley stepping up to help her in. Once she sat beside the Emperor, the other men resumed their seats, the lords with the help of the two footmen.

The plates before them were empty, and it was clear that the men waited for her to join them. "I apologize for not having been here sooner and making you wait, Your Imperial Highness. My maid tried to do me a kindness by letting me sleep in longer after yesterday's excitement," she said sweetly, silently telling herself that she would make it up to the lady's maid later for throwing her before the carriage like this.

"Your maid obviously cares deeply for you," Xander said graciously and then signaled that they were ready to be served. Prepared hot plates were set before them with covers that when removed revealed a wonderful display of soft-boiled eggs with fried ham and scones with cream and jam.

Lydia's stomach loudly growled.

"Oh excuse me, my Lady," Lord Petre said, patting his belly to cover for her. "I'm an uncouth ruffian." The bright sunny smile did nothing to touch her inner darkness, but she intellectually recognized the effort.

"Now that we're all assembled, can we get back to the issues at hand?" Lord Dominique asked harshly even as he dug into his plate.

"Yes, quite," Xander said and he looked at Lydia. "The court is arriving today."

CHAPTER 41

REGRETS

Damian reined up his horse just as he crested the small rise above the Imperial City. He had ridden all day, from the moment the gray and pink sky had woken him with the woman still in his arms.

Even now with his arms aching and his ass protesting the long, hard ride, he could feel the weight of her as she slept against him. He could also see the image of her falling into bed with his brother. It had been all he could bear having watched from a secure peephole. The sound of her laughing for *him*, it was too much.

He had retreated to her room, unsure of what he would do with himself there once he arrived, or what he would do when... if... she arrived. It had been foolish. Of course, she would stay in her new paramour's bed. The Emperor's Mistress. The highest height a woman like her could reach. And his brother was handsome. Everything he himself was not.

And ... he could not blame Xander for desiring her as well. She was ... Lydia. Her smile, her confidence, her intelligence

most of all, the way she clung to him in her sleep, like a little girl longing to be safe. And he wanted that for her too, he wanted her to be safe, even though she did not seem like someone who needed protecting most of the time. Capable enough to handle anything.

She didn't need him.

Not the way he needed her.

He wanted her to be happy, but it was so hard to watch as that happiness unfolded.

He told himself he was leaving to give her space to build that happiness.

He wasn't escaping for himself, it was all for her. To not stand in her way.

Fisting his knuckles into his eyes, he forced away the tears, sniffing as he clucked the horse into motion again. These thoughts had plagued him since he left her that morning

The sun was low in the sky now when he pulled up to the gates outside the Imperial City. Unlike everyone else rolling in with carts and carriages, he turned at the last second, his visage safely obscured within a deep hood and scarf around the lower half of his face. Following a path cut across the ground, he went to the military door a half a mile on the other side of the city with its direct walls and path leading forthwith into the inner Imperial Grounds.

His military badge got him through with a wave and no one stopped him at the dozen inner gates that segmented the straight shot to the palace. Were there ever a siege on the capitol, this corridor would become a tunnel of death as each section could and would be closed off with twelve reinforced gates.

In the last third of that corridor of death, he turned off again, bringing his horse to a stop down a horse alley. Dismounting, he passed the reins to an approaching groomsman who took the mount after he flashed the badge again. From there, it was an easy thing to pass unseen through the wending ways that honeycombed around the corridor of death until he came to one of the secret entrances to the Undercourt.

"Alexandros!" he called as soon as he came into view of his hidden sanctuary. "Alexandros! Are you here?"

There was no answer and no sign of his friend when he pushed his way into his office. Of course, there was no reason Alexandros would be there waiting for him. If anything, the poor bird, having gone through several transformations and flights in short order...

"He's probably sleeping," Damian said to himself out loud.

No one answered. Yet, the fireplace had burned down to a small pile of coals because, of course, it was. Edith had headed out to Summerbourne Castle ahead of them, and Damian felt pretty sure he had piled the fire high and had not thought to bank it or remove the copious number of logs he had a tendency to throw on.

Instead of rebuilding the fire then, Damian sat down before it and leaned on his knees, hanging his head like the sad dog he was. As much as he hated it, he wanted to feel the cold now. Feel anything that didn't remind him of the warmth of her body and breath. But all it did was make it more acute the absence of her.

"Is this what obsession is like?" he asked, folding his hands as if in prayer. "Do you hear me? The gods of the Imperium? You granted me a great sacred gift, and then you took it away again? What lesson am I supposed to learn in that?"

"Damian?" a small voice squeaked out. At first Damian couldn't figure out where the voice came from until before his eyes, the pile of smoldering wood shifted and a long elegant head lifted out of it.

"Alexandros!" Damian jetted forward to land on his knees as close to the fireplace as he dared. The heat wasn't much, but it was enough to burn human flesh.

The phoenix within shivered, the light he naturally gave off having dimmed to nearly nothing, showing that it had been the source of the light that Damian had mistaken for cinders.

"What are you doing?" the forgotten prince asked.

"Dying, I think. I never seem to remember that part from life to life, so I can't be entirely sure." The phoenix shuddered again, and for a flicker, the light went out entirely only to flare back defiantly.

"What do you mean you are dying?" Quickly Damian grabbed up more tinder from the box nearby, throwing it onto the few actual coals that remained. The fire flared, and Damian sucked in a huge breath of air in a loud vocal gasp before leaning forward to blow the coals back to life.

Heat blazed as wood bits caught, and Alexandros fluttered his wings to help the fire resettle all around him. That was when Damian could see it; the golden blood burbling from a wound in Alexandros's chest. As it pumped out, the volatile substance doused the wood around him, stimulating the fire to greater heights.

Lifting his hand to shield his face, the fire grew so high from the combination of wood and phoenix blood that sharp pain from the heat pierced at his palms for being too close.

"Alexandros! You have to tell me, who did this to you?" Damian shouted as the fire roared loud enough to drown his voice.

"I am so disappointed," the phoenix said, his head lolling back and forth as he struggled to stay conscious, words slurring. "I really wanted to be ... a secretary ... for much longer than that. It's simply not ... fair. I'm not ready to start over."

Desperately, Damian grabbed more wood, throwing them onto the fire as the flames consumed the fuel too fast. "You're not going to die! I'm not going to let it happen!" he shouted. He would need more wood.

Bolting to his feet, Damian went to his bedroom and the other fireplace, scooping the various logs waiting there into his arms.

"There is no point... Damian... this is a mortal wound," Alexandros said as soon as he returned, dropping the pile of logs with a heavy clatter beside the fireplace. "My blood is already igniting."

"As long as we keep the fire going, you won't burn up. You can heal. I've seen you do it before."

"They stabbed me to my heart... I told you..." the head flopped down out of the fire, Alexandros's eyes closed.

"Told me what? Told me what, Alex! No! Don't you die on me, do you hear me? I can't lose you too! Alexandros!"

The eyes blinked open, as the phoenix tried to lift his head at the top of his swan-like neck, but he continued to waver. "You just have to tell the truth. It's really that simple. Promise me. Okay? Promise me you'll tell her."

Damian couldn't speak, his eyes were clouding over from the smoke and his tears. He continued to feed wood into the fire, which seemed to burn away as fast as he could throw it in. If he didn't keep feeding it, all that would be left would be the bird within being consumed entirely.

"Damian, I know you are afraid... but she might choose..."

Alexandros's head flopped back onto the floor then, his skin glowing and crackling as the fire crept up his veins, igniting the inside of his own body.

"No, no, no, no," Damian kept repeating. Standing up, he seized one of the chairs so he could smash it onto the floor. If Alexandros died, he would lose his connection to the phoenix forever, burned away by the fire along with his friend's body. Already he could see through the flesh of the phoenix's body, the creature's heart lighting up with each beat. It would burn down and burn down until all that remained was the calcified remains of the egg. And his friend would be gone.

Damian couldn't give up.

Not now.

CHAPTER 42

CHANGE OF PLAYERS

Lydia welcomed the distractions of preparing for the court's arrival. As long as she focused on the next task, she didn't have to think about anything else. For most of the time, she relied on Edith and Kinley's expertise, and only needed to sign or approve those decisions, releasing the money or the promises of money to cover it.

"Can this place really hold so many people?" Lydia asked.

"It is a castle; it is designed for this," Edith assured as she swept away with the next bunch of signatures. "The baggage carriages have arrived, milady. We are expecting the rest of the court by early afternoon, and lunch is prepared out back."

Lydia smiled as she caught the last of Edith's instructions before the housekeeper disappeared.

Before she could get comfortable having a moment of respite, Lord Petre appeared at the doorway to the library. "Our great and wonderful sun of the Empire requests your presence, oh, moon of this fair summer's court!" he declared, gesturing and bowing with all the theatricality his little speech required.

Now that did brighten her dark mood. A little at least.

"We have barely had an acquaintance, my Lord Petre, and already I think you will be one of my favorite people," she said earnestly, coming around the desk to take his proffered arm.

"We cousins must stick together," he said with a wink. He led her through the hallways and up to the Emperor's guest floor as the servants moved up and down all the stairs with unfamiliar luggage into the other wings of the castle, using every available guest room as they went.

"While we have a moment like this, I hope you do not think it too forward of me to ask, how are you holding up?" Lord Petre leaned in so that he could say his words at a polite volume. "You have been off to the races since we arrived, I think."

She squeezed his arm appreciatively. A million polite platitudes went through her mind and out again. The weight in her chest bore down on her heart, and she found she couldn't say any of them.

"My life was so simple only a few weeks ago," she said softly.

Petre's steps slowed to a saunter, and he laid his hand over hers. "You're acquitting yourself astonishingly well," he said with a pat.

There was so much she wanted to say, to dump on this complete stranger, simply because she needed someone, anyone to talk to about everything that had happened, but she didn't dare. The stakes were too high.

"Thank you for your kindness" was all she did dare.

"It is alright if you do not know where you are," he added, looking at her sideways as he continued. "Sometimes it's only in the darkest darks that we can see the guiding stars."

"What do you quote sir? It sounds familiar, but I cannot place it."

"I quote nothing," he said giving a crooked grin that just made him seem more charming. "Sounded pretty good though, didn't it?"

"So you are a poet?"

Lord Petre shook his head. "Honestly, I am probably more lost than you. I have no idea where I fit into this court, and right now I am my cousin's minder in these troubled times."

"Well, Damian trusts you," she said, remembering her... who knows what, vouching for this lord.

She felt him flinch under her hand on his arm. Then he cleared his throat. "You know..." he struggled for a title.

"I know," she affirmed, letting him off the hook.

They were silent for a few more steps while Petre worked it out. "I see," he said, nearly whispering. "I see now." Then he chuckled. "So you are one of his agents too. You are part of the Undercourt."

"I believe I am," she agreed, grasping at any connection to Damian still.

Now Petre pitched his voice down to a true whisper, speaking quickly. "Then you know about the attempts on his life."

She nodded as her reply.

"And about the envoy coming in two days," he added.

"The what?"

"The envoy. So you don't?"

Looking back and forth in the hall, he pushed her gently into an alcove of windows, then pulled the curtains partly closed to obscure them further.

"First, let me clarify," she said as he checked one last time to see that no one saw them. "I know about his impending marriage to the Queen in the Southern Kingdom."

"Good, what you don't know and what has been kept secret, which of course means that most everyone knows it, is that her envoy is arriving in two days to formalize the ceasefire and establish a date for the proxy wedding, in order to have it formally announced," Lord Petre said quickly. "Damian is right now back in the capital. He thinks he finally has the proof that it was Lord Dominique behind the *happenings*, back in the capital city."

"What sort of proof?"

"I don't know, but I've been certain it was Lord Dominique from the beginning. He's a conniving manipulator, always has been."

"Like *he* is the target of the assassination attempts?"

Lord Petre blinked.

Lydia measured Lord Petre's reaction carefully. She really wasn't certain if she could trust all this information he was suddenly freely giving her.

"What do you mean?" her co-conspirator finally stuttered out, grabbing her shoulders.

"Someone is trying to kill Lord Dominique?" a new voice said.

They both froze. Just beyond the curtains, Lady Regina stood closer than she should have been able to get without either of them noticing.

Achingly slowly, Petre dropped his hands and straightened, tucking them behind his back into the stance of a noblemen. Lydia didn't move at all, only regarded Regina with the same cool serene gaze she regarded her.

Lady Regina spoke first. "I came over to greet you both and thought I was interrupting a lover's secret tryst only to find something even more dire is afoot." If the woman had a fan, she'd be fluttering it.

Neither Lydia nor Petre said anything, so Regina shifted to regard only Lydia. Quickly, she curtsied politely. "Thank you for the invitation to your home, Countess," she said tactfully.

Lydia's eyebrow quirked. *It makes sense,* she realized, *She may come from a powerful family, but technically I have the higher rank. I am a countess in my own right.* Still, she curtsied in return. "You are most welcome."

"I am given to understand that there is lunch prepared?" Regina asked, shifting to continue down the hall. Lydia seamlessly fell into step with her, Petre trailing behind them both, still remaining stoically silent.

"Yes, we have prepared a meal outside for all so they may eat as soon as they arrive once they are settled in. I am headed that way now once I attend to the Emperor," Lydia reported.

"I wish to pay my respects to Xander as well," Lady Regina said boldly. Lydia resisted reacting to the use of the Emperor's familiar name, but Petre practically strangled behind them.

"Are you alright, Lord Petre?" Regina asked innocently, pausing to look over her shoulder at him.

She would have been formidable in the Crimson District, Lydia thought.

"Lord Petre, may I ask of you a favor? Could you go and see that the others in Xander's retinue have been herded toward the food and out of the maids' ways?" Lydia asked.

"Of course, my Lady," Petre said, bowing formally, and poignantly not looking at Regina. There was a deeper history there than Lydia knew, but recognized the signs of it.

"He truly is a sweet man," Regina noted as he disappeared.

"I have known him only a short time, but he has a turn of phrase I find quite pleasing," Lydia agreed as they resumed once more strolling the halls.

"There are many things about his words that are pleasing. Pretty words have dropped many a drawers in this court." Regina chuckled, and Lydia joined her.

"It seems I have much to learn."

"Well, you better learn fast if you are going to survive long as the Emperor's Mistress," the noblewoman said. She said it in the same politely mocking tone, but Lydia heard the edge and threat underneath it all just fine. "I must say I was surprised to hear how fast you abandoned one brother for the other." Lydia started to speak to that, but Regina continued over her. "I cannot argue with it of course. Anyone would make that same choice, but it saddened me to hear it."

"One cannot take blame for where the whirlwind takes them," the former courtesan said instead.

"Hmm, true," Lady Regina said. "I am not naive enough to believe that we have much control over which choices we actually get to make in our lives."

The women passed into a hallway lined with paintings. These were of the Imperial family, and Regina led her straight to one of a beautiful woman seated on a bench in a garden with a boy standing next to her.

Lydia would bet all her teeth it was a portrait of the First Empress, Damian's mother, though the boy in the painting would have been of her first son, Damian's older brother, long dead.

Regina brushed her fingers along the bottom of the frame. "The mistakes come when we roll the dice before rigging the game first."

"Or when we play the games at all," Lydia added.

"Hmm, yes, I suppose so, but it is a little late for that isn't it?" Regina regarded her again, her meaning clear. "I may no longer be destined to be the Crown Princess, but I am still a formidable player and could be a wonderful ally to someone such as you, who has the Emperor's ear. And his bed."

Allies abound this morning, Lydia thought. "I will consider it," she said. Then their attention was drawn to loud cheers coming from the opposite windows. Approaching to look out, both women could see Xander coming amongst a gathering crowd around the luncheon pavilion.

"I see we shall find our man outside now," Regina said.

There must have been some shade of Lydia's true feelings on her face because the noblewoman's posture shifted. "You know, there is a possibility of escaping—"

"Lydia!" Xander shouted from down below, having spotted them in the window. "Come down and dine with me!"

"At once, My Lord!" she called back, plastering her serenity back on. "Come Lady Regina," she said offering her arm.

But the noblewoman declined to take it.

CHAPTER 43

DEATH TO TYRANTS

It felt odd to sit next to Xander at the luncheon. Everyone in attendance was constantly glancing at her, measuring her with different agendas in mind. She pretended to see none of it, keeping her focus clearly on Xander... which was its own form of torture.

She used to be so good at listening to a patron, focusing on them and their interests, whatever they were. She could let their conversation go in one ear and out the other, all the while making the correct, appropriate remarks at the right time to show interest.

Yet, as Xander went on and on about how good he was at different sports, with much hooting and howling from the other men, all competing to entertain their Emperor, Lydia struggled.

She didn't even taste the fine feast laid out by her staff, though she studied each when Xander's attention had been pulled away. Roasted fowl of goose *and* pheasant, leg of lamb, a ham, a roast beef, a squab pie of all things, fruit tarts, cheesecakes, fruit compotes, cucumber finger sandwiches, bowls of sliced fruit, pastries,

Bavarian biscuits, and an endive salad with mustard vinaigrette. And that was just what she could see on this section of the table.

All she could think was how much she would enjoy it more if Damian were here.

If he could be here, we would never have met. He would have had no need of me, she thought bitterly.

Xander acquired her hand, and it took everything in herself not to rip it away. "Did you not hear me, my lady?"

She blinked, realizing she hadn't.

"Yes, Countess, what do you think?" one of his sycophants asked eagerly with such puppy-dog innocence she couldn't sense any malice in it.

"Honestly, I am not prepared to take a side yet. I don't think I've seen enough to make an informed judgment," she said. The men hooted and howled at her response with one shouting. "See, we're going to have to prove it to her now!"

I have a feeling this exchange is going to haunt me for months, she thought, wondering what the hell just happened.

Xander seemed entertained, however, and chuckled as he reached for the wineglass a serving woman just filled for him.

For some reason, the woman didn't step back, and when Lydia fetched her own wineglass for her to offer up to get filled, she froze. The woman stared down at the Emperor, her eyes wide, her nose flaring. In that same flash of moment, Lydia realized that, along the pitcher, the woman also held a knife.

Everything sped up then as the woman dropped the pitcher and lunged for Xander's unprotected throat. Lydia lunged at the same time going for the woman's wrist.

"Death to tyrants!"

Cheers turned to screams, and bodies startled. Xander seemed to think at first that Lydia had lunged in to hug him, but then he jumped up as the wine hit the ground near his feet. All within the same motion, Lydia slammed the woman's arm onto the table. The shock forced the weapon hand open, and the knife bounced and skidded amongst the crashing dishes.

Gasps.

Then someone screamed while others called out to "Save the Emperor!"

The serving woman Lydia held screamed and snarled like a wild animal, twisting her body to escape. The other men near the Emperor jumped on her to help hold her down, while someone, she had no idea who, pulled her away. She yielded, letting go. In the chaos around her, a voice cut through.

"Lydia! Where is Lydia!?"

Another person grabbed, pulling her away from the scattering pavilion out into the dull sunshine. Clouds were rolling in. It was only then that Lydia realized that it was one of the Imperial Guard who had grabbed her, bringing her over to where a group of them were trying to force a defiant Emperor away from the scene.

"We are not leaving until we find Lydia!" Xander demanded.

"Here she is, Highness!" the guard escorting her shouted, and the bodies parted to let her through. She found herself in his arms, crushed against him, and this time, she accepted the comfort.

"Are you alright? Are you hurt?" he demanded, pulling away again to look at her for evidence. But the guards weren't having it.

"We need to go now, sir!" a gruff one said. The people wearing Imperial uniforms circled tightly around them and Lydia had no choice but to go with the tide. Xander tucked her under his arm to guide her as they all ran alongside the castle. Then a closed carriage just materialized next to them, and she was shoved inside, followed by the liege of her nation.

The door barely shut when voices outside shouted.

"Go, go, go! Back to the Capital! Go!"

The carriage jerked into motion, and Lydia grabbed the bar attached to the wall and the seat to keep from being thrown. The carriage swayed like a ship on a hurricane sea as the horses went at a full gallop. To her shock, she realized that Imperial Guards were hanging on to either side of the carriage, their bodies blocking the windows.

There is no way they can hold on for the hours it will take to get to the Capital! she thought, but she could barely take a breath in to speak. Her mind raced, but her body could only react to the next stimuli.

"Lydia! You are hurt!"

Xander seized her arm and held it up.

Red drenched the back of it. She could only stare. It was blood. Her blood. She didn't feel it, but she could see it pouring out of her.

"I... I must have cut myself on the knife ... when I grabbed her ... somehow," Lydia said mechanically. She couldn't think of how she could have been cut. She hadn't felt it happen.

"Pull over! The Emperor's Mistress is wounded!" some voice ordered.

The voice sounded distant, like it was being shouted down a tunnel.

"Absolutely not!"

"I order you to stop! We need a doctor!"

There were more shouts, but the words became nothing. She watched with a detached, quiet space as another body came into the space. A cloth appeared and pressed into her arm. She felt a dull ache with the pressure, and then the world disappeared for a moment, going to black.

Then the world came back, at least some of it. She saw flashes. Gunpowder? A man dropping to the ground outside the carriage.

Xander shouted as the door tore open on the side of the carriage. A gun pointed in. First at her then at Xander.

More shouting, but it didn't make any sense.

Xander held his hands up, but then another person opened the opposite door to the carriage and went for Lydia. Xander dived at them, which earned him a punch across the face with the butt of the gun. She saw his blood fly and stain the back of the carriage in a long red swath.

Then she fell back into the black.

She stayed there. It was quieter there. Calmer.

She wondered if she had died.

After everything I've done to do the contrary, I die just like that? I wonder what I was so worried about. It doesn't seem to have been that difficult. Everyone makes such a fuss about death and... I don't really feel anything. Just regrets.

Damian's face floated up out of that dark. Or maybe it was a memory? She had heard once that when you die you saw your life replayed for you, but Damian hadn't been there for most of it. It was a bit of surprise to see him at all. Even more surprising was how much she wanted to see him some more.

She heaved a big sigh. Then paused.

The dead don't sigh. Do they?

If I'm not dead... if this is not the end... if the gods would just give me another chance... I won't be such a coward this time.

"I love you, Damian," she tried to say.

And then the world came back, light and sound returned in a rush; she still felt numb, detached from her body, but she could lift her head.

She was no longer in a coach.

Someone had tied her to a chair. Her arms were behind her.

The room she occupied was dark but for a single candle on a table nearby. And that candle seemed to struggle to stay lit. A draft blew through, threatening to snuff it out. Somewhere she heard water dripping.

She *felt* cold. In fact, now she felt everything. Her wounded arm lanced with pain as she shifted against the ropes. Her joints felt like she creaked similar to a clockwork automaton. Mouth dry. Eyeballs dry. Bladder far from dry.

"Hello?" she croaked out.

Another body moved on the opposite end of the room. It too sat in a chair, closer to the table. The light cast more clearly on his features.

"Ah. I see you are awake now," Lord Dominique grinned and crossed one leg over the other.

Chapter 44

IMPRISONED

*Trigger warning - strong language

"Where have you brought me you bastard?" she demanded.
He started chuckling more, bordering on laughter. Then he turned his face toward the candle as it almost guttered out. As the light fought back, she gasped at the sight of his face. His eye had swelled shut and streaks of blood and sweat, or maybe tears, streaked down from it as well as a bit of blood dried around the folds of his ears.

"I would proffer, lady, that you have as much to do with my being here as I do with yours," he said bitterly. "Though looking at the state of you, I'd say we are both in a whole load of trouble."

"The most pressing question still remains: Where are we?"

"I would argue the most pressing question is who brought us here? Followed by what do they want with us?"

"We will just have to agree to disagree then," Lydia said and spat some granules of dirt that had worked their way into her mouth. How many floors had she bounced or dropped on before she had ended up here? "Since I must make a guess, I would say we are in the Undercourt."

Dominique scoffed at that. "The Undercourt is just a myth and legend."

"Well, you would know best," she said dryly and tried to wriggle her arms again to see if she could get free. Immediately, sharp, horrible pain lanced up her arm, so much so that she couldn't hold back her cry.

"What is it?" Dominique demanded, the circumstances overriding his defense mechanism of sarcasm and false shows of control.

"My arm," she groaned, trying to force herself to breathe through the pain.

"Yes, you've been steadily dripping a nice pool behind yourself for a bit now. I've actually been concerned you would never wake up." Steeling her breath, Lydia cocked her head back to examine the aforementioned pool of blood. "You're right. It is an alarmingly big puddle. Explains why my head is swimming so much," she added as she straightened back to forward and experienced the world spinning a topsy-turvy. She swallowed and forced herself to focus. "If we are in the Undercourt then that means we're beneath the Imperial Grounds."

"We could be in any dungeon in a hundred castles anywhere!"

She knew he could be right, but something within her told her he was wrong. She also knew she didn't care.

"Hello!" she shouted at the top of her lungs. "Hello! Hey! Hey! Heeeeeeyyyyy!"

"What are you doing? If they know we're awake they'll kill us," he hissed.

"Don't be an idiot," she said, with complete disregard for his station.

He stared at her with saucer-wide eyes, his mouth dropping open dumbly.

She continued screaming. "Hey! I am awake, so where the hell are you!"

At last, the door opened. Lord Dominique even yelped like a little boy, and with the change of air pressure in the room, Lydia got a tang of urine blown at her.

How brave, she thought, but ignored the quivering noble to face down the small crowd of thugs who had entered the room. They didn't say anything either, only eyed her with expressions ranging from hostile to lustful to contemptuous with varying degrees of all three. Two of the men came around to stand behind her, and she forced herself to drop her shoulders. Any whiff of fear could set dogs like these off, and the Duke's son was throwing out enough fear for the whole room.

At last, the final person entered, and Lydia was only a little surprised to see her.

Regina pulled down the hood of her cloak and regarded Lord Dominique coolly, completely ignoring her other prisoner.

"You could not even hold on to your dignity, Lord Dominique. I believe you were poorly named."

"Regina," he snarled. "How dare you do this to me!"

She slapped him so quickly and so soundly that it whipped his head to one side. Lydia would have thought such a blow would hurt, but Regina showed no signs of discomfort at all. In fact, she seemed to have no expression on her face whatsoever.

"You are going to pay for everything that you have done. And once I am done with you and I let you die, the God of Vengeance will take you and do far, far worse," she said so matter-of-factly, it was as if she were merely reciting facts.

"What the hell have I ever done to your fat ass?" he roared.

She slipped something out of a pocket in her dress, which was a simple one that would be worn around the house. She pulled the object over her fingers and then backhanded Lord Damion. He cried out and blood spurted. In the dim light, Regina flexed her fingers and Lydia could make out the bronze knuckles she had slipped on, coated in blood.

"You all think you can play this game, and I really wouldn't care but you took something from me. Something I cannot get back. I will have revenge."

"Oh my gods, you sound pathetic," Lydia cried out loudly, throwing her head back.

Regina's attention snapped to the courtesan, her eyes narrowing. Then she snapped her fingers. Two of her ruffians grabbed Lord Dominique, while another started punching him liberally. All the while Regina kept her eyes on Lydia, moving with snake-like smoothness to the defiant woman. Lydia did the same, keeping her eyes on the real threat in the room.

"And then there is you, little whore."

Lydia slit her eyes and grinned. "Oh yes, that I am. I am most definitely a whore."

Somehow owning that fact to Regina unmoored her a second, for she opened her mouth then wrinkled her eyebrows in the first hint of an expression. Instead, she fingered the bronze knuckles on her fingers, rubbing at the blood-slicked metal with a thumb.

"If you're going to punch me, let's get on with it," Lydia sneered, haughtily.

"You are not worried about damaging your pretty face?" Regina asked.

"I've taken a punch before. I highly doubt you could do much even with your little toy there. Who knows, I might even like it," she replied suggestively.

Regina's lip curled. "I see the only reason he kept you around was because he had no other choice. You are most definitely not his type, whore."

"If you're his type then I'm glad I'm not, cunt," she lobbed back. Regina flinched. Apparently being called any sort of name was shocking to a refined, if murderous, lady such as her.

Finally, the noblewoman mastered herself. "I had half a mind to return you to Damian, as my gift to him, among many I wish to bestow, but I'm not so sure how my gift will be received considering your true nature."

"Why? Do you plan on fucking him yourself?"

The revulsion crossing her face was unmistakable, no words were needed. The sounds of Lord Dominique's beating cut into the silence between them.

"That is enough!" Regina commanded, her voice ringing out with queenly authority.

Lord Dominique wavered in his chair, his face bloodied, and after all that, he surely had some cracked ribs. But Lydia couldn't worry about him, she needed to worry about herself.

"Do you really not fear death?" Regina asked, studying Lydia.

It took a great deal of will to look away from the lord's battered form. "Oh, I fear death very much. It has visited me many times," Lydia said in a soft voice. "It is always used by those who fear the most."

"You have seen too much," Regina whispered. "You are innocent in all this, in the sins done against him, but if I let you go..." More calculations ran behind her eyes as she nibbled on her lower lip. "But if I do kill you, he will truly hate me forever. And that, I could not bear." She closed her eyes, a wave of exhaustion passing over her face, a weariness from life's trials that Lydia herself recognized. "It does not matter. He will know soon enough what I've done for him."

Regina gestured to her thugs. One produced a knife and stepped behind her. Lydia closed her eyes and focused on her breath, forcing herself to keep calm. Then pain lanced through her arm, and she hissed as the ropes fell away.

"Dammit, she's covered in blood," the man with the knife behind her cursed, shaking her precious liquid off his hand.

"Bind her up and get her out of her. Return her to her master," Regina said, spinning about to go back to her real prey, Lord Dominique.

Roughly, Lydia was hauled to her feet, and the world spun woozily. The light got brighter then darker, and she felt herself falling uncontrollably. She had no control, and she let herself go, hoping that at least when she hit the floor the world would resolidify itself. Her body didn't hit that ground, however. Instead, she continued to float in a world of alternating light and dark and she wondered if maybe now she had died. She felt like a ghost, disconnected from everything around her.

Hopefully, she would end up where she was going soon.

CHAPTER 45

IN THE ASHES

*Trigger warning - thoughts of suicide

Damian stared at the ashes, tears making tracks down his dirty face. He had burned everything he could. If he had had an axe, he would have destroyed the desk he now leaned against. As it was he burned all the drawers and everything else that had not been too heavy or too fixed to remove.

It had been for nothing. Lying amongst the ashes of his fireplace, he stared at the large gray egg that had once been his friend. It was the size of an ostrich egg and over its ashy surface, thin veins of lava-like threads pulsed as a heartbeat. Everything else of Alexandros was gone, except for a single pinion feather that Damian held in his fingers, turning it to watch the sheen reflect in it. He had no idea how long he sat there staring at it.

"There is nothing left for me now, is there?" he said out loud, hoping that Alexandros's voice would come and contradict him. But all was silent now.

"I have lost everything," he whispered, letting those words be real, not just truth in his head.

It took a while longer, but he decided to stand up.

The world wavered around him a moment. He had no idea how long since he had eaten or drunk anything. It didn't matter. Such things were for men who planned on continuing. He went toward his door, which would lead him out to the greater Undercourt, to a little pit he knew of. He wouldn't have to do much, just let go and let nature take its course.

He paused briefly, looking back at the fireplace, wondering if he should really leave the phoenix egg there, lost to the world above.

"You will be fine," he told it. The gods would take care of the small creature forming within. "Maybe you'll find someone worthy this time." Though that might be true, he had no idea. "Edith and Kinley will find you," he added, dismissing his guilt.

He intended to throw himself into that pit at last and be finished. There was no more Alexandros to stop him, after all. It would feel so good to just let go. He almost believed that.

But as he pushed his door open to leave, it stopped partway. A foot appeared, blocking his way. A small, woman's foot.

Urgently, he pushed his way out of the door to find Lydia lying against it. His speeding heart stopped as he took her in. Her skin was ghostly pale, and her eyes were closed with dark bruises beneath them.

She's dead! he thought until he touched her, seizing her face. She stirred, lifting her weak arms as if to fight him off, but she had no strength to do even that much. One of her arms was badly wrapped and stained red. She had no shoes.

"No, no," he cried and scooped her up into his arms. Her head flopped onto his shoulder.

The world was a series of steps after that. He brought her through the ruin of his office to his bedroom, onto the bed, which had been the other thing he could not destroy as a whole. He muttered a soft grateful prayer that it hadn't occurred to him to burn the mattress when he had ripped down the curtains. Now he laid Lydia there. She had started shivering after he picked her up into his arms, and his words went from blessing to curses as he realized he had burned all the blankets.

He needed to get her warm and address her wounds.

He needed a doctor and medicine.

He needed... He needed other people.

"I need you, Lydia."

He rushed away back to his office and scooped up the ashen egg. It was the only thing generating heat at that moment. Yet it generated too much heat, and he dropped it with a hiss as it burned his fingers. Taking off his shirt, he wrapped that around the phoenix egg and brought it to Lydia who was holding so deathly still.

"Lydia, please," he begged as he slid into bed with her, pressing the egg against her body, manipulating her arms to hold it close against her chest. Something in the heat of the egg seemed to wake her, and she curled around it.

"Damian?" she whispered in a small voice, and he tucked a strand of hair back from her face before kissing her with shaking lips.

"I'm here, my love," he said, pressing his forehead against her. "I'm so sorry."

"You left me behind." She started to weep, and his heart shattered.

"Oh no, no, I..."

There were no protests. That was exactly what he had done.

She clung to the egg as she clung to life. He had to keep going.

"I'm sorry," he said as he got out of bed. "I will return."

Then he ran full out to the bathing room. Seizing the towels that had survived his burning fervor, he also grabbed a bucket and scooped up some of the hot spring water there.

He had to get her warm. Get her well enough to bring her to a doctor, or well enough that he could leave her to get a doctor.

Returning to her side, he dropped his equipment by the side of the bed and took the badly wrapped arm carefully into his hands. To his relief, Lydia's face had a tiny bit of color in it as she continued to lie there with her eyes closed. As he pulled away the bandages, she winced and tried to pull her arm away.

"No," she mewed out.

"Shhh, it's alright. I'm not going to hurt you," he assured.

Her eyes tried to blink open. "Everybody hurts me," she said with bitter certainty, but she let him have her arm back.

"Lydia, can you keep talking to me? You don't have to tell me what happened, but just keep talking please."

She didn't respond at first, and he thought she had passed out again, but then she said, "I have to tell Damian that I love him."

His heart stopped.

Tears slipped down her dirty, blood-flecked face.

"Why are you crying, Lydia?" he asked, refocusing on the back of her arm. She had a long cut there, but it was hard to see under layers of dried blood with bits of cloth stuck into it. He dipped one of the towels in the water at his feet and began to gently wash. "Please, Lydia, keep talking to me."

"He can't love me. Nobody loves me," she said, sounding like a child.

"Why not?"

"Because all he sees is my beauty. I hate it."

"You hate your beauty?" That thought struck him hard.

"Nobody ever sees me. All they see is what they want to see. All they see is a thing. I'm not a thing!" she opened her eyes into slits again, looking at him, begging him to understand. "I would scar my face if it meant they could see the real me, but then how would I live? Why do I have to live like this? Ow."

She blinked then and looked down at her arm to see what he was doing as if she were just becoming conscious. Then she looked around, blinking. "Where... where am I?"

"You're here with me," Damian said gently, trying not to startle her.

"Damian?"

"Yes, it's me," he said, brushing her cheek. "You're going to be alright."

"I feel so cold," she said.

Gently, he pressed the shirt wrapped egg toward her. "Cling on to that."

She did and laid her head back. "I'm so tired."

"Don't go to sleep, not yet. We need to get you help," he said. "Keep talking to me."

"Hmm," she said. "This must not be very attractive right now."

That statement made him so angry. "Stop talking like that now!" he barked louder than he should. She froze, and he cursed himself a fool. "You need to stay alive right now. *That* is what is important. Just stay alive for me. Please."

Unable to meet her eyes, he examined her wound carefully. "This should have been sewed," he muttered. "At least it's clotted now." He took up one of the towels and tore it into strips so that he could start wrapping the wound back up. "We will need disinfectant, but the doctor will have it."

"Another scar," she said, regretfully. "This one will be harder to cover up."

"You have a scar?" he asked, "I haven't seen it..." but then he paused in his wrapping, dropping the puzzle piece into place in his mind. "That is why you will not allow me to see you naked."

The expression on her face was reluctant, sad, and resigned. With a sigh, she tried to sit up weakly.

"What are you... don't," he said, pressing her back down.

"Then you'll have to cut my clothes off me," she said, "I need to get out of these. I'm wet."

He nodded and fetched scissors from the sewing basket Edith used to mend his shirts. She indicated her collarbone. "Here. Start here."

Chapter 46

CONFESSIONS

*Trigger - descriptions of past sexual and physical assault

He did as she requested and worked, slicing through the fabric, destroying the dress to free the woman. Once he had cut past her torso, through the dress and then the corset, she pulled the cloth away herself. At first, he couldn't figure out what she wanted him to see. Then she pulled the flesh of her breast up toward her center, exposing her ribs on the other side. And the scar.

It was twisted and ugly. A long line that started near the top of breast flesh and curved down the crest, as if someone had tried to carve off...

"Oh gods," he breathed. She looked away ashamed, but his fingers reached for it to trace. Just before he touched, he paused. "May I?"

She closed her eyes, pressing her lips together hard, but nodded.

Gently, he touched the puckered skin.

"How could anyone have done this thing to you?" he asked.

"How? Easily. With a knife and two of his buddies holding me down. Laughing."

"But why would they do this?" he insisted. Carefully, he went back along the thicker flesh, feeling every nuance of the knife long gone.

"I was just a whore. Not a person. Just someone who didn't matter that they could destroy for their pleasure. I had already fucked two of them, but I got mouthy with the third. He kept calling me names, and I took exception to it. It was all the baiting he needed."

"It wasn't your fault." He busied himself cutting away the rest of her wet and smelly clothes.

"I know. They could have done it no matter what I did. I've seen women desecrated begging for mercy, cajoling, or defying. It doesn't seem to have anything to do with us. There is no way to know sometimes which way a patron may turn. Sometimes the sweetest and most innocent will hide a darkness. One has to simply trust their gut about a person."

"And what did you see when you looked at me?" he asked, standing up to go to the wardrobe. Somehow, in his frenzy and fever to save Alexandros, he had not touched anything that belonged to Lydia.

"You know what I saw. I keep telling you, but you don't believe me."

He pulled out one of her cloaks that she had left behind, it was a heavy winter one. "Yes, well. I keep thinking you're just trying to be nice."

She snorted. "I'm not nice. Nice doesn't get you very far and can never be trusted."

"Then what do you trust?"

"Kindness," she said, then nodded at the cloak now covering her. "Like this. This is kindness."

"How did you survive? Did someone save you?" he asked, as he helped her slip the rest of her ruined clothes off.

"Yes, though I have no idea who. One minute I was screaming, and next, the man cutting me, his head flew off. The other two tried to escape but didn't, and I was left on the floor bleeding and crying until my street mother came for me."

"Your street mother?"

She blew out an aggravated breath.

"I am sorry, we do not have to talk—"

"No, no. We've come this far." Lydia licked her lips. "I never knew what her real name was. And she wasn't actually my mother, but as orphans on the street, we banded together with those who would help us survive. Street mother, she had us run around fetching things, bring back what we stole, and guided us in the ways of the street. She could make the things we stole turn into food, and we never questioned about doing that for ourselves. And then she got me into whoring. Shortly after," she paused and gestured once more to her scar, "this happened... I don't really know how she heard about it, but Georgiana took me away from street mother. That's when I started my education to become a courtesan."

Damian gathered up the remaining destroyed clothes and tossed them into his equally ruined office so she wouldn't have to keep smelling them. Then he retrieved a fresh cloth and proceeded to wash her.

"How are you feeling?" he asked.

"I think I'm going to make it," she said softly, and she did look much better. She still cuddled the egg against her, still wrapped in the remains of his shirt. Strangely to him, not wearing a shirt, he didn't feel cold.

"I will get you fire and food soon, but I will have to leave you for a moment. And get a doctor!"

"I can manage," she said, though he could tell she didn't want to be left alone.

"I will make you comfortable first," he said and proceeded to cleanse her with the water.

"You still haven't said anything." He looked at her and she continued. Her cheeks pinked, which he was relieved to see. "About the scar."

"What about it?"

She blew out an aggravated breath. "About how it ... looks?"

He laughed. "I love every inch of your body," he assured her, and he meant it.

She narrowed her eyes at him. "I don't believe you."

He cocked his head at her, then shifted her breast flesh covered in her cloak aside so he could lower his face to the scar.

"What are you..." but he didn't let her finish that sentence.

Tenderly, he pressed his lips to the flesh, and she gasped a breath in. He didn't just stop there, he continued all the way around it to the other end of the mark. "This is a symbol that says you survived. I love it," he whispered as he lifted up to gaze down on her face so she could see his sincerity. This time she cupped his cheek, rubbing her thumb along his skin.

"I know you think what happened to you is a curse, but—"

"There... there is no curse," he said, pressing her hand against him there. "This is just my face."

Her eyebrows furrowed together. "I don't understand."

"It's not a curse or anything. No magic spell was put on me. I didn't do anything to have this happen, other than simply being born into the Imperial Family." He took a deep fortifying breath. "When they say 'the Family Curse' what they mean is a disease of the body passed down through the generations. Once every other generation, it manifests, but in this case, it had skipped my father's generation and manifested in me. And later than it should have. The only reason I survived was because of my bond to Alexandros." Unconsciously, he laid his hand over the egg bundle, still radiating warmth.

You were right, my old friend. I should have just told her sooner. He had no intention of hiding anything from her again, but it was too soon to speak of what else he had lost. He would soon, but there was time.

"Are you alright enough for me to go and get food and warmth for you?"

"Can I close my eyes now?" she asked, snuggling the egg closer.

"Yes," he said, though it stroked a chord of fear within him. Yet she looked so much better. Still tired, but with more color in her and she was warm again. *The phoenix egg could have healing properties?* he wondered silently.

She smiled at him as he left, and it only made him hurry faster so that he could return to her side quickly.

Lydia hugged the warm bundle close, already missing Damian now that he was gone.

"He'll come back. He promised to come back," she whispered to herself.

They always say that, the street mother's voice cackled, but it was easier to quiet her today. The warmth in her arms made it easier. In fact, the longer she held it, the better she slowly felt, like sacred healing was emanating off whatever it was within the cloth wrap.

And even if I die now, I will have no regrets this time. I told him the truth. She recalled the feel of his fingers on her ruined body and the touch of his lips on her scar. Despite how bone weary she felt, it still sent a shiver through her.

"I'm here my love," he had said to her, and she believed him.

He would return.

She had no idea how long she had drifted off, but soon she felt his body slide into the bed with her, coming underneath the large cloak to join her. The skin of his chest pressed against hers adding to the warmth instead of taking it.

"Damian?" she asked, when the whisper of concern that it might not be him nattered.

"It is me," he said, pressing a kiss to her temple. "Don't worry my love, help is coming. Rest until it arrives."

"Do you still think I'm beautiful?" she asked sleepily.

"I'm learning to look past that," he answered.

"Hmm, good," she said and snuggled her body back against his.

CHAPTER 47

PIECES FALLING

"But where is the Emperor?" Lydia asked.

"He's fine, I checked," Damian said.

Lydia stared down at the mark across the back of her forearm. Where there had been smooth skin, now there was a puckered scar, similar to the one by her breast. The only difference was, this one had come into existence over the course of a couple of days. Her original one had taken her weeks to fully heal.

"This is remarkable," she said, lowering her arm back down, tucking it under the quilt Damian had brought her. She wore a soft nightgown as well, and a roaring fire burned in the fireplace. Beside her, he sat fully clothed, fussing with a bowl of soup that had been brought down from the kitchen.

"What is remarkable is that you disarmed the assassin all by yourself with only that to show for it," he said before blowing over the surface of the brown liquid in the bowl. They had been talking since she woke up, her filling him in on everything that had happened after he left her at Summerbourne.

"So they... his guards took him and left me for dead in the carriage?"

"That is what my report says. When the carriage was attacked, their first priority was to keep the Emperor alive and whole. You were superfluous and wounded. I understand that Xander screamed for you the whole way back to the palace."

She sniffed. "I suppose there is some comfort in that. At least he felt guilty for leaving me behind to die."

"It wasn't his choice—"

"Yes, yes, I understand all that," she said, waving at him to give her the soup. She was starving.

Instead, he leaned forward, offering her a spoonful of the soup hovering over the bowl. At first, she wanted to scoff at the gesture, but the solid earnestness in his eyes persuaded her otherwise, and she took the food from his hand. The soup was warm, thick, and delicious.

"Have you told him that I am alive and well?"

"You're not well," Damian corrected. "It's only been two days, more or less. Edith and Kinley will be returning to us today. They are going to murder me when they see the state of you."

"If it wasn't for you, I wouldn't be alive," she said and ate another spoonful.

"If it wasn't for Alexandros..." he said soberly.

She cocked her head to one side, noting his dour expression. "What do you mean? I haven't seen hide nor tail... or feathers I guess of him."

Damian sat back. Settling the bowl on his lap, his eyes stared off. *No,* she realized, *not staring off.* Staring at the warm bundle still resting on her lap. She started unwrapping the shirt.

"Careful. Don't touch it, it'll burn you," Damian cautioned.

Heeding the warning, she kept her fingers on the cloth, pulling it away to reveal the egg within. She gasped, staring at the ashen gray surface and the veins of glowing red and orange threading it. "What happened?" she asked.

He shook his head. "I don't know. I found him dying. It was clear to me that someone stabbed him, but he died before he could tell me who or what happened."

"I'm so sorry," she whispered.

"In one small way, I am grateful. I don't think you would have survived without it. Phoenix eggs are known to have healing properties, though I wasn't sure it was true until now." He nodded at her new scar.

"But Alexandros's life?"

"It's gone. Everything he was in this life is gone. And whatever they become in the next life won't feel or think the same as they did, even if they remember everything. This is what it means to be a phoenix."

"So we can never know who killed him," Lydia concluded. She stared down at the patterns though, a singular thought pushing forward, unrelenting in its certainty. "It was Regina."

Damian blinked once, then his eyebrows furrowed hard. She could see he knew it too, now that she said it aloud.

"We have no evidence," he said.

"No we don't, but..." and she proceeded to tell him everything that she saw and heard. "I don't even know if Lord Dominique is still alive," she said with a pang of regret. "I don't know for certain how this is all related, if it even is."

"Regina's animosity toward House Cathor was always on principle because they were rival to the Imperial family," Damian said. He had started pacing during her story and continued now from one end of the bedroom to the other in a quick military march.

"So why would she move against him now?" Lydia asked, scraping the last of the soup from the bowl into her mouth before setting it aside. "To protect your brother maybe? His people are trying to assassinate Xander, so she's trying to assassinate Lord Dominique?" She thought about Regina's face and the tone of her words when she last spoke to her. Pressing her hands against her eyes, Lydia shook her head. "No, that isn't the impression I got from her. She said she was getting vengeance. That doesn't make sense, it isn't the word you would use for something that hasn't happened yet, it is what you would say for something that has. So what has happened to her?"

Damian stopped pacing. "Me. She lost me. She lost her chance for the Imperial throne, to become empress." He met her eyes. "It is the one thing she has wanted her entire life, and when my disease manifested itself, Alexandros saved my life but the damage was done. I was removed from succession."

"But then why not just get Xander to marry her instead. I know that might be callous but logically it makes sense."

"Xander despises her, and with the possibility of an alliance with the Southern Kingdom always in play, he avoided her."

"So he spurned her," Lydia stated, while he went to his office and then came back again with empty hands. "I burnt all my paper! I need paper!"

"Use a charcoal stick from the fireplace," Lydia said, swinging her feet to the side of the bed.

He rushed back and returned.

"There," Lydia said, pointing at a blank spot on the light-colored stone walls.

He rushed up and wrote Xander on the wall and circled it. Then added Dominique as he talked. "Dominique was with me when the disease manifested itself. We were at the siege of the Highborne Keep, and one of the more popular rumors was, of course, violating the sacred shrine there got me cursed, but it was Dominique's people who attacked and pillaged the place."

Then he wrote Alexandros.

"Being bound to the phoenix was supposed to save me. And he did, but could not restore what had already been lost."

He wrote throne.

"Then there is the throne."

"But you were removed from succession," Lydia repeated.

"Yes, but for a little while, there had been a plan," he winced now, as if it pained him to remember it. "That I would be made Emperor anyway and then try to conceive an heir with Regina.

But she couldn't bring herself to touch me. It was all too painful." He shook his head. "And currently there is no heir. It would not be an enormous leap to reinstate me if something should happen to Xander. Many of the noble houses and cabinet ministers would still support me, despite everything that's happened to me."

Lydia's heart beat hard. "Regina said that you would be grateful for what she's done for you. But wouldn't killing Alexandros hurt your claim?"

He growled. "You're right, it doesn't all fit together."

Slapping his hand against his impromptu chart, he turned. "I need to go speak with Regina."

"And what are you going to say to her when you do? If we're right and she's done all this for you... If she is trying to kill your brother and if she killed poor Alexandros... And it's all for you..."

"I'm tainted by association. Even if it isn't true, no one will believe I didn't orchestrate any of this. If I show my face anywhere out there now, I'll most likely be arrested or killed. Or one then the other." He kicked the end of the bed, then seized the pole to lean his head against it. "But I can't let her kill my brother."

Lydia shook her head. "And we won't, but we have to find her."

Damian nodded. "I'll put the word out through the court. Someone will know where she is. God, it used to be so easy to just go to her quarters and find her."

"Come to me," she ordered, extending her hand.

Dropping the charcoal stick on the ground, he obeyed and came to sit beside her on the bed. It felt so natural for their arms to come around each other, their heads pressing together. They stayed that way for a long time, simply holding and being held.

"I don't know why I was so afraid," she whispered.

"I was scared too."

"Do you think everyone goes through this? When they fall in love?"

"I don't know," he admitted. "But it all seems so natural, maybe."

"Whatever happens now, let's stay by each other's side."

"If that is what you want, my Lady."

Chapter 48

FUGITIVES

They were bolted awake to the sounds of banging at the door. Gasping, Lydia grabbed up the egg to her chest, still wrapped in its cloth nest. Damian grabbed up Lydia as they both sat upright in their bed.

"Open the door in the name of the Empire!" the authoritative voice barked on the other side of their bolted bedroom door. The banging continued.

"We need to run," Lydia hissed and got out of bed. Damian jumped up on the other side and ran to the door, throwing down a bar she hadn't seen before.

"That will hold them," he said, and spun in place to grab up his clothing from the floor.

Lydia deposited the egg on the sideboard, the nightgown she wore spinning around her in time to catch a bundle of clothes Damian tossed her. They were her breeches and page shirt.

"Your brother couldn't have ordered your arrest?" she asked, while Damian stepped into his black pants.

Yet, the grim look on his face didn't reassure her. Instead, he went to the wall and pulled down a sword and scabbard, then snapped up the belt from inside a cabinet underneath.

The banging at the door stopped a moment, just as Lydia got the breeches on and Damian had buckled the belt with sword around his waist.

They both held still, listening.

Then *bang, bang, bang*!

The pounding had turned rhythmic.

"They're battering the door down!" Damian hissed, sliding the leather strap through the other side of the buckle, then bolting forward to grab Lydia's boots. "Finish dressing later; we have to move!"

"Wait, you need a shirt!" she said and managed to grab his along with her own and her corset, which would definitely take more time to cinch than they had.

The door started to splinter.

Without another word, Lydia slapped the clothing at Damian's chest, which he grabbed while she scooped up the egg. He held the door for her with his free hand to let her through into the office. They paused for nothing more as the pounding at the door haunted their escape. Once down the long hall to the other barred door, a nasty crack stopped the pounding rhythm.

"They're through!" Lydia hissed.

Damian was already lifting the double bars off the other door, while she clutched the egg to her chest, her nightgown swirling all around her as she looked back and forth between the danger and their escape, trying to will the bar out of the way.

An eternal few seconds later he had the bar up and out, dropping with a loud reckless clatter just as shouts filtered through the bedroom to the office.

"Go, go!" Damian ordered, holding the door and she went through.

"Stop!" a voice barked as Damian pulled the door shut.

Lydia was already running up the slope, finding her steps by intuition. Then Damian roared behind her, and she spun around in time to see the ruins on this side of the door collapse. The whole cavern groaned and shook, knocking her down onto the stairs. Still she clung to the egg.

"Damian!" she cried, sure that the tumble of rocks had swallowed him up. She stared into the dark, seeing very little now that the gaslight by the door had been drowned. All she could smell was dust and grit, everything was silent but for one or two rocks still trying to settle.

"D... Damian," she whispered fearfully.

"I'm here." He coughed, and she felt his presence in front of her.

"Oh thank the gods," she prayed and wrapped her spare arm around him in the dark. He held her back, continuing to cough, then pulled away to spit.

"We need to keep going and get out of here. I don't know what I've done. There could be more of a cave in."

He pressed her boots at her in the dark and they traded egg for boots so she could pull them on. Slipping the cloth around the egg away, faint light illuminated his skeletal face. To anyone else, it would have been haunting in the dark, but to her, it was the face of the man she loved, and she was relieved to see it.

"I'm sorry, I lost your shirt," he said.

"You did too." She nodded at his bone pale bare torso. She stood and took the long edges of her nightgown, rolling it up and knotting it at the side. "That will have to do until we find something better," she said.

He smirked.

"What?"

"You look like a pirate," he said, grinning.

"Har de har har." She took the egg back so he could keep his hands free and turned to head up the stairs in order to hide her own smile, relieved that they were both still alive after the harrowing escape.

It wasn't until she reached the first juncture that the reality of their situation came back. "What are we going to do now? Where can we go?"

"To the Emperor," he said resolutely, and he took her hand to guide her down a new route. "We need to be careful. This way isn't the safest. Nobody knows of it but me, and I found it by accident and nearly died for the trouble."

"Charming," she said dryly.

"I don't understand, how can we see him, but he can't see us?" Lydia whispered. Damian touched the strange mirror they looked through.

"An Imperial secret," he whispered. "There are mirrors like these all throughout the palaces, the better to spy on the court. Only I know they exist now."

"And now I," she said softly.

He put his arm around her and kissed her temple. "You can know all my secrets," he whispered.

She leaned into him, "Right now I'm simply weary." The journey to get to the Emperor's chamber had been uneventful, but trying, and a hell of a lot of climbing, made more awkward by the egg she still protected. They had managed to cut what remained of her nightgown to form a sling, which she used to tie the egg to herself. Still she cradled it with her arms, fearful it could slip out.

"We could run," he suggested softly. "Run away and hide. Escape this place."

"Then we would be running forever," she said. "And your brother will definitely fall in time without you. The Empire. All of it." That thought filled her with dread. "Things in this Empire may not be good, but they could definitely get much worse."

Damian grunted in agreement.

They continued to watch Xander in the dimness of his room. It was fully night in the world outside the Undercourt. The Emperor paced the floor much like his brother would, stopping in front of his roaring fire to stare into it, before swinging back to walk the length of the room. Two servants stood at the ready to serve him which meant Damian and Lydia could not enter the room without being seen or an alarm raised.

"The Emperor is rarely ever alone," Lydia noted. "But... but I have an idea."

She untied the egg sling and passed it to Damian. "How do I get into that room?"

Her love hesitated only for a moment. "This way." He stepped to the side of the mirror, running a hand along the wood there. Pausing halfway, he slid it down and pulled out a thin metal handle, locking it into place with a click.

They both held still, waiting to see if anyone inside the room noticed the click, but there was no reaction. Slowly, he opened the door, and she passed through wordlessly. Curtains framing an alcove window obscured the secret door. Through the glass she could see that they were on the second floor.

Running her fingers through her hair, she took a fortifying breath, then pushed the curtain to the side to peek out.

"Xander?" she asked in a frightened, small voice.

Immediately, his head snapped up, and the servants startled.

"Lydia!" Xander dashed to her and she made a show of stumbling in with a pathetic whimper. His arms wrapped around her. "Oh thank the gods, you're alright! You're alive! I'm so sorry!" He whipped around to the two footmen, standing there shocked. "Get her a blanket hurry! And some wine! A doctor!" he ordered.

One footman rushed off to obey, but the other dithered, unsure.

"But, sir, how did she—"

"Go now!" the Emperor roared, and he guided Lydia to the chair by the fire. He knelt down before her, rubbing her legs as if to warm her up. "I'll take care of you. I promise. You're safe now."

She nodded, visibly shaken. "I knew I had to get back to you."

"Wine! Do you want something to drink?" He bolted to his sideboard to slop some in a glass for her. "How did you get back by yourself? It must have been terrifying?"

Damian's hand appeared from the curtain and ripped the glass away from his brother. Xander startled back, slamming his hands against the sideboard, making the glass there rattle. Unperturbed, Damian took a drink from the freshly poured glass, his eyes murder as he stared at Xander the whole time.

"Brother," Xander said, "W-what are you doing here?"

The forgotten prince turned back to the sideboard and refilled the glass. "I think you and I need to have a talk, brother."

"Guards!" he screeched, and Damian brought up his sword obscured by his leg to Xander's neck.

"Call them off now or you're dead," Damian hissed.

Xander's eyes were wide as blue disks.

"Your Imperial Highness?" a call came from the next room as the door banged open in the Emperor's suites.

"I kill you now and the succession is mine. Lydia is mine. But we can still fix this if you call them off now!" Damian hissed.

"G... get me a doctor!" Xander shouted, turning his head to the door.

He didn't see Damian duck back behind the curtains with a sword. Lydia herself stood up, using the chair as if she were struggling to stand as the guards burst in. Xander pointed at her as if the sword were still pressed to his throat, and he couldn't move.

"She needs a doctor. My physician, quickly!"

"No, please! No guards!" Lydia cried cowering behind the chair. "Make them go away, my Xander!"

The guards looked to the Emperor confused. "Y-you heard her! Get out! Get out!! Keep everyone else away!"

Obediently, the young guards did as they were told, and as soon as they had backed out and shut the door, Lydia rushed to lock it, then the Emperor's bedroom door.

"Now, let's talk."

CHAPTER 49

SEE THE TRUTH

"My advisors told me you betrayed me," Xander defended, staring daggers at Damian as he re-emerged from behind the curtain.

The older brother returned to the sideboard and poured another glass of wine. "Or did they say they suspected. And then told you it would be a good idea to just do away with me rather than risk a rebellion," he shot back.

"Would you have taken the chance?"

"If I had wanted to kill you, I could have done it several times over very easily as you have just seen." This time Damian took the glass of wine over to Lydia who sat back into the armchair to receive it.

"You stay away from her!" Xander barked, but both of them ignored him as she took the wine with a grateful smile. Then to drive the point home, Damian brushed his hand through her dirty hair affectionately.

"So what is it brother? What has changed that you would send your guards to kill me, after everything I've done for you?"

"Everything you've done for me? Pray tell, what have you done for *me*?"

"I have been your most loyal and staunch ally, I gave you life, security, and even, the throne. I graciously left the line a succession with no bloodshed. It was a *peaceful* transition. Something unprecedented in our family since our grandfather's grandfather! I even let you have the woman I cherished more than anything, even my own life, for the sake of this empire and her! How have I not done enough for you?" He was shouting at the top of his lungs by the end, completely heedless of who it may alert or summon to them.

Lydia strained to listen for the sounds of pounding on the locked doors, but for now, none came.

Xander glared back at his brother. "You knew I couldn't do it," he growled back softly. "You knew I couldn't be half the Emperor you were, and it would just be a matter of time before I failed. I can see everyone: watching me, measuring me, comparing me to *you*. To the Emperor *you* would have made. You *gave* her to me?" He gestured at Lydia. "I *saved* her from *you*. From your cruelty and your manipulations. You just put me in place to show how much better than me you'd be so that when they finally couldn't handle any more of my failures, you would come sweeping in, and they would beg you to come back. Even with that face of yours, you know that if you gave a snap of your fingers, they would all come running back to the Imperial Phoenix!" He sneered on the last. "Even the actual Imperial Phoenix chose you over me!"

"Not anymore. The Imperial Phoenix is *dead*," Damian said, his voice low and pained.

Xander stood there shocked. "What do you mean, 'It's dead?'"

"Damian," Lydia asked, standing up worried, "Where is the egg?"

He gestured to the hidden passage.

She went quickly behind the curtain. Xander moved to go with her, but Damian blocked it, unwilling to show the secret hidden there. She found the egg in its sling at the back of the narrow secret passage and, careful not to touch it, she gathered it back up to hug to herself.

When she returned, she pulled the secret door closed, and it blended seamlessly with the wood, two foot wide, framing the window. Xander's eyes returned to their round state when he saw the bundle in her arms.

"Let me see," he begged.

She glanced to Damian who nodded once, keeping his eyes on the floor as if he couldn't bear to look.

Gently she pulled back the sides of the cloth sling to show the ash gray surface and the veins of lava, glimmering along its surface.

"The gods in the heavens," Xander swore softly and stretched his fingers to touch it. Neither of them stopped him. He hissed sharply as he withdrew his burned fingers.

"How?" he asked. "How did this happen?"

"I don't know," Damian admitted. "I found him in the midst of dying. I was not able to save him. They will be reborn someday, when the next person they are to bond with touches them. That person may not even be born yet. It is the duty of the Imperial family to guard them now until then." A sharper look of guilt passed over Damian's face, and for a brief moment, Lydia was sure there was something more that he wasn't telling. Something she would ask him about later.

Xander dropped his singed fingers, exhaustion weighing on him. He trudged himself back to the fireplace and dropped into the chair. "I don't understand. Who would commit such a grave sin as to murder a phoenix?"

"I think it was Regina," Lydia said. Both brothers looked to her.

"Why do you think it was Regina?" Xander asked.

But she shook her head. "I don't know. I don't have any evidence, simply, something in me says, it was Regina. I just see the truth."

"Lord Dominique was found dead today," Xander said levelly. Damian's head snapped to him once more, his eyes wide now at the implications of that. Lydia simply felt pained.

"Now, I do know that Regina is responsible for that. She was beating him to death when they brought me to you," Lydia confirmed, nodding at Damian.

"You would testify to this?" Xander asked.

Lydia nodded.

"Is his death publicly known?" Damian demanded.

Xander's hands were shaking. "Not yet. The ministers are trying to keep it quiet for now. There was a note pinned to him. 'Death to all those who have betrayed the true Emperor.'"

Damian lifted his head, his mouth opening in understanding. "Hence why they believed it was me." He turned and started pacing. "Then yes, arresting me would be the right move, and I would have been a fool not to see it coming and still been in my hiding place in the Undercourt."

"But I still don't understand how Lord Dominique could have betrayed you? Regina knows the truth about your face."

"Lord Dominique was the principal figure in charge of negotiations with the Queen to the South, arranging the ceasefire and marriage conditions."

Damian pounded his fist against the wall. "And Regina is one of the war faction who would see such an alliance as a betrayal to all those who have fallen in battle. Even if it brought us all peace and prosperity. It was something she refused to forgive and something she and I could never see eye to eye on."

"And she would kill Xander to clear your way to the throne," Lydia said. "But I still don't see why she would kill poor Alexandros?"

"I received word from him that he discovered something," Damian said.

"Yes," Lydia cried remembering. "Petre told me that was why you left."

"Where is Petre now?"

"Being held by the Imperial Guard in his quarters," Xander said. "We thought it prudent considering his connection to you."

"Dammit, Xander," Damian growled. "You push away and make enemies of everyone who is trying to help you."

"How was I to know? With his close connection to you!"

"Do you believe me now?"

The tension held between the two brothers, neither willing to give the other an inch.

Then suddenly, Damian dropped to one knee. Bowing his head like a knight before his liege, he rested his hands there.

"What are you doing—"

"You are our Emperor," Damian said, cutting him off. He looked up, his eyes full of righteous conviction. "You," he whispered. "There can be no one else, and there will be no one else. You don't see it, and you don't understand it, but you are the Emperor this country needs to lead us. Ever since you were a little boy, you have been so good. I was told to stay away from you, that you were my enemy, but you were my baby brother. My bubber."

The childish name would have sounded ridiculous any other time.

But it reached Xander, making the angry young man seem like that small little boy from so long ago. Lydia could see it then. The family trauma these two survived, struggling for a different life. To not be rivals but to be brothers.

"You have what it takes to break this cycle," Damian insisted. "You can lead us to a different future, a better one than our father drove us to. I am too much like our father. I *can't* lead us there."

"You really believe that?" Xander asked in a small voice.

Across his chest, Damian slapped his fist in a knight's salute. "I am with you all the way."

Xander collapsed then, dropping to his own knees and throwing his arms around his brother, crying. Damian blinked in shock, but then he too put his arms around him.

"Never doubt me again," Damian choked out, and Xander nodded vigorously.

All Lydia could do was snuggle to the egg, feeling its warmth penetrate her to the core while tears rolled down her face.

CHAPTER 50

AN UNEXPECTED MEETING

Xander's hands shook as they waited in a side room of the theater. Lydia laid her own hands over his, squeezing them tightly. "This is going to be alright," she assured. "I'll be by your side. I promise. And Damian will be watching above."

"What if our subterfuge doesn't work?" he asked softly. "What if she still manages to get to me?"

"That is why we changed the venues. She won't think to find you here," Lydia said soothingly, indicating the theater at large.

"There is still no word of her?" he asked, adjusting his cuffs.

She shook her head. "No, not yet. Damian is still looking."

"This all seems so very surreal," Xander said, running his finger along a rack of costumes, the fine fabrics glinting in the lamplight.

"It is, but then my own commitment ceremony to your brother, when I became his Endowed Mistress, was also very surreal," she said, smiling warmly at the memory of it.

"You liken it to a marriage, sister?"

"It is a commitment, of my own choosing. It is the closest the likes of me will ever have," she said. "It does not make it any less precious to me."

Xander regarded her a minute. "If you wish it, I would grant you permission to marry, Countess," he said.

She shook her head. "Thank you for the gesture, but neither of us are willing to risk your position, Your Imperial Highness."

"Xander, please. When it is just us," he insisted.

"Well, straighten up then. You want to impress your bride," she said as she came over to adjust his silky cravat. He snorted. "The woman in question is just a proxy."

"It's still a promise. With this commitment, you are ensuring all our futures."

Xander brushed her hair back from her shoulder. "Still, I harbor some regret that you will not be by my side."

She narrowed his eyes at him warningly. "I will be by your side the whole way, brother," she said.

"You know what I mean," he said.

"And you will never speak of such things to me again, are we clear?"

His own eyes narrowed for a moment, the Emperor in him coming out, but then he relented. "You are right, sister. Forgive me."

There was rapping at the door. "Excuse me, Your Imperial Highness. All is in readiness," one of his ministers said, bowing at the door. Like all the others had, he eyed Lydia mistrustfully but didn't dare say anything. No one seemed to understand what to make of the mysterious Countess of Summerbourne or her connection to the Emperor.

She stepped back from the Emperor, folding her hands demurely in front of her.

"We will be there momentarily," the Emperor acknowledged. He turned to Lydia. "Any last words?"

"You look magnificent, Imperial," she said. "Try not to sneeze."

"Thank you, I will take that advice to heart," he said dryly, but his eyes twinkled.

"There, I think you are ready," she proclaimed.

He offered her his arm, and she took it.

Outside, the Imperial guard fell into place around them accompanied by two of the ministers ahead and behind. While the Emperor wore the white and gold of a bridegroom, Lydia wore the red and yellow of the Phoenix. They passed through the backstage of the opera house, empty now for this special, secret occasion. The performers themselves were supposedly doing a command performance for the court with a lookalike sitting in for Xander. So far everything was going according to plan.

At last, they reached the stage, which had been left dressed in the mythical imperial throne room of the First Emperor. Still, looking out over the room full of empty chairs, Lydia counted the various Imperial Guard stationed around the room. There was nowhere for an assassin to hide. Yet she did not feel settled or secure. Her eyes drifted up to the highest point in the hall. Higher than seating to above the ornate carved angels along the top. She saw nothing up there; if one did not even know it was there, no one from below could see anyone at all.

On the stage itself, another party entered from the opposite side of the stage. A woman stood in the middle, dressed similarly to Xander, as a bride in white and gold. She wore a hood and cloak over her face obscuring it from view and was surrounded by her own guard. They met together in the center of the stage, over the painted mandala of the Imperial Sun.

First, both of the parties except the Emperor and the Queen's proxy bowed and curtsied to each other.

Then one of the ministers stepped forward beside Xander. "May I present Emperor Magnus IV, the Divine Sovereign of the Imperium."

A woman from the Southern Kingdom's envoy stepped forward and gestured to the woman beside her. "May I present the proxy for Her Royal Majesty, the Queen Regina Emeralda of the Southern Kingdom touched by the hand of god."

The woman pulled down her hood. She was beautiful. With hair like gold, she stood with a cornet woven through it. Her eyes were green as emeralds, and her small status stood regal.

Beside her, Xander's breath caught.

"The ... proxy?" he asked, looking at the member of the Queen's envoy beside the woman.

"Until I am officially welcomed into your kingdom, we thought this best," said Queen Emeralda said with her southern accent and a wicked little smile. "But We did wish to meet the man who would be Our husband."

She offered him her hand, and Xander took it eagerly, pressing his lips to the back of her fingers. Lydia found herself very glad that she had not actually had any attachment to their Emperor, for she could see she would have lost him to his new queen immediately. As well it should be.

"And is this the Emperor's Mistress, I have heard so much about?" the "proxy" asked, turning her cool emerald eyes to Lydia next.

Lydia in her turn bobbed to the secret queen. "I am the Countess of Summerbourne, your majesty. I am the Endowed Mistress of the Prince Regulus, the king's brother. I am here to stand as witness on his behalf to this joining of peace and love."

The perfect eyebrows of the secret queen popped straight up at that declaration. "Endowed Mistress?" She looked to the herald of her envoy a moment, who looked as confused. "We do not know what this means?"

"Not quite a wife, more than regular mistress. I am committed to the Prince Regulus," Lydia explained unashamedly.

"A concubine?"

Lydia inclined her head. "If you like, Your Majesty. Though it would be best to address me as a countess."

The secret queen *hmmm*'d in her throat. "Then you will be as my sister-in-law." She then nodded accepting it. "Well then, husband. Shall we begin?"

"Yes," Xander agreed, staring at her, mesmerized. He offered his hand again, and she took it as they both turned toward the bishop who had been waiting in the center of the stage in front of the crest of the sun. Soon the chanting and the exchange of vows and promises began. Lydia drifted to the back of the gathered few, witnessing the exchanged vows quietly.

Still, the hairs on the back of her neck rose. Something was not right, yet her glances around the room only showed the Imperial Guard and nothing else.

She turned to eye the Emperor and his new wife. They only seemed to have eyes for each other. The alliance was so close to being finalized, they had only to sign the agreements that were currently being laid out on the tables. Without those signatures, the vows exchanged would have little meaning.

A strong desire came over her to go to the hidden area and see Damian, to be assured that all was well. The gathering had dispersed into smaller groups now that the ceremony was complete, and Lydia went over to Xander to give him a kiss on the cheek.

"I am going up to see your brother now," she whispered.

He nodded. "Tell him I would speak to him later," he said, then turned back to receive the congratulations of one of his advisors.

Lydia faded back, nodding and acknowledging a few of the ministers who sought to curry favor by acknowledging the new Countess of Summerbourne, but she managed to ease her way out of the stage area.

With renewed alacrity, she found her way to the backstage stairs that took her to the secret passage that led her under the audience. It was dark down there but for two old lanterns throwing dim light, but the dark didn't bother Lydia anymore. She knew where she was going, and once she reached the far end, she squeezed past the pipes that brought her into a natural alcove that connected her into the Undercourt. She found one of Damian's long ladders there, that took her up to the highest balcony, through a forgotten crawl space. Her dress and slippers were getting dirty and weren't the best for the task, but she did not give one wit about it.

Some unnamed dread urged her forward.

Chapter 51

A FUTURE FOR US

Damian watched from above, his hands braced on the edge of the unseen balcony as the figures on the stage below moved about. They were preparing to sit down and sign all the official papers. He had been as surprised as his brother at the Southern Kingdom queen's secret appearance, pretending to be her own proxy, but he could understand her motives. If his brother's reaction to her was any indication, they may just have a chance at the new future they were trying to build.

Yet he grew concerned when he realized that he could no longer see Lydia down below. His eyes continued to drift to her all during the bishop's ceremony, pulled by the bright colors of her dress. Now, the assembled were coming around a small table to sign everything. Then the secret meeting would end, until the city could welcome their new Empress publicly a few months from now. Only then would the alliance be consummated, and nothing could stop it from happening. So far their plan had worked perfectly, but he still waited for some hint of one of Regina's assassins to appear.

"I thought I would find you here," a voice said softly over his shoulder.

He froze, every muscle and nerve on end as he turned to look toward the source of the voice.

Regina stood there, dressed in breeches and leather, clothes he would never have thought her ever to wear even when taking exercise.

Realizing she could see his face, he turned away, tugging up his hood.

"No, there is no need for that," Regina said, and he paused his fingers still gripping onto the edge of his hood.

"What are you doing here?" he demanded.

"Same as you. To do what needs to be done," her voice sounded as warm as ever. "I see it all now, our destinies have brought us here."

His breath came fast as he sensed her approaching behind him. "Damian," she said. Her hand slid up over his shoulder, squeezing. He longed to take it, all of his feelings for the woman he once loved swirling up inside him. "I am so sorry. For everything."

Roughly, he pulled away from her. "Did you do it? Did you kill Lord Dominique?" he asked. Anger burned through him, but not for that.

"Yes, I did," she said simply as if what she had done was no more grave than butchering his favorite cow.

He closed his eyes, struggling to believe her confession even from her own lips. "Why, Regina?"

"You know why. And soon I will make everything right again, and you can help me."

There was a thump of something hitting the floor, which forced him to look. Planted between her feet was the butt of a rifle. "The man I hired has failed me, and we are running out of time. They are hunting me Damian. If we don't remove the Emperor now, there is no future for us."

"What do you think you are going to do with that?"

"We can do this together," she said, caressing the stock with her fingers. "Like the first Emperor. We will slay the usurper by our own hands, and then by divine right, we will claim the Imperial Throne. We can finally get everything we deserve. Together. We both know what's down there, and it will only take two shots. You can be Emperor, and we can take the Southern Kingdom, ours by the divine right of conquest. And me," she stepped up and set her hand over his on the balcony. "You can have me back by your side. Your Empress."

"Regina..."

"You can even keep your whore. She can bear our heirs, I will claim them as mine. Don't you see? This will be perfect. We can set everything right again." She reached up to cup his damaged face, her eyes pleading with him to understand. "We can finally be happy."

He jerked away from her touch like it was acid. "No."

She blinked once, struck by that word. "No?"

He shook his head. "No, Regina. I will never be the Emperor, and you will never be the Empress."

Fury filled those black eyes. He could tell that it had never occurred to her once that he would say no. She had stretched for every obscure legal precedent she could to make her plan work, but it had never occurred to her that no one else would support it.

Before she had a chance to decide her next move, he seized the rifle from her and threw it away.

"No!" she cried, her hand moving as if she could recall it back to her with a thought.

"This is over, Regina," he tried to say but her head kept shaking.

"No, no, I've done this for you. Don't you understand, everything I have done for you—"

"You did this for yourself," he snapped. His eyes landed on the butt of the pistol in her belt at the same moment her hand landed on it.

He rushed her to grab it at the same time as she drew it. They fell back together, struggling for the gun, while he tried to pin her down to the ground.

"No! I will kill you!" she tried to roar, but he covered her mouth with his hand, to muffle her shouts so those below wouldn't hear anything. She bit him hard.

The plan: they were so close to succeeding. Any disturbance or hint of betrayal would destroy everything. Then a sharp blow hit him from behind. The world went dark with white bursts of stars and he lost connection to his body for a moment. He fell onto his side, and too late, he tried to sluggishly catch Regina as she struggled up. The pistol was still hers.

"No," he said weakly, as Regina's ally stood over him, holding up the butt of another rifle, preparing to bring it down on him. All he could do was raise his hands to try to shield his head.

Then there was a bang.

"No!" Damian cried, reaching out to Regina as if he could stop the shots from her gun from ending everything he had ever fought for.

Instead, the form above him jerked. Red spread across his front and then he collapsed on top of Damian. He could see Regina, just over the dead man's shoulder, lifting and aiming her gun, but she was hesitating, scanning for a target.

Somewhere was a ka-chunk of a cocking sound.

"No!" he shouted again, but Regina didn't stop.

Then there was another blast. This time Regina fell forward, then flipped out of sight over the balcony.

He stared at the space she had occupied only a moment before, listening for some hint of what was happening below. There was an odd crash of meat hitting wood, then nothing. No screams. No alarms. No sense to be made of any of it.

Desperately, he shoved the body on top of him to the side, scrambling for his own feet. Immediately, he locked eyes on Lydia standing a few feet away, breathing heavily as she lowered the rifle, letting it point at the ground.

Damian then scrambled over to the balcony's edge and looked down. Laid out over two rows of seating was the bloody corpse of Regina, her dead eyes staring with her mouth open. A stab of pain went through his heart, and he looked away, unable to bear to see it and unable to wipe it from where it had scarred his mind's eye.

At last below, he could hear shouts, the Imperial guards converging on the body below.

It wasn't until Lydia came to his side, dropping the rifle on the ground that he found his voice. "She's dead," he said, numb. "Oh gods. I couldn't stop her."

"It's alright," Lydia said, squeezing his arm before pressing her head into his. "It's alright, now."

"Where... where is the Emperor?" he asked, gripping the balcony edge to steel himself to look over again.

"She was too late, they were already leaving when the first shouts went up. The queen had departed first. I don't know if they heard or saw any of it, but once the shouting happened, they were already getting Xander out of here."

"Gods, I don't deserve such luck," he said, shaking his head. "I don't deserve you."

She took his face then and kissed him hard. All he could do was reach for her in turn, letting her tongue slide through and wash away his fear and pain and panic. They had done it. They had stopped the assassination, and this was the proof of it. They were both alive and safe. He felt strangely calm as they pulled gently away to look at each other.

But they weren't entirely safe yet.

"We need to go," she said, and he understood. He could hear the Imperial Guard trying to find their way up to the hidden space, shouting orders for Damian and Lydia to stay where they were, to find answers. He wasn't sure how long it would take for them to get up there, but he and his Lydia had best be gone by then.

Taking her hand, they retreated back to the ladder and down once more into the Undercourt where no one would find them.

Chapter 52

VOWS RENEWED

Lydia laid back to float in the warm waters of the bath, leaning her shoulders against Damian's chest as she floated.

"At least the baths were not destroyed," she commented, making plans to simply live there forever. Her hair flowed about her freely, and she felt once more as an ancient woman, hiding in the bowls of the Earth, before the First God of Light cracked open the way to the surface and let all of humanity out.

It had been several days since Regina's demise. Whether her passing was fortunate or not was a matter of debate, but only more time could pass before they could tell. The court was obsessed with the scandal, but it had caused very little disruption otherwise. The current story, seeded with some well-placed gossips, was that Regina had tried to escape with a lover, and it had all gone wrong, resulting in a murder-suicide of the unfortunate lady. Who this lover was morphed depending on the telling. Other rumors flew, entirely on their own, that she had been murdered by the Ghost of the Undercourt. There was even a less popular rumor that she was not dead at all, that someone who looked a lot like her had died, and she had escaped the Imperium, unable to bear the rejection by the Emperor in favor of his love for his new mistress. Those few who favored this rumor even claimed that the funeral for Regina was all staged with a sham body since the casket was never opened to reveal the lady to public.

The Imperial House neither confirmed nor denied anything, only extended condolences to the House Laon.

Not a word was spoken anywhere about the Emperor's secret marriage. The ruse had worked, and any hint of the truth was overshadowed by Regina's scandal. And soon there would be an official announcement of the ceasefire and the dismantling of the war front. It would be another year before the official, public marriage could be performed.

"Will we be able to continue living here?" Lydia asked, trying to let all the issues of the outside world drift away in the water. Those things were too far away to be a concern of the Undercourt.

"It will take some time, but I have had an engineer through, and he believes this area is stable, so we may rebuild this part of the Undercourt if you like. Make it more of a home for us."

"Are you sure he can be trusted? This engineer?" Lydia asked, surprised to hear someone would be let into their secrets like that.

"He will be paid very handsomely to repair this place and then even more handsomely to disappear to a foreign country far, far away, along with any and all workers. Our secrets will be safe, and no one needs to die for them."

Lydia smiled and accepted. "That is what it needs to be then."

His arms came up around her body and pulled her back against him. She laughed, his lips attacked her neck, tickling and delighting her at the same time. In the water, she split her legs apart and accepted him into her body, her laughter shifting to moans. The water sloshed around them, taking on a new rhythm, but it was all very awkward. Not at all conducive to the satisfaction that she sought.

"Turn me around," she ordered, and he did, spinning them about in the water so she could brace against the side of the pool, while he took her from behind. His face buried into her hair, and she held it there with her own hand sliding through the strands.

"You are never leaving me again?" she gasped.

"Never," he promised, speeding up his thrusts into her, taking her, possessing her, as much as she possessed him. Her voice matched each thrust, crying out with no fear of being heard. She could hear his gasps and grunts, firing up her own.

"You want me," she declared, the idea of that heightening her pleasure. She spread her legs wider as the water sloshed violently, he shifted into an even more delightful angle.

"Fuck! I want you," he growled in his throat, his hands coming around to grip her breasts, his thumb seeking out her scar. "My Lydia."

"My Damian," she squealed, covering his hands with her own, increasing the pressure on her aching breasts. "Fuck me harder."

"Yes, my wife," he said and applied himself. She came all at once, gripping down on him with every fiber in being, letting her voice ring out in the bathing chamber.

She felt him pump inside her, riding his own release, and she welcomed it as she laid her cheek down on the cooler stone, trying to catch her breath. Their coupling had been almost too fast, but she could hardly argue with the results. While she had wanted it to last longer, she knew there would be many more opportunities to come. And only when she wanted it. When it pleased her to do it.

Wrapped in sensations of bliss, she melted once more into the water, and into his arms, resting against his chest. Gently she cupped his cheek and kissed it. "My husband. In every way that counts."

"Do..." he swallowed, still not having caught his breath. "Do you think you will be satisfied with me? I cannot make you my wife in truth."

"Hush," she warned. "What is marriage, my love, if not an agreement between two consenting people to live together, to be with each other, to share in everything, happiness, sorrow, pain, and triumph? At its most fundamental is that not all that marriage is?"

"I can see your point."

"And you are as free to make that choice as I?"

"Yes. I give you all that I am freely."

"And if you keep loving me like that, I cannot see why we should be any less married. I need no one else to agree to it," she said pleasantly. "And this is better than what we had before. I am a woman of independent means now. I spend my time with whomever I choose."

"And you choose me?"

"As you choose me, my prince."

He chuckled, and she could feel him nod his head. "Yes. Yes, this is better." He kissed her shoulder. "This is better."

They floated like that for a while, savoring the feelings of each other.

"You don't have any regrets, my love?" Damian asked. Clearly his brain was still stewing, but she decided it was simply who he was and what he did, and she might as well accept it now.

"Well, only one," she admitted and looked over at the side of the pool. The egg rested there, nestled in its own basket upon a nest of tiny satin pillows.

A wave of pity flowed through Lydia, and she pushed away from Damian to go to the basket. Hopping up beside it, she sat gazing down at its beautiful colors.

"For everything we've been through, we still don't know why she killed Alexandros," she said sadly.

Damian crossed the water to float at her knees. "It doesn't matter now. We will keep them safe until they are born again."

Without thinking, she went to brush her hand over the beautiful shell. "Oh Alexandros..." she whispered.

"Don't!" Damian tried to warn her, tried to grab her hand away, but it was too late.

She flinched but her fingers were already resting on the smooth surface. Some part of her mind could tell that it was raging hot. Pure power flowed into her from the shell. It should have been burning her flesh away. Yet, it didn't. Instead the veins pulsed brighter, with blinding shards of light.

"Lydia!" Damian cried just as the egg flashed, bursting apart under her hand. She barely had time to cover her eyes with her other arm. There was a *fwoosh* in the room, like the air had been sucked out, then reversed, whirling back into the space.

And then it was over.

The dim light of the torches in the bathing room danced quietly as if nothing had happened. In fact, all was quiet. Lydia still sat on the edge of the pool, though much of the water seemed to have been blasted out; it was significantly lower, nearly to Damian's hips. He stared up at her, his eyes perfect circles in the blackness around each one. Then they both jumped as the water started up again, the spout spilling its warm waterfall into the pool once more.

"Lydia," Damian breathed, with a level of understanding she didn't have yet.

Slowly, she raised her hand to search for damage, only to look at her whole, healthy skin.

"Lydia?" Damian asked again. He touched her knees, eyes searching for some sign of harm.

"I'm alright," she assured. "I'm alright."

Then a small creaking sound caught both their attention. Sitting amongst several pieces of shell in the basket, was a small glowing, yellow and orange ball of fluff.

END OF STORY

Book Club Questions

1. Why did you first think Damian hid his face when he first met Lydia?

2. Why do you think Lydia agreed to become an endowed mistress?

3. What was your initial impression of the emperor?

4. Who did you suspect was trying to assassinate the emperor throughout the book and how did that change? Or why did it not?

5. What was your impression of Lady Regina? Did you think she knew who Lydia was?

6. Why do you think Xander wanted to steal Lydia away from Damian?

7. When do you think Lydia fell in love with Damian? When did he fall in love with her?

8. Why did you think Xander suspected his brother of attempting to kill him?

9. Where do you think Lydia and Damian's relationship goes from here?

10. What was the biggest surprise at the end?

Author Bio

Author Megan Mackie writes something for everyone—she's written cyberpunk, urban fantasy, paranormal demon romance, speculative fiction, post-post zombie apocalypse, steampunk, and mid-grade science fiction. She's also a contributing writer for RPGs Legendlore and Legendlore: Legacies by Onyx Path.

She's a popular figure at comic cons across the country, so if you come across her, ask about the Lucky Devil series and prepare to get your mind blown.

Whats the news, Barman?

Sign Up for Megan's Newsletter!
https://www.meganmackieauthor.com/newsletter

Also check out her free Wattpad novel!

https://www.wattpad.com/1423396171-i-can%27t-get-the-vampire-rogue-to-romance-me

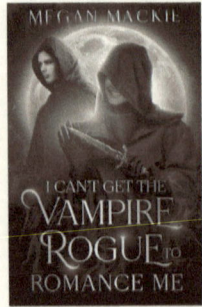

It was all fun, until she got sucked into the game.

Other Books By Megan Mackie

Urban Fantasy/Cyberpunk

The Lucky Devil Series
The Finder of the Lucky Devil
The Saint of Liars
The Devil's Day
The Digital Mage
Demonic Inc. – Coming Soon

The Saint Code Series
The Lost Constable – Coming Soon

Mid-Grade Science Fiction

The Adventures of Pavlov's Dog and Schrodinger's Cat
Maxwell's Demon
The Ship of Theseus - Coming Soon
Sniffy the Virtual Rat – Coming Soon

Post Post-Zombie Apocalypse

Dead World
The Prisoner of the Dead
The Journey to Naraka – Coming Soon
The Damned Road – Coming Soon

Superhero

Working Masks
The Vilification of Aqua Marine
The Indemnification of Black Heart - Coming Soon

Epic Fantasy

Silverblood Series
Silverblood Scion

www.ingramcontent.com/pod-product-compliance
Lightning Source LLC
LaVergne TN
LVHW040041080526
838202LV00045B/3434